P9-BZH-269

Reviewers comment on Bunn's previous Marc Royce novel, *Lion of Babylon*

"Description is so vivid you can smell the food and choke on the desert sand. . . . Bunn's fans will leap for this precise and intricate tale of cross-cultural friendship and loyalty in the heart of the Red Zone."

Publishers Weekly

"This exciting, action-packed thriller features a strong sense of place in its depictions of the people and politics of the Middle East. It is sure to please [Bunn] fans and win him new ones."

Library Journal
*Selected by *Library Journal* for the 2011 Best Book Award

"A fast-paced, gripping thriller, *Lion of Babylon* is rich not only with adventure but also with visual details and dramatic, snapshot insights into the Middle East, its traditions, history, and people."

Phyllis Tickle
Former Sr. Consulting Editor at *Publishers Weekly*

"A phenomenal read. *Lion of Babylon* is far more than simply a great thriller. This book delves into a series of crucial issues, and does so with a sensitivity that left me literally stunned. Bunn tells a story that grips the reader and refuses to let go. . . . The descriptions are beautifully crafted, the characters vibrantly drawn."

Keith Hazard
Deputy Director (ret.), CIA

"It is a terrific book, deeply moving with new insights into important connections between the world's faiths. . . . I have long admired and appreciated Davis's work and I will say I think this is his finest."

Jane Kirkpatrick
Novelist and Speaker

Books by Davis Bunn

* with Janette Oke   † with Isabella Bunn

RARE EARTH

DAVIS BUNN

RARE EARTH

BETHANYHOUSE
a division of Baker Publishing Group
Minneapolis, Minnesota

© 2012 by Davis Bunn

Published by Bethany House Publishers
11400 Hampshire Avenue South
Bloomington, Minnesota 55438
www.bethanyhouse.com

Bethany House Publishers is a division of
Baker Publishing Group, Grand Rapids, Michigan

Printed in the United States of America

Library of Congress Cataloging-in-Publication Data

Bunn, T. Davis, 1952–
    Rare earth / Davis Bunn.
      p. cm.
    ISBN 978-0-7642-1017-4 (hardcover : alk. paper) — ISBN 978-0-7642-0906-2 (pbk.) 1. International relief—Kenya—Fiction. 2. Refugee camps—Kenya—Fiction. 3. Mines and mineral resources—Kenya—Fiction. I. Title.
PS3552.U4718R37 2012
813'.54—dc23   2012004411

Cover design by Kirk DouPonce, DogEared Design

12 13 14 15 16 17 18   7 6 5 4 3 2 1

This book is dedicated to

Michelle and LeRoy Yates.

Dedicated in service,
wise in counsel, strong in love.

RARE
EARTH

Chapter One

Marc Royce arrived at the latest African crisis by way of a United Nations chopper. He was a last-minute hire, taking the place of a man who had trained hard for the role. Marc had little chance of success. Even his survival was in question. He had spent a week in Nairobi hearing this a dozen times and more each day. He was not welcome, he was not wanted. The four UN staffers sharing the chopper shunned him. They knew Marc was employed by Lodestone, a U.S. company contracted to bring in emergency supplies and do so for a profit. The UN staffers might need his company, but they still treated Marc like a pariah. They chatted among themselves and studied the rising tide of mayhem below them. They did not even acknowledge his presence. Marc was having too good a time to care what they thought. He was headed back into action. It was enough.

Up ahead, a new calamity had struck a region already devastated by drought, famine, and civil war. A volcano near the border between Kenya and Uganda, dormant for centuries, had erupted. Marc had been awakened in Nairobi two hours before sunrise with frantic orders to go out there and make things happen.

He ignored the glares as he shouldered his way in tight to the window. He was not going to miss this first airborne glimpse of his job. The base of Mount Elgon was just visible to his west, but the peak was lost to the ash cloud. Directly ahead of him was a ribbon of fire running from the volcano's new fissure. The hillside was now split with veins of smoke and fire, a wound of violent hues.

As they swooped in for the final approach, Marc studied the advancing lava flow. Ahead of the molten rock was a flood of people and vehicles fleeing the ruined city of Kitale. From his perch, Marc could see the remnants of a shantytown that crawled its way up the once-verdant slope. The city had been flattened by the earthquake that had preceded the eruption. Where the lava had not touched was only dust and rubble. Kitale was no more.

They landed in a dry riverbed west of the city. The UN relief workers jumped down and departed without a word. Marc had no idea where to go. All he had was a set of vague orders, printed that morning at Lodestone's airport office. He showed the sheet to the chopper pilot, who grinned at his confusion. "How long have you been at this job?"

"Eight days."

The copilot slipped off her headphones so she could enjoy the show. The pilot asked, "What kind of training did they give you?"

"I've had a week in Nairobi."

The pilots exchanged a glance. "And before that?"

"I was an accountant. In Baltimore."

The pilots were laughing out loud now. "Why don't you just hang tight, let us fly you back to the Nairobi airport. You can catch the big silver bird back to sanity-land."

"Thanks, but I've got a job to do."

"Man, you've got *no* idea what you're about to get yourself into." The pilot pointed out the sun-splashed windscreen. "This place will *kill* you."

Marc shouldered his backpack. "Any idea where I check in?"

The two pilots pointed him toward a tent at the border of the landing zone, then dismissed him with a pair of mock salutes.

Were it not for the ash floating like brittle snow, the September air would have been pleasant. The temperature was in the upper eighties, the morning sky a chalky blue. But every now and then a black cloud streaked above Marc's head, vague shadows that promised danger to come. And off in the distance was a constant low rumble that thrummed through Marc's boots.

Inside the tent, Marc found controlled chaos. A woman worn down by fatigue and stress inspected his orders. "You're another mercenary?"

"I'm the new supply officer for Lodestone."

"What I said." She shot out a hand. "Passport."

Marc had it ready for her. She checked his face against the photo. Then she keyed his name into a computer, squinted at the screen, and pointed at the dusty chaos. "See those supply trucks?"

The field beyond was a mini-city of supply mountains and rumbling trucks. "Yes."

"Four are headed for the French camp named here in your orders. Go check in with the dispatcher." She inspected him again, her gaze glinting with dark humor. "Don't expect looks and a smile to get you very far out here."

13

"What smile?" Marc replied, but the woman had already turned away.

The four trucks were piled high with cornmeal sacks and water purification systems and medical supplies. Marc knew because he had been given the manifest by a sweating dispatcher who scarcely even glanced at Marc's credentials. The man was simply glad to find someone willing to take responsibility for the load.

The lead truck was a Volvo with three hundred thousand miles on the clock. The others were in even worse states of repair. Marc's seat was patched with duct tape. The springs dug into his back with every jouncing dip. The driver was a good-natured Angolan whose name Marc had not caught. They shared the truck's cab with two other young men, one of whom was stuffed into the rear crawl space. Two more rode perched on top of the load.

The driver spoke a few words in Marc's direction, laughed at Marc's lack of understanding, and turned on the radio. The volcano formed a hissing overlay that drowned out the music, so the driver slipped in a tape. The men drummed their hands in time to the tune and chattered constantly. The air was compressed, the men's fragrance an earthy spice. When they turned west onto the main highway, Marc finally released his smile. He was headed in the one direction he truly relished. Toward action.

The manifest he held was stamped with the emblem of Marc's company. Lodestone had recently become one of the largest suppliers of humanitarian equipment in Africa. Theirs was a specialty service. Their clients included every major aid agency, along with the United Nations. Whenever and wherever a crisis erupted, the agencies turned to firms like Marc's to deliver emergency supplies, and do so fast.

But there was a problem. One so large it had rung alarm bells eight thousand miles away. Which was why Marc had been brought in. An outsider who some thought had no chance of success and even less of survival. Before departing for Nairobi, Marc had been repeatedly warned of unseen foes who would make it their business to assure he never made it back alive. Marc had responded that he would have had it no other way.

Now that he was isolated by smoke and fire and turmoil and Africa, Marc wondered at his habit of landing in impossible situations.

Traffic along the main road to Eldoret moved at a crawl. Directly ahead of them were crude donkey carts piled with farm implements and children, with goats tied to the rear gates. The animals fought the ropes and bleated as they were pulled forward. Marc's convoy remained on the road for over three hours and covered less than ten miles.

They then turned north on what was little more than a rutted dirt track. A pair of waist-high signs with Red Cross camp names were the only indication of life ahead. A squad of bored soldiers kept the traffic from making the turn, motioning it farther west with languid African gestures. After exchanging a few words with the lead driver, the soldiers stepped aside.

The vista consisted of scrub and the occasional thorn tree. To their left, the world was lost behind a curtain of doom. Occasionally they came upon crumbled patches of asphalt, but most of the road had long been washed away.

They traveled through much of the day, crawling along at a brisk walking pace. Marc figured they might have covered twenty miles.

They were far enough from the volcano not to see many cinders, which was good because the region looked bone-dry to Marc. Now and then the wind shifted just enough to fling ash their way, blanketing the low brush with a false snow. The driver started coughing and motioned for Marc to roll up his window. The cabin quickly became a fetid sauna.

They passed through a forest of skeletal trees, bleached a yellowish white by the drought. When they emerged on the forest's other side, Marc watched as a dozen specters appeared on the road ahead of them. The women were dressed in tribal robes coated with ash. They had wrapped the edges of their headkerchiefs around their faces, leaving only the eyes exposed. When the truck blew its horn, the women stepped aside slowly. They carried bundles of firewood and viewed the passing truck through eyes red as live coals.

Just as they arrived at the camp's border fence, the wind started pushing in from the east. As the air cleared they rolled down their windows and breathed deeply. The driver beeped his horn once. The camp guards pulled back the main gates, and they trundled inside. Tendrils of ash blew from the ground, bitter flurries that stung the eyes and left Marc's mouth tasting of old smoke and sulfur. The camp was impossibly quiet, the earth blanketed by several inches of volcanic powder.

The camp was a massive shantytown, an endless sprawl. Dwellings were built from corrugated siding, plastic sheets, canvas tarps, thorn brush, anything. Some had miniature fences surrounding bits of land, Marc assumed, for chickens or other animals. Children stood and watched them pass, their feet and legs turned the color of old bones.

They rounded a slight bend and came upon a wall of packed humanity. The people blocking the road pressed out of the way, their motions slow and grudging. They entered the camp's central compound. The horde encircled them, twenty or thirty people deep. Marc heard a soft rumble, like another volcano threatening to erupt beneath his feet. Only this one came from the people who now surrounded the trucks.

The driver and his mates muttered nervously.

"Stay cool," Marc said softly.

The driver glanced over. It was uncertain whether he understood Marc's words. But Marc's tone and expression were enough to calm him. His death grip on the wheel eased slightly.

Inside the throng was an empty space, perhaps two hundred yards across. This central zone held an administrative building of unpainted concrete blocks, a chapel and schoolhouse, a medical clinic, a bunkhouse and mess hall, and a trio of godowns, the local word for an open-sided warehouse. The entire area was rimmed by people.

A squad of soldiers in sweat-stained uniforms stood before the godowns. Four people in white gowns watched their truck through the clinic's mosquito-netting walls. Otherwise there was no movement. Just the wall of dark faces and scowls and red-rimmed eyes.

Then a woman came bounding out of the admin building. She appeared to be in her late twenties and was attractive in a disheveled manner. She had a coltish manner of running, her long legs weighted by heavy lace-up boots. A rubber band only partly managed to control her dark brown hair. She gripped Marc's windowsill and addressed him in frantic French.

"Sorry," Marc said. "Do you speak English?"

The woman demanded, "Where are the soldiers?"

Marc waved at the trucks. "We're just delivering supplies."

"I spoke on the radio with the colonel. Last night and again this morning. I forget his name." Her accent was almost comically French, drawing the *r*'s from somewhere deep in her throat and making *z*'s of each *th* sound: *Ze radio wit' ze colonel.* "He promised more soldiers."

"The base camp is sheer chaos," Marc replied. "No one said anything about soldiers. I never saw an officer. I flew in; they told me to come here."

The woman released his window so as to pull her hair away from her face. Marc realized she was doing her best not to cry.

She took a pair of raspy breaths, then said quietly, "We are all going to die."

Chapter Two

When Marc stepped down from the truck, the surrounding throng greeted him with a low growl. He pretended not to hear anything, though his belly quivered from nerves.

Fear added tremors to the French aid worker's voice. "How can they send me more supplies and no staff? I am the only person here with authority. I cannot control the situation."

Marc opened the truck's rear gate and unhooked the bungee cords holding down the medical supplies. He pulled out the nearest crate. "Take this."

She did so only because he shoved the container into her arms. "Did you hear a word I just said?"

Marc pulled out a second one and started across the ash-covered earth. He kept his voice calm. "I would advise you to be quiet."

She hurried to catch up. "How *dare* you say such a thing. You have *no* idea what I've—"

Marc smiled cheerily. "Your tone of voice is making things worse."

The medical clinic was an identical concrete block structure to the chapel and admin building and bunkhouse, only it had been expanded by hooking open-sided tents to three of its four exterior walls. Marc slipped through the mosquito netting lowered to keep out the ash and asked, "Who speaks English in here?"

An attractive young nurse in a sweat-stained uniform said, "I do."

"May I ask your name?"

"Kitra."

"I am Marc."

The aid worker behind him clearly disliked being ignored. "You Lodestone people are all the same. You think you can buy your way out of any crisis."

Marc replied, "I know you're scared. But we can get through this intact." He realized the nurse was backing away from him. "What's the matter?"

Kitra was dark-haired with eyes of emerald fire. "You are from the Lodestone group?"

"That's right."

Her face now held an acrid mix of fear and loathing. "Get out of this tent."

"Look, I'm here—"

"Leave!"

A pair of medical staffers started toward him. Marc set the crate he was carrying on an empty bed and raised his hands in submission. The French aid worker watched in bitter triumph as Marc retreated.

A tall African in a dark short-sleeved shirt and pastor's collar was waiting for him. "Perhaps I can help. I am Charles Matinde, camp chaplain."

Marc gestured at the faces glaring through the screen. "What just happened in there?"

"The aid supervisor, her name is Valerie. She is very frightened and most certainly out of her depth." The chaplain's English was precise and heavily accented. He was in his forties, tall and slender in the manner of a long-distance runner. "As for the nurse, she has a personal issue with your company."

Marc asked, "What about you? Do you have a problem with Lodestone?"

"Certainly not." Charles indicated the crowd of people. "My concern is for them. My question is, can you help?"

Marc liked that answer as much as he did the chaplain's steady manner. "Who else is in charge here?"

Charles motioned toward a middle-aged African who leaned against the side of the nearest godown. He cradled an AK-47 with such ease it was almost possible to ignore the readiness to his stance. "Sergeant Kamal."

"Is the sergeant to be trusted?"

"He does not have enough men. He complains. But yes, I think he is a good man, and his men agree."

"Does he speak English?"

"A few words."

"Would you come translate for me, please?"

Valerie emerged from the medical tent, clearly displeased with how Marc was circumventing her authority. She fell in beside them and continued with her complaints. "I was promised more staff. I was promised security. We do not have any way to protect the supplies we have now."

The sergeant scowled at Valerie, adding his own displeasure to Marc's. The woman went silent. Sergeant Kamal wore a khaki uniform with blue stripes on his lapels and sleeves, denoting a soldier in the UNHCR brigade. When the chaplain introduced them, Marc drew himself up to full height and gave the man a parade-ground salute. "Please extend to the officer my sincere respect for keeping things under control."

The sergeant underwent a remarkable transformation. Gone was his sullen rage, which Marc knew was a noncom's customary response to threats of any kind. The sergeant smiled, revealing a mouth crammed with overly bright teeth.

Marc said, "Ask Sergeant Kamal when the last time food was distributed."

The chaplain replied without asking. "Not since the volcano erupted."

"I need the sergeant to respond and feel included."

"Ah, of course." Charles spoke with the sergeant in what Marc assumed was a local tongue. He then replied, "Three days and counting."

The aid worker snapped, "How could I *possibly* deliver supplies when I have no idea of what or who represents which refugee family? We have *thousands* of new refugees arriving every *day*. We were promised machines to make IDs. We were promised staff to make proper records. We were promised *guards*."

Marc turned to the aid worker. "Your assistance is no longer required."

Valerie gaped at him. "*Comment?*"

Marc said, "You would help us a lot by returning to the admin building."

The chaplain actually smiled.

"How *dare*—"

"Are you able to find it on your own," Marc said, "or should I ask the sergeant for an escort?"

The sergeant tracked Valerie's angry retreat with cynical approval. He turned back to Marc and nodded once.

Marc asked, "How many able soldiers are we talking about here?"

"Sixteen," Kamal replied through the chaplain. "One understrength squad."

Marc scanned the area. The tension emanating from the anxious crowd was a palpable force. It felt to Marc like a finger slowly drawing down on the trigger. "We don't have much time."

"No," Charles quietly agreed. "We do not."

He liked the pastor's calm. It was the manner of someone who had long since given up worrying over everything he could not control. Marc sensed the sergeant held the same attitude, so long as his superiors gave him direction and at least a hope of survival.

The godowns, whose tin roofs were supported by concrete block pillars, were crammed to the gills with supplies. The third was empty. Marc knew without asking that the sergeant had massed the provisions into as small a space as possible to keep from overextending his squad. Marc asked, "Which godown holds your oldest perishables?"

The sergeant used his machine gun to point at the godown to his left. Charles translated, "The mealy sacks have begun to smell."

"Okay, here's what we do. We pull the trucks up to the empty godown. You take your men off the warehouse there and direct them to stand guard while we off-load the trucks."

The sergeant understood immediately. "You will let them steal everything?"

"First of all, the supplies were always meant for these people. Nobody is stealing anything. Secondly, we don't have enough men to guard three godowns."

The sergeant looked at the surrounding throng for the first time. "And they are starving."

Marc released the faintest wisp of wrath. "That is absolutely unacceptable."

The sergeant turned back, approval clear in his dark gaze. Charles translated, "Kamal asks how long you will be staying."

"One day beyond as long as it takes," Marc replied. "Let's get started."

Marc joined the guards standing around the trucks. He held a Nambu machine pistol that belonged to one of Kamal's soldiers who was down with gut rot. Marc had never liked the Nambu. The gun was exceedingly ugly, with a pig's snout of a barrel and a curved clip long as his forearm. The clip was oversized because when the weapon was switched to full automatic it threw out bullets as fast as metal rain. The gun was polished with years of handling, but there was no rust and the trigger was firm. Marc had no doubt it would fire well. But he had no intention of using it. He carried it as a show of authority.

Because the camp was about to blow.

The camp was run by the largest French aid agency. Africa's crisis camps were segmented by agency and nation, to avoid language confusion and duplication of either action or personnel. But when the volcano had erupted, the nation's minister for refugees had ordered the camp's directors to take over three other camps whose own administrators were trapped in Kitale and presumed lost. Valerie had been the lone aid worker left in charge, and was overwhelmed.

Valerie was obviously accustomed to having any number of staff do whatever she wanted. Only now there was no one around for her to manipulate, except for the pastor and the sergeant and a pair of overworked male nurses. Kamal scowled whenever she came within range, and his men were more than happy to follow his lead. The camp elders utterly despised her. Charles viewed her with amused condescension. Marc had no idea what opinion the medical personnel had of Valerie. He had not been permitted back inside their tent.

Since the other administrators had departed, the camp had swelled from nine thousand to somewhere around thirty thousand people. This Marc learned from the pastor. Charles revealed a sharp but gentle wisdom that matched the silver threads woven through his close-cropped dark hair. The man possessed a quiet dignity that Marc found genuinely appealing, especially as it remained untouched by the current crisis. As Marc separated the medical supplies and water purification systems from the foodstuffs, he asked, "Think maybe you could find the camp elders?"

"That is simple enough." Charles gestured toward a cluster of older men standing to the right of the main road. "All but one is there. The other is laid up in the clinic."

"Will they speak with me?"

"They will listen. As for talking . . ." Charles gave an eloquent shrug. "They stopped speaking to Valerie the day before yesterday."

Marc stopped by the nearest godown and hefted a sack of grain. The elders watched in unblinking silence as Marc and the chaplain walked over. A deep voice roared from somewhere to Marc's left. The sound was followed by a chorus of rumblings. Marc could hear the pastor's breathing, quiet gasps like he had just run a hard mile.

Marc set the grain down at the elders' feet and said without preamble, "I offer my solemn apology for the hardships they have faced. I thank them for the order they have maintained in the camp despite the situation."

Charles translated in the same tight breaths, nervous punches of a few words each. The elders made no sign they heard him.

"My aim is to relieve the worst need for food, and then set up an equitable system to distribute the other goods."

Charles seemed to have trouble finding enough air to shape the words. When he was done, Marc said, "Tell them the left godown holds food, and everything can be taken. Now."

Even before Charles finished translating, the youngest of the elders turned and lifted his staff high overhead. He was a slender man in his late thirties, with the motions of a tiger and features to match. There was no doubting his authority. He pointed at the godown and called. The cry was taken up by a hundred voices, a thousand. All but the elders erupted in a tide of ash-colored robes.

"*Non, non, c'est ne pas—*" The French aid worker had the good sense to scream her objections from the admin building's front step. She shrieked once more at the sergeant, who paid her no more attention than Marc or the elders.

The people rushed the godown from all sides. The native truckers stood on their vehicles and chattered nervously as the UN soldiers formed a line between the left godown and the other supplies. But the people made no attempt to break through the phalanx.

When Valerie realized no one paid her any attention, she seated herself on the top step and smoked and sulked. Marc ignored her and kept his attention on the crowd. The people cleared the warehouse with the speed of locusts. There were a few squabbles, not many. The youngest leader protected one woman whose sack was being tugged at by a pair of teenage girls. The sergeant ordered two of his men to shield a trio of children struggling with a carton. From inside the medical station, patients rose on their beds while the staff stood and watched.

Children began dancing about the central compound. Packets of Plumpy Nut flickered mirror-like in their hands. Plumpy Nut was a true success story, a combination of Western ingenuity and African need. The product required no refrigeration, was crammed with vitamins and proteins, cost less than thirty cents a portion, and suited the locals' tastes. Marc had tried it in Nairobi and thought it tasted like peanut butter laced with boiled ham. But the children loved it. And that was what mattered most.

Then it was over. The tension was released. The camp went quiet. Marc remained where he was, stationed by the elders, until woodsmoke rose and blanketed the camp with the fragrance of cooking grain.

Chapter Three

The afternoon was quiet, the hours very full. The central compound remained ringed by thin wisps of woodsmoke. An hour or so after the grain was distributed, the wind died. The southwestern sky was dominated by a giant pillar of ash. It rose from the earth, a looming menace of biblical proportions.

Marc prowled the compound, mostly so the people would become accustomed to his presence. He and the soldiers and the truckers sorted through the goods filling the other two godowns, both those he had delivered and the piles already in place. There were no manifests that he could find, so he borrowed pen and paper and clipboard from the medical tent and fashioned lists of his own. Three times he went back to the medical tent, twice to deliver supplies and once more to ask what else they required. The nurse named Kitra scowled at him every time Marc came within range, but made no move to bar his entry.

While the medical staff discussed what to add to their growing wish list, Marc tracked Kitra's movements. The nurse had the rare ability to remain alluring even when exhausted and stressed, like now. Marc did not mind her hostility, for he knew the reasons. In truth, he knew a great deal about her. She was, in fact, the reason he had come. Sooner or later he was going to have to confront her. But not yet.

The oldest foodstuffs Marc shifted into the now-empty warehouse. The soldiers huffed and discussed the task among themselves, but did not object. The truckers followed the soldiers' lead. Just as they were completing the task, the chaplain emerged from the medical tent with a two-page list of supplies. "We managed to contact the doctors. They added materials required by the other camps where they are working."

"Good idea." Marc copied the items to his manifest, then handed the medical staff's list back to Charles. "Tell them to hold on to this, so they can check their order against the incoming supplies."

"They will ask when these items should arrive."

"Soon. I hope." He rose to his feet. "You mind translating for me?"

Together they approached the truckers. Marc handed the manifest to the lead driver, then extracted two hundred dollars from his money belt. "Tell him there's another five bills for him and his workers if he can deliver this stuff in three days."

Charles did so, then replied, "He says, the problem is not him and not his trucks, but the depot bosses."

"Tell him to hang tight. I'm going to make a couple of calls and get him a name." Marc moved over to the sergeant and offered another cash payment. "Tell Sergeant Kamal, he and his men were a pleasure to work with. This money is my way of saying thanks."

The sergeant made the money disappear. "This is payment for what we have done, or what is yet to come?"

Marc grinned. "I am liking this man more and more."

Charles asked, "Am I to translate this also?"

"Sure thing." Marc crossed the compound, climbed the stairs, and knocked on the admin building's doorframe. He could see the French aid worker seated behind the desk on the room's opposite side. But Valerie gave no sign she was aware of him. Marc pushed open the screen door and entered. "I've shifted the food with the closest use-by dates to the empty godown."

She continued to stare out the main room's rear window. The back area was dominated by a massive baobab tree. Beyond that stood a lone concrete hut, housing the generator and fuel tank. Marc could hear the generator's low throbbing through the open window. When Valerie gave no response, Marc crossed the room. "I need to use your satellite phone."

Marc hefted the heavy apparatus off her desk. She glared at him, but did not speak. The device was warm and slightly moist. Marc assumed she had just finished a call, probably complaining to someone about what he had done. He wiped the phone on his shirt and dialed the number at the top of his own manifest. He made his request, got the required name, cut the connection, and replaced the phone. "I'm thinking it would be a good idea to delegate responsibility to the elders. And Charles, if he'll do it."

"You are here a few hours and you think you know everything." She plucked a cigarette from the pack on her desk. The large central office stank of stale smoke. "How positively American."

"Is there a photocopy machine or printer that works?"

"I want nothing to do with you or your questions." She lit her cigarette and blew a long plume toward the rear window. "Your superiors at Lodestone must be very proud."

Marc searched the offices and found a new printer-scanner in the second room. He took out his passport and made fifty copies of the page with his photo. When he returned to the front room, Valerie was still there, still blowing smoke at the baobab tree beyond her open window. Marc left the building without another word.

Charles seemed to have been waiting for him, which Marc took as a good sign. Together they walked to the collection of three ramshackle huts that made up the elders' compound. The buildings were identical to all the others Marc saw, made from plastic sheeting and ragged tarpaulins and dried tree limbs and thorn bush. The trio of structures opened into a small inner yard where chickens pecked. The elders remained seated on little stools as Marc and Charles entered. The center stool was occupied by the youngest of the group, the man with a predator's latent force.

Marc handed over all but one of the photocopied sheets and launched straight in. "There are bound to be weaker and older members of this community who might not receive their share. I want you to take responsibility for getting them food. I'd suggest you use these printouts. One of you sign a photocopied page and have Charles do the same. Sergeant Kamal and his men will hand over a sack of grain for each signed form."

The young chief took the pages, inspected them, and entered into a solemn discussion with the others. Twice Charles interjected a few comments of his own. The elders studied Marc intently.

The discussion went on for some time. Then the leader called out. Swiftly a pair of stools were brought. The chief gestured for Marc and Charles to seat themselves. A clay pot of some mildly fermented cow's milk was brought. It tasted like month-old cottage cheese and smelled far worse. But Marc followed Charles's example and smacked his lips over the putrid drink.

The formalities observed, Marc said, "I need to know what problem to attack next."

The elders seemed to have been expecting this very statement. There was a brief exchange, a low murmur as the clay pot made its way around the circle. Charles translated, "The younger women and the widows and the lonely grandmothers. They have a problem."

"The most helpless," Marc said, showing he understood. "The ones with no man to protect them."

"The camp lacks many things, but the most serious need is cooking oil. There is firewood. The forest you see beyond the camp boundary has mostly died with the drought. But many of the women refuse to go. We are hearing tales." Charles hesitated. "This is a sad thing."

"I am listening," Marc said. He did not know what he was going to hear, but already his gut burned with live coals.

"The elders suspect some of the men wait for the young women and demand sex in exchange for granting them passage. Some of these maidens refuse to enter the forest. They are starving, even when they now have grain."

Marc stood and made a process of dusting off his pants, trying to hide his rage. "I will see what I can do."

The elders had the same red-rimmed eyes as everyone else in the camp. They studied him carefully. The youngest finally spoke. Charles translated, "They wish to know your name."

"Marc Royce."

"They ask if you are a chief in your homeland."

"Sorry. No." He turned to leave. "Just an accountant."

At a signal from the young chief, Charles remained where he was as Marc rose and departed. Gathered in this circle were eleven elders from five different tribes. Two were in fact not officially elders at all, merely those selected to speak. Only one was a true chief, of the Luo. He was the youngest, not yet forty. His name was Philip. Philip had taken this new name when he had turned to Christianity. His clan had been animist for over a thousand years, worshiping the sun and certain trees and the hill known in English as Kilimanjaro. Charles held this one in something akin to awe.

The elder from the Ndebele tribe asked, "Truly, this newcomer is a man who looks at numbers?"

"Why would he lie?" another replied.

The clay pot was passed from hand to hand. Only a few drank. Among the tall tribesmen of the Rift plains, the pot would have been spiced with fresh cow's blood. When it came to Charles, he dipped his nose into the pot's opening, then passed it on. As a child, he had become physically ill merely from the odor. He still found it faintly nauseating. But he had learned to mask his distaste. He said, "Marc Royce genuinely cares for those affected by this latest trial."

"I sense this as well," Philip said.

The fact that Philip had spoken in agreement ended the discussion. One of the older men asked him, "Do you think he is the one?"

"I only know what I dreamed," Philip replied. "You have all

heard this. Many times. Since the night a month and more before the eruption."

"Tell us again."

"A man arrives on a chariot. He enters through the camp's front gates in the day's high heat."

There was a respectful murmur, a rumbling deep in the chest. A Kikuyu elder called for a smoke. His senior wife approached, drawing a long-stemmed clay pipe from a pocket. She used a curved knife to pare shavings from a compressed plug of native tobacco. She lit a twig and puffed deeply before handing the pipe to him.

Philip continued, "He halts the chariot and enters through the gates on foot."

"This the newcomer did not do," an elder said.

"Perhaps his entering on foot suggests a deeper meaning," Charles offered. Any who are offered the pot might speak as an equal. "A symbol."

The eldest among them responded, "But a symbol of what?"

"Humility, perhaps," a third said. "Or a desire to be accepted."

There was no impatience, no need to press forward. The elders counted time by a different clock. The story was less important than understanding what role Marc Royce might play in the days to come.

When the others went silent, Philip said, "Where he stepped, the ash disappeared. Grass shoots rose from the earth. And then I was lifted up. High as an eagle's flight I rose. And far as I could see, all the earth bloomed. Trees whose limbs are now white as old bones bore fruit. As I awoke, I heard the maidens and the children singing the harvest song."

"It cannot be this one," the eldest murmured. "A man who

35

dwells in a room without windows and eats numbers as we would mealy bread. This one cannot bring the rain. This one cannot save our land."

"I saw what I saw," the young chief replied.

"Did you see his face?"

"I did not."

The eldest among them held up one arm. His senior wife stepped forward and helped the man to his feet. He took the clay pot a final time, drank deeply, and smacked his lips. He leaned heavily on his cane as he started toward his hut. He said as he departed, "This new one will stay only as long as he can take money from our plight. He will count his winnings, and he will leave. Numbers are the white man's fascination. He must fill the forms. He must count the heads. And when he goes, we will be as we are now. Seeking to survive another day."

Chapter Four

The sunset was spectacular. Even the elders emerged from their huts to observe the pyrotechnics. The volcano's plume became a fiery staff that challenged the heavens. To the southwest the descending ash formed a veil of glistening jewels.

Throughout the camp Marc could see people watching. The medical staff gathered by the screens and murmured softly. Marc could not make out any faces, but he noticed Kitra's slender form among them. Only Valerie, the French aid worker, remained unmoved by the sunset. Marc could see her sitting in the admin building.

The mess hall was a long lean-to attached to the bunkhouse. Marc ate dinner with the others, but remained isolated by more than the generator's constant grumble. Kitra ate with the medical personnel. The only time she showed an awareness of his presence was when one of the technicians stopped by Marc's table. Kitra smoldered the air with her expression.

After dinner Marc joined the drift toward the chapel. It was dark enough now for the candle by the sacristy to offer a soft defiance to the shadows. Sergeant Kamal and two of his men came. Camp dwellers filled the pews and then pressed in on all sides. The faces surrounding the chapel's perimeter gradually faded into the night.

Kitra and one of the other nurses were among the last to arrive. Marc noted with surprise as she joined in with the formal response and opening prayer. From her file Marc knew she was an Israeli Jew. He forced himself not to stare, and tried not to worry. For the file to miss such an important point left him worrying over what else might have been gone unnoticed.

Charles looked very regal in his white robes. He spoke every sentence first in Swahili, then in another native tongue, then in English. Marc prayed for a time and afterward stared over the heads of the parishioners at the southern reaches. The volcano painted a sullen red glow beyond the horizon. Now and then it emitted a deep rumble, a drumbeat more felt than heard.

He found himself thinking back to his last assignment, rescuing a group of Americans and an Iraqi who had been abducted in Baghdad. He recalled another dark-haired lady, with flashing eyes and a beautiful daughter and a heart big as the desert sky. Marc did not miss her so much as wish he had been ready to give what she had hoped to receive. But in the weeks that had followed his departure from Baghdad, he had come to realize he was not yet ready to love another woman. He no longer ached with the loss of his own wife. But as he sat and watched the Kenyan night envelop the gathering, he offered a silent prayer, asking God if he was ever meant to love again.

When the service ended, Marc waited until the last villager departed before approaching Charles. "I need to ask your help once more."

"Let me remove my robes, and I am ready." The service's formal tone remained in his voice. "Are you a believer?"

"I am."

"Then we are joined by more than concern for the people of this camp, yes?"

In the candle's dim glow, Charles resembled a mystic from some ancient age, only partly connected to the harsher realities of here and now. "I'd like to think so."

Sergeant Kamal chose that moment to emerge from the shadows. Charles listened to the man's rough burr, then translated, "The sergeant says he has a problem and hopes you can help."

"If I can, I will."

The pastor motioned them into the second pew. Marc seated himself next to Kamal while Charles slipped the white robes over his head and carefully folded them. His black T-shirt was stained with sweat. Marc asked, "Would it be impolite to ask how a sergeant commands a camp's guard?"

Charles seated himself so his legs extended into the aisle and he could face them. He spoke swiftly, then translated Kamal's response, "There were a captain and two lieutenants. All had families housed in the UN military compound on the volcano's eastern slope. They left to get their families to safety. They have not returned."

"His men are fortunate to have Kamal."

"As is the camp," Charles agreed.

Kamal nodded his thanks for the compliment and then launched into a longer discussion, which Charles translated, "He needs more men. Right now he has enough to patrol the central compound only. He keeps two men on the main gate, but otherwise the camp is not secure. The elders cannot maintain order in the camp without soldiers to give strength to their words."

"How many more does he need?"

Kamal responded before Charles had completed his translation. "Ten for perimeter patrol. Twenty for the camp. Split into units of five."

"I'll see what I can do." When Kamal started to rise, Marc said, "We have another problem, one that cannot wait."

As Marc described his discussion with the elders about the dangers the women are facing, Kamal's features took on a bitter cast. He replied, "We have suspected this. But without more support, there is little we can do."

Marc said, "I have a plan."

Marc used the rudimentary shower, then dressed once more in the same sweat-stained clothes. He selected an empty bunk in the men's chamber, stowing his carryall in the trunk at the bed's foot. A lone ceiling bulb burned midway down the central aisle. Five ceiling fans drifted in lazy circles. Marc pulled the mosquito net around his bed and lay down. He could smell the bitter odor of disinfectant and hear bugs strike the screen by his head. In the distance, the generator chugged. Gradually the day's tension released him. He watched the fan's lazy orbit until he fell asleep.

The night was strong and black when Kamal touched his shoulder. Marc slipped from the bed and followed him from the bunkhouse. They were joined by two other soldiers and Charles. Five was the standard number for nightly patrols. Any more would attract attention. Marc had disliked the idea of bringing the pastor along. But his plan required a translator.

They took the central road and padded toward the main gate. Their boots squeaked softly in the ash. There was no moon. The camp was draped in a gentle myth of calm. Somewhere to his left a baby cried. Marc saw no one, but felt eyes on him at all times.

Marc had no idea if the soldiers could be relied on. He disliked entering an ops situation with an unknown team. His life could well depend on them following orders. The sergeant seemed trustworthy enough. But Marc had only observed him within the central compound's relative safety. If they faced a free-fire situation, which he imagined they probably would, he would have to take great care.

They collected the two men on gate duty as they passed. At a signal from Kamal, they left the road and drifted into the woods. The trees all appeared dead to Marc, the limbs leafless and silver-gray in the starlight. But Marc had been in other arid places. He knew how such vegetation adapted to the absence of water. When rain fell once more, the entire world could flash into colorful and abundant life. Marc followed in Kamal's footsteps, ducking under the occasional limb, and thought how much his own life resembled this landscape. Blanketed by ashes of regret and loss, waiting for that faint blessing of rain. Waiting.

They were in position before the first light of dawn touched the east. The volcano's rumble seemed stronger out beyond the camp's relative safety, a noise filled with anger and phlegm, like the earth was clearing its throat. Kamal handed out energy bars and encouraged his men to drink. The two men off gate duty looked very tired after a night without sleep. But they joined in the soft banter and showed Marc feral grins. Wanting him to know they were ready.

Kamal squatted down on Charles's other side. His voice was a soft whisper, the sound of a hunting cat waiting on prey. Charles translated, "He misses the birdsong at dawn."

"It is quiet," Marc agreed.

"The birds and the rest of the game began leaving four years ago, when the rains failed. Each year the dawns have grown quieter."

"Four years without rain."

"Yes, so long. Now, with the volcano, the elders ask if the land will ever live again."

"Your family are farmers?"

"Since the time before time." Charles's translation matched the sergeant's rolling plainsong. "On a plateau above the Rift. We grow millet, corn, melons. Even a few almond trees. Some coffee. Good land."

"And yet you became a soldier."

Kamal flashed a rare grin. He was the only one of the team whose smile did not come easily. "One can love the land and not the life."

"There is much wisdom in what you say."

"Someday I will go back. Raise fat babies. The land is good for children."

"I wish you success with your dream."

"And you? What is the dream of a Western man in Africa?"

"To be here."

Kamal's hand swept slowly over the vista of dawn-lit ash. "I am thinking yours is a strange dream, to stand in the shadow of doom. I mean no offense."

"None taken." It became increasingly easy to ignore the pastor's translations. The American and the sergeant spoke in a cadence that was both friendly and extremely African. "I meant, I wish to be here. Helping others. Doing good in dangerous times. It is where I feel most alive."

One of Kamal's men hissed a soft warning. Charles confirmed, "Here they come."

Chapter Five

The slender shapes only took on true form when they were close enough for Marc to hear their voices. The women spoke anxiously, like the chirp of dawn birds. There were several dozen of them, most in their early teens. They remained close together, not quite touching, their fear evident in their unsteady gaits.

The elders had done their job well. The previous evening, Marc and Charles and Kamal had approached them and explained the plan. How they needed a number of young women to go out with the dawn, enough from various parts of the camp to attract attention. The elders had responded with only two questions, and one command. The questions had been, would Kamal give his solemn oath to protect the young women, and would the American be with them. The command had been, only use their firearms as a last resort. Kamal had balked at the order, but the elders had remained adamant. Guns had decimated their world and way of life. Unless some attackers fired first, there would be no guns. Reluctantly Kamal had agreed. His men would carry only pistols, and keep them holstered.

Behind the girls came a second group, moving slowly. In

the gathering light, Marc saw that many were little more than children. With them came the widows. The old women set the pace, some leaning heavily on the young ones.

And behind them lurked the wolves.

Marc saw them rise up like phantom beasts on two legs. Kamal hissed to his men and pointed.

The closest girl heard Kamal and froze in the process of picking up a dead branch, her eyes wide and glistening in the gray dawn. To Marc she appeared like a nymph of a mythic age. Their eyes locked. Her defenseless terror gripped him so tightly his rage ignited.

Then one of the small girls in the second group spotted the predators and squealed.

"Now!" Marc rose and bolted forward. The young girl screamed, but he was already past her, threading his way through the group, heading for danger.

Kamal appeared at his right, flying gazelle-like, his boots pushing up tiny clouds of ash. The sergeant found the breath to shout an order. Marc assumed he was telling his men to spread out.

The wolves paused, caught off guard by the soldiers' sudden appearance. Two attackers bolted for the camp and safety. But that still left a far larger group than Marc's paltry band. The leader of the gang yelled words that required no translation. Marc took aim straight at him.

The leader crouched in hungry anticipation and yelled a second time. His voice was hoarse. His two closest mates took up station on either side. Marc's initial thought was confirmed. These were not merely young toughs. They were either former soldiers or criminals. They were trained for the assault.

But they did not appear to be armed. Which was as Marc had expected. Why bear guns when their prey was simply women from the camp? To carry arms would mean revealing themselves to the guards by the gate.

Two of the attackers facing Marc hefted staves from the deadwood littering the ground. The leader motioned at Marc and crooned softly. His mates laughed and whistled and made smacking sounds.

Marc knew they expected him to hesitate, to show caution at their greater numbers. Instead, he bulled straight in. There was a brief instant when surprise registered on the leader's face, a tightening of the skin, a warping of the scar rising from his jawline. Then Marc struck.

He slipped easily under the right-hand attacker's swing. He was then too close for the staves to do any good, as they risked striking one of their own. He uncoiled so fast the leader probably did not even see the two strikes, a fist to the point over his heart and another to the jaw's hinge. The man was unconscious before he was fully aware of having been hit.

Marc used the leader's body as a shield against the left-hand attacker, and aimed a kick for the most vulnerable point, the throat. He let the leader drop and twisted the stave from the attacker's fumbling hands.

Swinging around, his entire body a whip, he aimed a blow at the now-uncertain man to his right. The attacker blocked the strike with his own stick, but barely. Marc did not care. The important thing was to have this man also become aware of the ferocity he faced. Fear would do the rest.

Marc channeled his momentum and recoiled back around. He rapped the man to his left on the forehead, then spun a second time, aiming at a new attacker. But this man had already given up the fight. He tried to flee, but Marc leaped and tapped his rear ankle, tripping him. Marc bounded forward and rapped the man's head.

Only then did he become aware of the din that surrounded him. Women screaming, men shouting and struggling, the dawn obliterated by clouds of swirling ash. Marc stepped over and assisted Kamal in dispatching his third adversary, and together they hurried to shield one of Kamal's men who was down.

And then it was over.

They brought their captives back to the camp roped in a long line. Marc and Charles walked at the head, Kamal at the rear. Villagers gathered about both sides of the camp's main road and shouted, especially the women. A few made as to strike the men, some raised sticks and plucked rocks from the ash. At a signal from Marc, Kamal and his men forced the camp dwellers to keep their distance.

The roped captives were settled in the dust before the empty godown. Guards were posted, mostly to keep the villagers from attacking. Marc watched as Kitra approached the men and examined their wounds. Marc knew the Israeli nurse expected him to order her away. But he liked her compassionate care, shown even to these brutal men. There was a rock-solid core to this woman. Marc left the prisoners under her care and the soldiers' supervision. He took a long shower, then dropped into the bunk and shut the mosquito netting. The last image he had before the night's burdens pushed his eyelids down was Kamal grunting his way into the bunk next to his.

He awoke in the early afternoon, famished. Kamal was already gone. Marc rose and went in search of food. He found a grinning cook, who offered Marc all he had ready, a bowl of gruel sweetened by lumps of brown sugar and condensed milk. It was one of the finest meals Marc had ever eaten.

Marc recharged his tin mug and returned to the compound. The captives were slumped in a circle, surrounded by women who eyed them with the patience of vultures.

Charles found him there and indicated that the elders wished to speak with him. Marc followed the pastor through the ring of villagers. As before, the men were seated in the open space encircled by their huts. The same clay pot of rancid brew was passed around. The oldest leader, a true ancient with skin more yellow than brown, asked through Charles if Marc would care for a pipe. He declined. If the elders were aware of the oppressive heat, they gave no sign. Marc sat on his little stool and flicked his hand at the flies and waited.

Finally the youngest of them spoke. Philip was dressed like the others, in a motley collection of western clothing and bare feet. But his eyes were bright, his voice deep and direct. Charles translated, "Philip wishes to know what you intend to do with the prisoners."

"Is he the leader here?"

Charles did not translate his words for the elders. Instead, he replied, "Philip is both a chief of his tribe and a district chief. The regional chiefs are appointed by the government in Nairobi. Unlike many regional leaders, Philip is honest. What is more, he does not put the interests of his own tribe above the others represented here. Because he is the youngest, and because the region has been destroyed, his position could be a matter of great conflict. But these elders respect and honor him. As do I."

Marc nodded that he understood. "Please tell him that I would welcome his counsel."

Philip spoke, and Charles translated, "Tradition says you must give these attackers to the women who have been wronged."

Marc replied firmly, "That will not happen."

The chief showed no anger at being refused. If anything, he seemed to approve of Marc's response. "The women expect it. As do some of the elders."

"I am sorry. But these among you are going to be disappointed."

One of the other elders muttered, but Charles found no need to translate it. Marc asked, "You say his name is Philip?"

"He became a believer, then led his entire family to Christ. Soon after, his parents were killed in a traffic accident. His father was a chief before him. Philip's conversion was a great scandal. But he himself called it a gift from heaven that helped him recover from the death of his parents and accept the call to take their place as chief."

Marc studied the young man seated across from him. There were distinct differences between the elders that went far deeper than merely the shades of their skin. Philip had the features of an ancient warrior, as though carved by a heritage that predated civilization.

Charles went on, "Philip is of the Luo tribe. His clan has always been animist. Not all the Luos, you understand. But all of his village. Philip did not order his clan to follow his choice, or expel the witch doctor. He built a church and then invited a missionary pastor and his wife to come live in their village. When the pastor objected to the witch doctor, Philip told him that their clan had worshiped the trees and the sky for over a thousand years. The pastor had been there for a month. So it would be up to the pastor and Philip and their families to live the message of Jesus, and let the people make up their own minds." Charles smiled. "Nine months later, the witch doctor moved away."

Marc met the chief's gaze. "So Philip too has gone against tradition over vital issues."

When Charles had translated, he responded with a question of his own. "Philip wishes to know if the Lord Jesus ordered you to come."

"I would like to think," Marc replied, "that Jesus guides my every step. But I am human enough to know that there is too much of me in everything I do."

This youngest of the elders studied Marc a long moment, then rose to his feet and offered Marc his hand. "Philip says that you should do with the prisoners as you see fit. He will speak with the women."

Chapter Six

Half an hour later, the women dispersed. One of the chief's wives had emerged and spoke softly with those gathered. Afterward the women simply drifted away, one by one, until only a few children and a homeless pie dog remained.

Marc soon noticed a distinct change to the compound's atmosphere. People were not especially friendly. This was, after all, a refugee camp in a time of severe crisis. But the central area and its personnel seemed to accept him as one of their own. The medical staff no longer took their cues from Kitra and froze him out. When he approached the empty godown where the soldiers had established their guard station, they made room for him with easy familiarity.

Soon after, the elders sent Marc the gift of a live chicken. The soldiers laughed so loud and hard they drew stares from the medical tent. The chicken was a scrawny beast with mangy gray feathers and fierce red eyes. The cook accepted it with a cheery offer to stew it all day and all night. The soldiers assured Marc it would remain tough and tasteless as boiled boot.

A nurse and a medical technician joined Marc for lunch. They fumbled through a discussion of the food and the camp in broken English. The nurse translated a sign over the access slot where food was served: *Eat! Drink! You need 2,000 calories and 3 liters of liquid each day to do your job!* Marc understood the sign's purpose. He also felt the guilt of being seated beneath rotating fans, eating hot food, drinking clean water while around him people faced the daily terror of starvation.

As the medical team left the dining hall, the technician called back through the screen wall and noise erupted from his mates. The nurse translated, "A UN chopper arrives."

"When?"

"Soon. Perhaps this evening, but more likely tomorrow. There are many camps to visit. They are excited because it brings mail and perhaps a new doctor." She gave a coquettish smile. "You will not be leaving us, I hope."

Marc thanked her and rose with the others. He headed for the one individual not looking his way. He would have liked to give Kitra more time to see him for what he was, not the company he represented. But he had no idea what change the inbound chopper might bring. This connection was suddenly urgent.

Kitra blanched at his approach. "Go away."

"We need to talk."

"You are the *enemy*."

A departing nurse called over a question in French.

Marc leaned in closer, ignoring how Kitra recoiled from him. "I'm here because of you. Your five emails and the phone messages about your missing brother. They got through."

Her loathing turned to fearful confusion. "What are you saying?"

"Your brother was not kidnapped by Lodestone. People have checked. From the inside. I'm here because we think his disappearance is tied to something much larger."

"Words," Kitra said. But the heat was gone from her eyes and her voice. "I have been lied to by so many. Better than you."

The nurse spoke again in French. Kitra glanced over, uncertain now, and waved the nurse away. Marc went on, "Think about what you have seen. I brought food. I helped get it to the people in need. I showed the elders and Charles respect. I have—"

"Serge was taken eight days ago. Why are you so long in coming?"

"Because we had to see if there was a link."

"So in truth you are not here for my brother." Her tone was hard. "You do not worry over him at all."

Marc slid into the seat opposite her. "Think about it. I have been inserted into a critical situation. After an investigation that has stretched across three continents. No matter how much you love your brother, even you have to accept that more is at stake than one man's disappearance."

"I am still thinking you are the enemy." But the words held a dullness, as though she was repeating a mental litany that had lost all meaning. "A wolf trying to bleat like a lamb."

Marc waited.

She stared out beyond the screen entry, then said, "We will go and sit where the others can see. And you will tell me why I should trust you, even a little."

The wind picked up as they rounded the dining hall, blowing straight from the north. They sat by the baobab tree that dominated the compound's rear area. Giant roots protruded from the earth, forming an irregular circle of benches. Kitra made a process of selecting her place. Marc stood where he could be clearly seen by everyone inside the medical facility.

"What do you intend to do with the prisoners?"

"I am open to suggestions."

"You must move them into the shade. Give them food and water."

Marc turned and walked to the empty godown. Charles was away somewhere inside the camp. But Kamal caught the meaning of Marc's gestures and ordered his men into action. The attackers, reduced to limp submission, were resettled inside the godown's shade and offered canteens. Marc returned to the tree.

Kitra greeted him with, "Why you?"

Marc took that as an invitation, and settled himself on a root facing the woman. "Recently I helped rescue other kidnap victims."

"Here in Kenya?"

"No. They were taken in Baghdad. We recovered them in Iran."

She somehow managed to shrink further inside herself, a dark-haired woman enclosed in a fist of grief and loss. "Is this a joke?"

"I'm not suggesting your brother's disappearance is the same. I'm just trying to say that I'm good at my job."

"I'm afraid to trust you." Her words were softer than the wind rushing through the leaves overhead. "I'm afraid to hope."

Kitra's expressive features and thick hair lent her a distinctly Mediterranean flair. Her eyes were rounded by tragedy so great she looked perpetually ready to weep, if only she could find more tears.

Marc hesitated, then quoted, "'What good is it, my brothers and sisters, if someone claims to have faith but has no deeds? Can such faith save them?'"

Kitra looked at him. Really looked.

He went on, "You and your brother are here living your faith through deeds. So am I. Sooner or later you are going to have to accept the fact that I'm not your foe. There is too much evidence to the contrary."

"But you work for Lodestone."

"For the past two weeks."

A single tear emerged and trickled down her cheek. He had not noticed how her skin bore a faint sheen of ash until the tear washed a channel clean. "And before that?"

Marc stretched out his legs. "It's a long story."

Chapter Seven

After Baghdad, Marc's life never went back to normal. In fact, Marc decided the best way to handle his situation was to stop trying to define what normal was.

For eight months after returning from Iraq, Marc lived in a state of limbo. He was officially on interim leave from the Baltimore accounting group. But only because Ambassador Walton had ordered it. Marc thought he would return to State Department Intel, where he had been before his wife's illness. Before Walton had fired him for taking unpaid leave. Before Marc had nursed his wife and then buried her. Before he'd meandered through days devoid of hope and purpose and passion. Before he'd woken up and rediscovered life again. In Baghdad.

As far as the other members of his accounting firm were concerned, Marc remained buried deep in some faceless Washington building, handling a chore so toxic that the full-time GAO accountants refused to touch it. The story planted by Walton's minions was so effective, Marc's Baltimore co-workers waited expectantly for his ultimate failure.

Marc had indeed been kept busy. Upon arriving back from Baghdad, Walton had dragged him to debriefings in the

Pentagon, the OEOB, Langley, even one in the White House basement. None of the attendees had ever been named. Marc had remained sequestered in one hallway after another, then brought in and questioned and dismissed. The one time he had asked Walton who they were, the ambassador had simply replied, "Deniability, son. It's all important in this day and age."

When his debriefings were completed, Marc had been sent out for refresher courses at Fort Benning's FLETSE training grounds—covert intelligence practices, surveillance, black ops, armed and unarmed combat, latest intel technology. After that, he had spent three months in the State Department warren known as the Iraq Desk. Then had come an unexpected, and unexplained, surprise; Marc spent ten weeks with the East Africa analysts at Langley. Every week or so, Walton checked in by phone, never for more than a minute. Just letting Marc know he was not forgotten.

Five weeks earlier, in the hour before dawn, all this had changed.

That morning, Marc had been contemplating a possible leap from the grid, Intel-speak for going rogue. Marc was increasingly tempted by the idea of leaving the safety of official duty and working for an independent contractor. He was tired of playing a cog in someone else's machine, waiting for the unseen hand to reach out and wind him up. He had been telling himself for weeks that it was time to take the jump. If only he could convince himself it was true.

The cellphone's buzz had cut short his internal debate. When Marc answered, Walton said, "I need you."

"When?"

"The car is downstairs." Walton cut the connection. Ever the conversationalist.

Marc took his time. He stretched and showered and shaved. He made coffee and drank a cup. He left the house just as his cellphone buzzed again. He did not bother answering.

The driver waited for Marc to slip in beside him, passed over a manila folder, and pulled from the curb. The only words he spoke were, "You have eighty minutes to memorize the file."

When they entered predawn Washington and turned onto Sixteenth Street, Marc wondered if they were headed for the White House. But they pulled up to the Hay Adams Hotel, where another dark-suited agent, a female this time, spoke into her wrist mike before telling Marc, "Suite six-nineteen."

The hotel was quiet. Two weary custodians pushed vacuum cleaners. The concierge glanced his way, noted the agent dogging Marc's steps, and returned to his computer screen. This close to the center of power, the arrival of another hard-faced staffer was not interesting.

The suite was a lovely rendition of the hotel's earliest days, when presidents slipped away from the new White House to smoke cigars and talk power off-the-record. The elm wainscoting glowed warmly; the parquet floors creaked a comfortable welcome. The high ceiling was domed and frescoed and crowned by a crystal chandelier.

A third agent ushered Marc into the parlor and slipped from the room.

Only when the door shut behind the departing agent did Walton say, "This meeting is not taking place."

"Understood, sir."

"Have a seat." Ambassador Walton had grown stouter in

the months since Marc had last seen him. The age spots on his bald pate were larger. The skin folded over his starched collar, and the voice was reedy. Only his gaze was the same, gray and fierce and laser-sharp. "Coffee and such at your elbow."

"I'm good, sir."

"This gentleman has a problem." Walton's cuff link flashed as he motioned to the stranger and said, "It's your show."

"I'm head of UN Internal Security, based in New York, with a second office in Geneva," the man began. "My team has been placed in an impossible situation. The ambassador thinks you may be able to help."

The man's accent was subtle, his English excellent. Marc's first impression was German; then he decided that was wrong. Dutch, perhaps, or Danish. His fluency suggested a combination of early years in this country and a natural gift with other tongues.

"I direct a component of the United Nations security. On paper, we have a large remit and almost unlimited authority. In reality we have become caged by protocol and a lack of funds."

Only when the man rose and began pacing did Marc realize how tall he was. Marc guessed his height at somewhere around seven feet. He favored his left leg, but at the same time paid it no mind, which suggested a well-healed wound that had simply become a part of who he was.

"Recently we have become aware of a possible internal problem. Corruption, bribery, collusion."

"All the things which, if revealed, would add ammunition to those who want America to withdraw from participating in the UN at all," Walton interjected.

"We have no direct evidence," the tall UN security chief

went on. "But it appears that someone with very real power is directing lucrative supply contracts to a corporate ally in return for kickbacks."

Marc named the group in the manila file he had left with the limo driver. "Lodestone Associates."

"Lodestone is a major provider of armed security services. They have an excellent reputation for training police forces. Another division has been involved for over a decade in supplementing UN security details when we become over-stretched. Three years ago they acquired a third group. Mede-vac helicopters, field hospitals, personnel. Last year they added a fourth."

"Emergency relief supplies," Marc said, mostly to let the man know he was on the same page.

"This is a logical move. They have the connections. Their forces are often first on the ground. They know the players, the people who would issue the contracts."

"But you suspect something."

"Their growth rate is astounding. In the ten months since Lodestone acquired the supply group, they have increased turnover almost tenfold."

When the man went silent, Walton said, "Tell him the rest."

The man slipped back into his chair. He picked up the injured leg and dropped it over his other knee. The chandelier took the sharp angles of his face and created deep caverns. Marc liked the man's strength, his disregard for his own dis-comfort. He said, "Now we are moving from what we know to what we fear."

"I understand."

"We have received some very troubling rumors from our

allies in the field. Lodestone may not be satisfied with merely winning new contracts. They may be attempting something far worse."

"Such as?"

"We have no idea."

Walton said, "One division helping another to gain new business is standard tactics."

"Not if their business is built upon graft and corruption," the man barked. "Not on my watch."

Walton offered Marc a tight smile. Marc nodded agreement. This man was one of their own.

"We suspect that Lodestone has become involved in other, more nefarious operations. Netting them hundreds of millions of dollars."

He stumbled slightly on that word, *nefarious*. Marc decided the man was definitely Dutch. "I don't get it," Marc said. "If they're involved in such huge ventures, it doesn't make sense that they'd worry about medical supplies."

"Explain," Walton demanded.

"The risk of discovery is the same. But if they're caught at this smaller game, they give you a reason to question their larger enterprises."

"I happen to agree with you," the man said to Marc. "And I wonder if perhaps more than medical supplies are involved in this new operation."

"They could use the legitimate operations to hide something dirty," Marc said. "What evidence do you have?"

"None. We do not know for certain what Lodestone is after."

The man rubbed a spot on his wounded leg, six inches above the knee. The trouser leg indented deeply. Marc decided it was a bullet wound. The man had taken a hit to his thigh, and come back. Marc said, "But you suspect."

"We prefer not to discuss what could be total speculation," the man replied. "We would prefer an outsider to go in with no preconceived notions."

Marc gave voice to what the man was probably thinking. "To maintain a major illegal operation over time, they will need protection from within the procurement system. Someone high up inside the UN may be shielding their activities from view. If they are indeed involved in illegal activities."

The security chief studied Marc intently. "What would you suggest we do?"

"Plant someone inside Lodestone. If a number of divisions are involved in an illegal operation, there's bound to be a trail."

The man lifted his gaze and spoke directly to Walton for the first time. "I concur with your assessment of this gentleman. He is precisely what we are after."

"Told you he was good," Walton muttered.

The man said to Marc, "You will be fitted into Lodestone's new humanitarian-supply division as an accountant. One of their principal subcontractors will suggest you as a field officer of merit. This division has outstripped Lodestone's current field staff. They are actively recruiting."

"Where am I going?"

"We have recently received word of an abduction. The missing man, Serge Korban, is an Israeli medical technician assigned to a French-run refugee camp in western Kenya. So far as we have been able to determine, Serge Korban has no direct connection to Lodestone. But his sister has repeatedly insisted that Lodestone is behind his disappearance."

"There's more," Walton said.

"There has to be," Marc agreed. "For the White House to have an interest, we've got to be talking about more than another case of bureaucratic corruption, no matter how big."

The unnamed security chief said, "We are hearing rumors of an international smuggling operation."

"One that could have serious implications for U.S. interests," Walton added. "At the highest level."

"Our problem," the security chief went on, "is that at present we have no hard evidence. None whatsoever."

Walton said, "We think it would be best for you to go in with an open mind. Check into this situation without bias."

"See if your findings tally with what we are hearing," the security chief added. "We simply want you to see if there is any evidence of wrongdoing, and what possible connection Lodestone might have to this Israeli's disappearance."

"Why aren't the Israelis involved?"

"Officially, they are," Walton replied. "A complaint has been lodged, both by their embassy in Nairobi and from the government in Tel Aviv. But nothing more."

"Which is understandable," the security chief said. "The only indication we have of wrongdoing comes from his sister. Kitra Korban serves as a nurse in the same camp from which Serge was abducted. We have also received a rather vague confirmation from our field agent."

"Can I make contact with your source?"

"Most certainly," the man replied, going grimmer still. "If only we could locate him. But he has been missing now for a week, and we fear the worst. I urge you to take great caution, Mr. Royce. Whatever it is Lodestone hides, they value it far more than the odd human life."

Chapter Eight

The next morning began with a dawn service in the make-shift chapel. The singing and the children were a joyful accompaniment to the sunrise. Kitra sat as usual on the front pew, silent and withdrawn through it all. Later on, Marc stood alongside the elders as the chief expelled the attackers. It seemed as though the entire camp joined together to make their trudging departure a walk of shame. He asked Charles, "Where will they go?"

Charles and Kamal shared bitter humor before Charles replied, "Kibera, most likely."

"Where's that?"

"A Nairobi slum. A terrible place." Charles blended his translation with Kamal's quietly spoken words. "Where they belong. Kibera has many gangs. They will be among their own kind."

Following the expulsion, Kamal's men fanned out, carrying a message from Marc and the elders. It was the first time soldiers had ventured through the camp since the volcano's eruption. They walked in pairs, their rifles slung. Marc was after strong men and women who were respected by their own, young people who resisted the temptation to give their anger free reign. Who yearned for more, even if they could not name the desire. That was how he had described it to the elders. He sought young people who could be trusted with the lives of the camp's citizens.

The elders brought their stools into the empty godown's shade and became part of the selection process. One of the wives brought out an extra stool. Philip motioned for Marc to make himself comfortable. At his signal, Kamal lined up the young people in two groups, male and female, and stamped the dust with his worn boots, barking out the questions Marc had asked him to demand of each person. Charles walked over to stand alongside Marc and translated. Marc did not speak. He pretended to study each person in turn. But in truth he wanted Charles and Kamal and the elders to make the choices. He hoped these people, and the other watching eyes, would begin to work together as one group.

During the selection process, Philip asked through Charles, "How many do we seek?"

Marc shook his head. "Perhaps we should use the guidance of a better man," he replied. "Twelve men and twelve women."

Philip revealed a rare smile and turned back to the selection process.

Afterward the chosen young people carted out all the boxes of forms from the admin building. The French aid worker squawked a bit, then retreated to her bunk and blew smoke at the ceiling fan. The group built a bonfire that illuminated a growing number of faces. The camp stood and watched the flames devour box after box of the hated forms. Only when the fire died to glowing embers did they turn away.

Marc ordered the two teams to issue foodstuffs and ensure that no family tried to obtain a double portion. Doing this

cemented both their authority and his own. And it freed up
Kamal's men to make regular patrols.

They were still at it when the chapel bell chimed for the
evening service. Marc was moving toward the open-sided
chapel when he heard a phone ring inside the admin hut.
Valerie answered what Marc assumed was the satellite phone.
A few moments later, the screen door opened. The woman
stepped onto the front stoop and gestured to him with the
bulky apparatus.

Valerie handed him the phone and said, "Now we will see."

Marc watched her disappear inside the admin hut's shadows.
"This is Royce."

"Frederick Uhuru here. Have you heard of me?"

"Sorry, no."

"Well, I have heard of you, young man. First from the aid
worker—what is her name?"

"Valerie."

"Yes, that one. Your camp was run by some very good people,
but they are now dealing with the crisis at another camp. You
have heard this already, yes? Then I heard from your medical
administrator. I have heard from this gentleman three times
now. He wanted to be certain that Valerie was not the only
voice speaking about you. His opinion of you is very high, Mr.
Royce. And growing higher by the hour."

"That's good to know."

"I am the UN administrator for this district. I was expecting
to be with you today. That will not be possible."

"Understood, sir."

The man had a good African voice, rich and deep, with a
timbre that made him sound ready to burst into song at any

moment. "I need you to stay on the job there, Mr. Royce. Do you understand what I am saying? I do not have administrative control over your movements. This is not an order. But I am officially requesting your assistance."

Marc listened as voices rose in song from the chapel, a distinctly African lilt that merged with the heat and the sunset. "I am happy to help out, sir."

"Do you have access to a map?"

"Just a second." Marc opened the screen door and stepped inside. Valerie was in the room to his right, stretched out on her bunk. She read a paperback book whose pages were so limp with sweat and the touch of many hands she could fold it back like a magazine. Marc crossed to the map on the office wall. "I'm looking at a detailed chart of this region."

Frederick Uhuru said, "Can you locate Camp Echo?"

The sat phone was bulky and fit oddly in his hand. The stubby antenna was as thick as his forefinger and the length of his hand. The entire apparatus weighed almost a pound, like a cellphone from the eighties. "Sorry, sir. I couldn't even tell you where my own camp is situated."

The phone's reception was good enough for Marc to hear the pleasure in Frederick Uhuru's laugh. "Ask the young lady for her assistance."

But before Marc could speak, Valerie walked into the main room, gave him a smoldering look, then stabbed the map with one finger. Marc watched her slouch back into the bunkroom, thinking that her ability to look attractive even when sullen was a distinctly French attribute. "Okay, sir. I'm centered correctly."

"Camp Echo is twenty-two kilometers to the south by east of your location. It should be marked."

"I have a yellow pin in that approximate position, but no name."

"Camp Echo is run by the Swiss Red Cross. Their supplies have been held up in Mombasa Harbor. It is my understanding that they are approaching starvation."

"We're hoping to receive a new supply shipment tomorrow."

"I have heard this also. I want you to share your provisions with them, Mr. Royce. Again, this is not an order. I can only give you my word that your company will be recompensed for their goods."

"Sir, payment is secondary here. If they need it and we have it, the goods are theirs."

The UN representative was silent for a long moment. "I shall look forward to making your acquaintance as soon as possible, Mr. Royce. In the meanwhile, it is a pleasure to have you on board. And, Mr. Royce?"

"Sir."

"Take care on the journey to Camp Echo. Bandits are active in your region. Uhuru out."

When Marc emerged from the admin building, Charles had concluded the evening service. The parishioners gradually dispersed, their voices melting into the gathering dusk. The western horizon was dappled with the final remnants of daylight. Marc remained where he was, surveying the shanties and their corrugated roofs. He listened to a child sing somewhere in the distance, the voice rising and falling in a distinctly un-Western cadence. Then he heard a growing rumble, a grinding of gears, and the tinny sound of a blaring radio. As the first star appeared, a dust cloud rose to stain the sky, and four heavily laden trucks pulled into the compound and halted.

The motors coughed and rattled and stopped. The engines ticked away the heat and stress of racing the night. The lead truck's door opened, and a weary driver beamed and laughed as Marc came trotting over. The driver gave an odd wave, unable to fully relax his grip on the wheel he no longer held.

That night and the next morning were spent dividing up the new shipment. Marc's teams of young people and Kamal's men and the medical staff all pitched in. Around midday, two empty trucks departed for the depot, with manifests for another load. Valerie hitched a ride. One of Kamal's men hoisted an overly cheerful salute as she departed.

When the two remaining trucks were loaded and the motors rumbling, Kitra and Charles emerged from the medical tent. Marc motioned for Kitra to join him in the lead truck.

As they passed through the front gates, he asked, "What can you tell me about your brother?"

Kitra pitched her voice loud enough to be heard above the engine. "Serge wanted to heal the land. That's all you need to know."

"He is also a believer? I mean—"

"I know what you mean, Mr. Royce. All my family are followers of Jesus."

"But you are Israeli, right?"

"Serge and I were both born at our kibbutz near Tel Aviv. My parents had emigrated, my mother from Paris, my father from Chicago."

"Serge is a doctor?"

"Electronic engineering. But he had trained as a medic in the IDF. You know this term?"

"The Israeli Defense Forces." Marc had worked with them on several assignments. "Good soldiers."

"Serge called them the best army in the world."

Marc heard the past tense and the hollow loss in her voice. "So you both volunteered to come help out here. Why Kenya?"

"Should Americans be the only people on earth who volunteer to help in foreign lands? Send out missionaries? Work with others at times of crises?"

Marc had the sense her words were masking something deeper. What that might be, or how he might uncover the hidden meaning, he could not tell. "I'm just trying to get a handle on what happened to him."

"Serge heard about villages being evacuated north of the volcano's eruption. But according to the lava flow, Serge was certain they were in no danger. The elders who arrived with the new flood of refugees confirmed this. Serge went to find out what was going on."

It was the first chance he'd had to see Kitra up close. Her green eyes were so dark they appeared almost black in the shade, but became translucent in the sunlight. It was a remarkable transformation, as though two sides of her nature were revealed in her gaze. Kitra was too strong a woman to be called beautiful in any classical sense. A vibrant energy radiated from her. As their truck lumbered and swayed, every brush of her arm created sparks. Or so it felt to him. Kitra gave no sign she either noticed or cared.

Kitra went on, "Serge suspected that corrupt bureaucrats were using this latest disaster as an excuse for a land grab. Ever since the national elections three years ago, the Kenyan power structure has been rushing to take advantage of the chaos and line its pockets. Serge assumed it was just more of the same."

"Your brother sounds like one amazing guy."

For some reason, his words finally released the tears. Kitra wiped dusty streaks across her face and struggled to keep her tone steady. "Serge lived to give voice to the voiceless. It was his defining trait. I'm certain that's why he was made to disappear. He tried to protect the innocent. He asked the wrong question. He made an enemy of the wrong man."

Marc's mini-convoy required three hours to cover the twenty-two kilometers. The terrain turned hilly for the last five miles, the going increasingly rugged. They held to tracks or game trails or, on a few occasions, simply cut across open fields. The roads were rivers of humanity and beasts, all headed in the opposite direction. The savannah was populated by giant acacia trees, their distinctive flat tops shaped like living tables.

At the crest of one rise, Kitra asked the driver to stop. She climbed down and motioned for Marc to join her. Far to the south rose the lone mountain crowned by fire. The volcano's smoke was a giant stain upon the arid blue sky. To his left, refugees crowding the highway formed a single dusty line, as though an entire nation was on the move.

Kitra pointed to the east. "That was where Serge was taken."

Where she pointed, a trio of candelabra trees flanked a deserted village. The towering trees and the vacated huts were chalky with ash. There were no animals save a few vultures. No sound save the wind, and a far-off rumble, soft and constant. Marc asked, "How can you be sure?"

"He called me. I insisted that he take the medical clinic's sat phone, in case his truck broke down."

The village was a cluster of huts blanketed by cinders. A central open space was flanked by two longer buildings, like meeting halls, or perhaps the residence of a chief. "Tell me what he said."

"He had just finished meeting the village elders. Serge called me to say a district chief had shown up. You know this term?"

"Like Philip."

"No, Marc Royce. Not like Philip at all. If all the district chiefs were like Philip, this land would be thriving, despite the drought and the volcano."

"Charles said there was a problem with other regional leaders."

"Charles knows what he is talking about. Many district chiefs bribe their way into the offices. They come to make money off these poor villages. Serge said that the chief who arrived was very angry that Serge was there, and furious when he heard about the questions Serge was asking." Her voice was very bleak. "Since then, I have heard nothing."

"Why did you accuse Lodestone of being behind the abduction?"

Her gaze was fierce. "Because he said that the chief came with a squad of mercenaries. He was very certain of this. Not UN soldiers, and not Kenyan. Private security."

Marc reluctantly confirmed, "Lodestone is the only group operating security personnel in Kenya."

"Yes. I know that. I checked."

"We need to find that chief."

"I've spoken with the only elder I could find from that

village. He claims the district chief has never visited them. Not once."

"Does that make sense to you?"

Kitra shrugged, the weight of too many unanswered questions pressing on her. "Serge would not have made it up. That is all I can say for certain."

"What else did Serge tell you?"

"Serge said the man who confronted him positively stank with greed."

When she stopped, Marc pressed, "I need to hear the rest."

"As he was saying that, the line went silent. The phone was still connected, I could hear him breathing. I called his name. Then he whispered that the mercs were hunting him."

"He said that? Specifically?"

The hand that swept the hair from her face trembled. "His exact words were, 'The mercs are tracking me. I just heard them ask where the Israeli was hiding. Two Anglos, six African.' He said they were coming his way. He said to tell our father . . ." She swiped her face. "Then nothing. Until now, nothing."

"You've tried to phone him back?"

"Of course I've tried. Morning and night I've called his line." The anger turned her voice coppery. "Lodestone stole my brother."

"You don't know that." His protest sounded weak to his own ears.

"Oh, but I do. And I am still frightened that I might be putting my trust in the enemy." She shut her eyes to the thought, and murmured, "What I would give to taste a clean wind."

Chapter Nine

They arrived at the Red Cross camp in the early afternoon. The first sign they had of their destination was a pair of flags dangling limply against a pale blue sky. As the gates came into view, Kitra pointed out a collection of huts near the entrance.

"Lebanese traders," she explained. "They hear when a camp is starving. They flock like carrion to rotting meat. When the refugees grow desperate enough, they will sell whatever they have, including children."

The Lebanese trading posts were flanked by armed guards, all of whom scowled as the trucks appeared. Refugees standing in front of the huts reached out in supplication as the trucks rumbled past.

Kitra explained, "This camp started during the AIDS crisis. Just as they brought that under control, the region was hit by a blight called black sigatoka. It devastated the two main staples, plantain and banana. Both crops will feed a family from a small patch of land, and both were vulnerable to the same disease. No one had ever heard of it before. In two years it wiped out every farm in this entire district."

The Red Cross administrators were pitifully glad to see

them. The camp director could not hold back his tears as they off-loaded the boxes of Plumpy Nut and cooking oil and sacks of mealy grain.

Marc left the others to finish unloading and started listing everything the administrator wanted with their next shipment. He did the same with the chief medic. Kitra approached him twice, both times to urge him to greater speed. They did not want to be caught in open territory after sunset. The bandits, she insisted, would not know the trucks were empty.

They reached the forest fronting their own camp's main gates just as the sunset was fading. Fatigue had long rendered them all silent. Marc had visions of a hot meal, a drink of water that did not taste of the road, a shower, and bed. But when the camp came into view, Marc knew that was not happening. Parked before the main gates was a United Nations helicopter, the white paint glowing almost gold in the dusk.

As they approached the chopper, Marc finally asked the question he had carried all the way back. "Why risk trusting me at all?"

Kitra turned from the dusty lane leading to the camp's heart, and replied, "Because you know no fear. Just like Serge."

He did not know how to respond.

"No, that is not correct. Serge was different. He was fearless because he was happy." The admission brought fresh pain. "He was defined by joy. And you, Marc Royce? What are you defined by?"

He did not wait for the truck to halt before climbing down.

Kamal stepped through the camp gates and said through Charles that the UN officials were with the camp elders. They assumed Marc and his team would be exhausted and had suggested they all meet in the mess hall. Marc rode into the central compound with Kamal standing on the truck's running board.

The water from the overhead cistern was blood-warm and soothing. He drained the tank, then dressed in fresh clothes and headed for the mess hall. He was standing behind Kitra in the buffet line as the screen door slapped open and a beaming burly man entered. "Marc Royce!"

"That's me."

"Stand easy, Mr. Royce. I know all about how tired a day on the road can leave you." He offered Marc a hand the size of a spade. "Frederick Uhuru. UN district administrator. May I join you?"

"Sure thing."

"Let us take this table by the window." The UN administrator was huge and solid. He was also clearly tired. Weariness and old sweat made his broad features appear almost greased. He wore a blue shirt with the UN insignia over the pocket, and navy trousers. A pair of young aides planted themselves by the side wall as Uhuru settled onto the bench opposite Marc. "The elders have some grand things to say about you and your methods, Mr. Royce. They are normally reluctant to speak of strangers. So reluctant, in fact, I am left with the distinct impression that you are a stranger no more." Uhuru's deep voice carried a lilting formality as he turned and waved over a group of newcomers. "Your camp's new batch of administrators arrived at HQ just as we were departing. We offered them a lift."

The UN administrator rattled off introductions, and Marc shook their hands, though his weary brain could not keep hold of their names.

Uhuru asked, "How would you describe the situation at the Red Cross camp, Mr. Royce?"

"Just as you told me on the phone. Organized starvation."

"Can your group supply both camps?"

"Not with what we have in Lodestone's Nairobi warehouses. I spoke with our HQ on the return journey."

"The Mombasa port is in a state of absolute chaos. Ten times the normal ship traffic has jammed the waterway. Mountains of goods wait to be off-loaded. And once they are, the roads are nearly impassable because of the refugees. Your people have transport helicopters, do they not?"

"Yes." Marc had toured the Lodestone hangar during his seven days in Nairobi. "And fixed-wing transport designed for short takeoffs and landings in the bush."

"Splendid." He lifted himself from the bench far enough to extract a ratty map from his pocket. "There are three more camps in this vicinity that face similar straits, Mr. Royce. I want you to take temporary responsibility for getting them supplies. They are here to the northeast. Your nearest landing strip is here in Eldora, the district capital. There was formerly another strip at the base of Mount Elgon, but it is lost beneath a blanket of volcanic ash. I know; I flew over it this morning."

Uhuru raised his hand and a young aide instantly handed over a pen and blank document. "I am hereby authorizing you to fly in sufficient supplies to keep these camps operational for the next ten days. No, let us be realistic and make it the next three weeks. And don't forget medical supplies, will you, Mr. Royce?"

Marc watched the man print out the instructions and knew he was being handed a blank check. "Absolutely not."

"Be sure and include as many Plumpy Nut packets as you have in stock. I am seeing too many children with swollen bellies. And I dislike that among my children. I dislike that intensely." Uhuru signed the document with a flourish, then ponderously pushed himself from the table. "Be so good as to accompany me, Mr. Royce."

As they left the mess hall, Kitra remained seated in the far corner, isolated by the shadows. She lifted her head and gave Marc a silent plea. Marc nodded once in reply and followed Uhuru into the dusk.

They crossed the central yard and started down the main road toward the exit gates. As they passed the chief's encampment, Uhuru lifted his hand and called a cheery farewell in what Marc assumed was Swahili. Two of the camp's elders responded in kind. The administrator's aides and one of Kamal's men followed at a discreet distance. Marc figured he would never have a better chance to ask. "I need a favor."

"Of course I will help if I can, Mr. Royce."

"One of the medics here has gone missing."

"I am aware of this. Serge Korban, yes? Nine days and counting. I fear his chances are not good." The declaration did not alter the man's apparent good humor. "Korban is an interesting name. Do you happen to know where he is from?"

"Israel."

"Ah. So many people are drawn to our country in times of tragedy. From so many places. And here you are, newly arrived, and already you have taken on the woes of the missing man's lovely young sister."

"Can you help?"

"I doubt it, Mr. Royce. I doubt it most sincerely. Serge

Korban had entered an official no-go area, and did so without proper authorization."

"He was investigating why a village had been displaced."

"A curious task for a medic, wouldn't you say? And you know what curiosity did to the cat." Their footsteps scrunched over the loamy earth. Marc felt eyes press on him from all sides. "I also want you to fly in tents. We need to establish satellites of existing camps to the west of here. Tell your Nairobi office to supply us with ten thousand tents, on a cost-plus basis. As swiftly as possible."

Marc did not know what to say, so he settled on, "Thank you."

"What brings you to Kenya, Mr. Royce? I find this most interesting. Is it merely a nose for profit, or is more at work?"

Marc sensed the piercing quality of an experienced diplomat, probing deep beneath the surface. "We were talking about tents. And Serge."

"We were talking about whatever it is that I wish to speak on. And I detect a reluctance to discuss your own motives." As they passed through the camp gates, Uhuru waved a hand in response to the guard's salute. Uhuru said, "I only ask because I wish to know what it is that drives my new fixer."

"I'm sorry, what?"

"Fixer is a long-established title in this line of work. A fixer does anything and everything for a profit. They make things work when everything else is broken down. Communications, transport, supplies, all gone. And yet a fixer makes the impossible happen. My first fixer, that was in Nigeria back in the eighties. The man made his reputation by supplying ice cream in the middle of a heat wave. The power was knocked out, the roads were melted, even helicopters could not fight the invisible heat drafts. Six weeks it had been like this, people driven mad by the heat and the lack of drinking water. And suddenly this fixer delivers five hundred gallons of ice cream. Six flavors. Ben and Jerry's. I will never forget the taste of that first bite. Marvelous."

"Can you ask about Serge?"

"I have never stopped asking." Uhuru swung around. In the glare of the helicopter's landing lights, a hard glint shone through his polished veneer. "You are new to this country, are you not?"

"I've been here less than two weeks."

"And already you are being offered an opportunity that many wait a lifetime for and never receive." A hint of angry impatience rumbled in the deep voice, echoing the volcano's distant rumble. "A word to the wise. You must learn to focus upon the opportunity. This is Africa, Mr. Royce. Opportunities such as what I am offering are few and far between."

As the rotors began whining up, Uhuru offered Marc his hand. He raised his voice above the engine noise and said, "The fixer I told you about is still there. His office remains just down the hall from the regional governor, though few can even remember how he won the treasured post. That is a fixer's dream, Mr. Royce. You and your company would be well served if you kept that at the forefront of your mind."

Chapter Ten

Marc stood in the camp's main office and spoke to his Nairobi headquarters via the satellite phone. The signal bounced over whatever communications satellite was closest, then back to earth. The voice on the other end was turned metallic and tense by the process. Boyd Crowder, Lodestone's chief officer in Nairobi demanded, "Cost-plus? You're sure he said that?"

Marc replied, "Those were Frederick Uhuru's exact words."

The generator chugged from the darkness out beyond the baobab tree. Lights from the mess hut illuminated the tree's knotted and twisted limbs. He heard insects strike the office window's screens, quick staccato drumbeats against the African night. Shadows flittered past his open window, bats chasing insects at impossible speeds.

Boyd Crowder repeated, "Emergency food and medical supplies for five camps."

"And ten thousand tents."

The line buzzed and crackled. Boyd Crowder was a grizzled veteran of many wars. Marc had seen the man on numerous occasions, first in their Washington headquarters and then during his brief layover in Nairobi. Crowder had served with the U.S. Army for sixteen years, ending his professional career as a full colonel. He had run Lodestone's Nairobi office for three years. Until tonight, Crowder had treated Marc as just another recruit.

Crowder said, "I'm pulling you out."

"Uhuru didn't say anything about my leaving the camp, sir."

"You answer to me, Royce. We're understaffed here in Nairobi. An order of this size is going to almost double our current turnover. You need to be back here coordinating these shipments all the way from supplier to the camps."

Much as he yearned for a hot shower and a good meal, the prospect of leaving only heightened his lack of answers. "Uhuru gave me the impression he wanted me posted here for the duration, sir."

"I'll call the UN's district HQ and square it with him. We need you back here ASAP. Be ready to move at sunrise. Crowder out."

The next morning Marc entered the camp chapel just as the first song began. As usual, most of the camp dwellers had arrived long before him, and filled the structure with noisy tumult. These services at dawn and sunset were the only times the camp showed any vibrancy.

When the singing began, people stood and swayed to the music. The volume was as amazing as the harmony. The words were all in Swahili, but Marc thought he recognized several of the tunes. The sun was well up over the horizon before the singing halted and the people dropped to the benches for Charles to lead the service.

Kitra occupied her regular place, the far left corner, up where she could slip away easily to the medical tent. She remained crouched on the bench, her elbows planted on her thighs and her face in her hands. When the service was over, several women leaned in close to Kitra and spoke to her with quiet intensity.

After everyone else had departed, Marc walked down the central aisle and settled onto the bench next to Kitra. Marc waited, content to remain as long as was necessary. There was a wind from the north, holding the night's chill a bit longer against the rising sun. The baobab's branches rattled. A child wailed in the medical tent and was quickly soothed. Marc found himself thinking back to his old church in Baltimore, the way he had sat through the services and the singing, often holding his late wife's photograph and wondering if he would ever truly live again. Do more than go through the motions of an endless line of empty days. He stared beyond the chapel's shadows, out the open side to where the corrugated roofs glinted in the sunlight. Ironically he felt at home here. Being comfortable with such upheaval probably meant there was something seriously wrong with him. But this was where he felt he belonged. Dealing with chaos, giving strength to the weak. Protecting those who were wounded and hurting. Just like now.

He said, "Tell me how I can help."

The words were enough to lift Kitra from her crouched position over her knees. Her hands came away as wet as her cheeks. "Last night I dreamed that Serge spoke to me from beyond the grave."

Marc reached over and settled his hand on her shoulder, as he had seen the local women do. Only later did he realize it was the first time he had touched her.

Kitra went on, "When I woke up, I felt as though he had come to me for a purpose. Ever since I've worried that I haven't done something. Or missed something. Or . . ."

Marc waited until he was certain she would not speak again, then said, "My wife died four and a half years ago. I used to have these long conversations with her, sometimes in church, but mostly in dreams."

She wiped her face with shaky hands. "What did she say?"

Marc recalled vividly the burden he had carried for over a year, that she wanted him to move on. But this was not the time to say such things to Kitra. "Usually I didn't hear the words. More like, the vacuum of her not being there had to be filled somehow."

Kitra's voice broke as she asked, "Is Serge dead?"

Marc tried to reply as gently as possible, but he did not mask the truth. "Uhuru, the UN administrator, doesn't give your brother much of a chance of survival."

She shuddered her way through the news. Marc waited with her. Finally she asked, "Should I leave here? Go back to Israel?"

Marc let his hand slip away. "I can't tell you that. Do you have family there?"

"My parents."

"Do they know?"

"It was the hardest call I have ever made."

"I'm sorry you had to endure that, Kitra. But I think it was important they heard the news from you."

She swallowed again. "I keep thinking Serge would want to find me here if he returns."

Marc recalled how he had himself been anchored by the home he had once shared with his wife, how he had spent four years clutching frantically at fading memories. He said simply, "I will pray for you both."

That was enough to calm her. "I am asking. What do you think I should do?"

"I spoke with Lodestar headquarters last night. They want me to return to Nairobi. I think you should come. The answers we seek aren't here."

She was silent a moment. "All right, Marc."

He started to rise, then, "There's something you said yesterday. I agree with the question Serge asked. Why should the administrators make a land grab here? I mean, after the volcano erupted. The village is blanketed with ash. The land is worthless."

"Who knows what they were after?"

Again Marc had the distinct impression she was holding back. He pressed as gently as he could. "Did Serge have any idea what might be behind this?"

The question lifted her from the bench. "This was once some of the richest agricultural land in all of Kenya. One day the rains will return and all this ash will be washed away."

Marc rejected that with an impatient shake of his head. Stolen farmland in Africa, no matter how valuable, was not going to interest the people who had sent him to Kenya. "There has to be something bigger. A diamond mine. Or gold."

She wiped her face with both hands. "Serge thought of that. The nearest known deposits of either are hundreds of miles away."

"Then what . . .?" Marc stopped at the sound of approaching footsteps. He turned to find Charles coming down the chapel's central aisle.

The pastor told them, "The elders wish to have a word."

Despite his solid Kenyan roots, Charles knew he would never sound like a born-and-bred Nairobi native. He had spent seven vital years in America, from his last year in high school through seminary. Upon his return to Kenya, he had found a great deal of hostility toward America, directed especially at rich black Americans who swaggered down the Nairobi streets and bought whatever they wanted and took pride in referring to themselves as *African Americans*. These strangers had no idea what the word meant, and made no attempt to learn. Charles shared the locals' disdain and did his best to distance himself from them.

Sometimes, when he was tired or stressed, the American mode of speech slipped back into his brain. Or when he was spooked. Like now. Because Philip seriously spooked him. There was an edge to the young chief, a deep brooding core of African blood . . . and something else.

Philip was two years younger than Charles. Yet there was a timeless dignity to the man and his demeanor. Charles knew the chief spoke fluent English. But in the presence of Marc Royce, Philip insisted on holding to Swahili. Why, Charles had no idea.

Philip told him, "Say to Marc Royce, I know he is leaving for the city."

Charles felt goose bumps as he translated.

Marc Royce jerked slightly in surprise, then asked, "How does he know this?"

When the question was translated, Philip replied, "The angels came to me in my dreams. They said this."

Marc nodded slowly, giving Philip's words the time they deserved. This American surprised Charles. He was extremely tough—Charles had seen this firsthand in the forest. And yet Marc also showed a genuine concern for people and their needs. Even strangers in a strange land, mired in poverty, trapped in a refugee camp. Marc Royce cared deeply. Of this Charles was certain.

Marc Royce asked, "God speaks to you in dreams?"

"Sometimes I am not certain whether I am asleep or awake," Philip replied, once Charles had translated. "Only that God's messengers have come. My task is not to understand, but to listen well."

"To listen," Marc added, "and then to act in accordance to the divine will."

Philip smiled. Charles felt a faint twinge of astonishment. Philip almost never smiled, and yet in the presence of this newcomer it had happened twice.

The chief said, "I see the word around camp is correct, that the faith is more than merely words for this one."

Marc asked, "How is it that you're so much younger than the camp's other elders?"

Charles told him, "I mentioned how his parents had passed on."

"I'd appreciate hearing it from him. Sometimes I learn more from how the answer is shaped than what the words actually say."

The elders on the other stools shifted as Charles translated. The senior Kikuyu said to Philip, "Perhaps I was wrong when I spoke the other day. About him not being the one."

Philip continued to speak through Charles, "All we have

is dignity. The other reasons for our authority, the land and the village and the heritage, all this has been taken from us. I treat the elders with the same dignity that I seek from them. Charles has told you that my father was a chief before me, and his father, back twelve generations. So long has our village existed. I was twenty-three when I lost my parents to the automobile accident. The village elders voted and placed my father's staff in my hand and moved his cattle into my kraal. That is the way of my people. And then the regional governor saw what we were doing, with new agricultural techniques, training our brightest in the universities, and seeking peace with all our neighbors, and I was appointed district chief as well. That was the year the drought struck."

"What can you tell me about your tribe?"

"We are the Luo. We once were river people, following the ebb and flow of the great river you call the Nile. Nineteen generations ago, my people were driven south by Arab invaders flying the flag of a new religion called Islam. We followed the Rift south. There in the valley we met a tribe we had never heard of before. They called themselves the Masaii, and to our astonishment, we shared the same tongue. We took this as a sign and searched out land of our own. The Masaii claimed the Rift, but the land above the great valley, it was empty and unclaimed. And so we came to be here. Centuries before the English arrived, with their papers and their stamps and their writing. And now, Marc Royce, pay careful attention, for I am about to tell you a great thing." He waited for Charles's translation, then went on, "Now there are people who claim the land of our village is not ours and never has been."

So it was with many of the wise ones in this land, Charles reflected as he translated. They took whatever question or comment was made and redirected it so that the matter they wanted to discuss became its heart, the central theme, the reason why they spoke at all.

Marc turned to Kitra and asked, "This was the village where your brother was taken?"

Kitra hesitated long enough for Charles to translate. It was Philip who spoke. "I will answer that, Marc Royce. Serge Korban was taken not from my village but from another within my district. So I consider his abduction a matter of personal importance. As well as a concern for these two friends, one who is missing and one who weeps for her brother in the night."

Kitra's swallow was audible. Charles saw Marc glance over, and saw too the emotions this strong man held in check. Marc then asked, "What does it mean, district chief?"

"As Charles has told you, I am both chief to my village, and chief to my district. The village voted for me, the government in Nairobi appointed me. I was one of the first chiefs named by the newly elected government. Before, there was much corruption. Many district chiefs paid for their office with bribes they later collected from the regions. As a result, the Nairobi government is hated by the people of this great land. The new government promised to change that. New district chiefs are to come from the region they oversee. They are to be respected. They are to be trusted. My people trust me, Marc Royce. And this is how I repay them. By clinging to my dignity in a camp where we have lost everything."

"How can I help?"

"To answer that, I must first know who you truly are. I must see to the heart of you. I must know whether you can be trusted with the future of my people."

The American then told them the most surprising tale. He described his background as an intelligence agent, the loss of his career through the illness and death of his wife. How he had been drawn back into service and sent to Iraq. Then his return to America, and the secret nighttime trip to the Washington hotel. He spoke of power beyond their imagination, of people connected to the White House, and questions for which Marc had no answer. Kitra's eyes grew round, for clearly she had known none of this.

When the American went silent, Philip flipped his father's oxtail whisk. "I thank you for your reply and for your honesty, Marc Royce. You have given us much to discuss. Go in peace. Help us find a way home."

If the American felt any offense over being dismissed, he did not show it. He and Kitra rose and departed. The silence gathered.

Philip looked around the circle, but none of the other elders chose to speak. He nodded, as though satisfied, and said to Charles, "You will go with them."

Charles objected, "My place is here."

"Your place is caring for the people of your church. This duty means you will accompany Marc Royce. And if he is to be trusted, you will share with him the secret."

Charles felt the thrill race up his spine. "You will allow this man to hold the future of your people?"

"Only if he is the one of my dream." The young-old man looked around the circle of elders, granting them the chance to object. But no one spoke. So he turned back and finished, "And only if he shows you a sign."

Once again the chief had managed to spook him. "What sign will that be?"

Philip rose with him, a rare honor. "You will know when God tells you."

Chapter Eleven

Marc stood just outside the camp's main gates, waiting for the chopper bringing Lodestone's chief. He squinted into the heat waves rising off the dusty earth and the bleached forest beyond, and recalled his job interview at Lodestone's Washington headquarters.

The interview had been handled by a mid-level company executive. Marc figured the guy had been hired away from the federal government. In Marc's previous line of work, they had called it the Washington side-straddle-hop. The interviewer wore an expensive jacket of some forgettable dark shade, flannel trousers, starched shirt, and crimson bow tie. He picked his way through Marc's résumé at an infuriatingly slow pace. Throughout that entire period, a second man leaned against the office's side wall and inspected Marc with a sniper's intensity.

The interviewer never introduced the second man, but from the security files Marc knew him to be Boyd Crowder. The colonel remained just beyond Marc's field of vision, inspecting Marc in silence. Two hours into the process, the bureaucrat asked why Marc was giving up the safety of Baltimore and his steady job to head off to the depths of Africa. The man managed to turn the question into a blemish on Marc's character. Marc replied that it was all there in his file.

Boyd Crowder spoke for the first time. "Forget the file," he said. "You didn't just take aim at a job on the wild side. Something happened. I want to know what that was."

Marc swiveled around to face this extremely tough relic of a life on the firing line. Marc replied, "A woman. And restless boredom."

"The lady left you high and dry?"

"That's right. She did."

Crowder showed a grim humor, until the bureaucrat found the appropriate line in Marc's file and asked, "You are recently widowed?"

"That is correct."

Crowder's mirth faded. "How long?"

"Long enough for the empty life to gnaw at me."

Crowder's gaze was not so much brown as copper, a hard glint that measured men with the same precision as he would a sniper's rifle. "So you think you've got what it takes for adventure."

"Either that," Marc replied, "or I don't have anything left to lose."

Crowder said to the bureaucrat, "Dump him in the deep end, see if he can learn to swim against the currents."

When they were done and Marc was leaving, he heard the interviewer tell Crowder, "This is a terrible mistake."

"The supplier has basically ordered us to take this guy on," Crowder said. "So we do as we're told and let Africa grind him to dust. Problem solved."

The four Lodestone choppers landed between the pale forest and the camp's main gates. Boyd Crowder was the first man to drop to the ground. His military fatigues were tailored tight to his triangular frame, the pant legs tucked into polished black jackboots. Three white scars snaked up his left arm, and another coiled around his neck like an albino tattoo. Karl Rigby, Crowder's aide and a silent blade of a man, followed three steps back.

Crowder handed Marc a plastic briefcase and said, "A man on the move in these parts needs to be reachable twenty-four-seven. Lodestone's supplying you with a new sat phone. The number's taped on the case."

The colonel made it sound like he was handing out medals, so Marc replied, "Thank you, sir."

Crowder's grin was as hard as his voice. "We had a lottery going, how long it'd take Africa to eat you up. I lost. I don't like losing."

Marc introduced Crowder to the new camp administrators. As they discussed the manifest Marc had prepared, listing the camp's most urgent requirements, Kitra stepped through the gates. She lifted her voice in order to be heard above the thrumming rotors. "Charles wants to come with us," she told Marc.

Marc wondered why the pastor had approached her and not come to him directly, but merely nodded and said, "I'll ask."

Crowder took in Kitra's form in three seconds flat. When Marc introduced them, Crowder said, "Your name's been flagged. Something about your brother, right?"

"Serge. Yes. Have you heard something?"

"Not a whisper. How long has he been gone?"

"Ten days."

"No ransom demand?"

Her lip trembled, but she held herself together. "Nothing."

Crowder dismissed his chances with a brusque shake of his head. "I'm sorry for your loss." He turned to Marc and said, "Where's your gear, soldier?"

"By the camp gates." Marc saw the look of bitter pain that Kitra gave the colonel before turning away. He found it difficult to keep his tone bland as he said, "The lady and the camp pastor need a lift to Nairobi."

Crowder seemed ready to argue, but he must have detected something in Marc's gaze, for all he said was, "We lift off in five."

The four transport choppers were adapted from their military roots, great elephantine beasts with little grace and no beauty whatsoever. Their payloads were held in place by nylon netting. Boyd Crowder directed Marc into the second seat between the cockpit and the mountains of gear. Kitra and Charles joined Crowder's aide and another soldier on fold-down seats by the bulkhead.

Once they were airborne, the volcano glowered angry and perilous, the column of smoke towering above the southwestern reaches. Crowder pointed out the chopper's front windows and said, "Kapenguria is the town at your six o'clock. Five klicks to the right is the Lenan Forest, the big rise there is the Cherangani Hills, and the Kiphunurr Forest is that stretch of green on the horizon."

Marc tried to implant the vista on the map he had studied. "What's up farther north?"

"Nothing but more Africa." Crowder gathered up the entire continent in one sweep of his scarred arm. "The city of Maralai sits up there on the Lorogi Plateau. The African plains begin just past the Samburu Hills and stretch all the way to the

Somali desert. Which is why all the refugees are streaming this way. And the government is letting them, on account of there's only one road through the whole savannah. You know what the savannah is, Royce?"

"Plains."

"Miles and miles of parched nothing. Drought has gripped that entire region for five years. The grass is eaten up, the rivers are dried up, and the animals are gone. From the Samburu all the way to the Suguta Valley. There's a new desert growing; they call it the Nachorugwai."

The chopper tilted into a banked turn, revealing the main road and the swarm of refugees. Beyond that stretched an endless yellow vista. It beckoned to him, this land. Marc yearned to do more than fly over with an angry man making light of the secrets on display.

Crowder leaned closer and let the drumming motor mask his words from the others. "The government's extended the evacuation order to include all the surrounding towns—Sodang to Kitale and beyond. We've been contracted to serve as security detail. Carry out the wealth of nine towns. Clear all the banks, the warehouses, the businesses, everything." Crowder grinned, one winner to another, totally unconcerned with the destruction or the lives lost. "There's a fortune waiting for pirates these days."

Marc had met such soldiers on every assignment that had taken him off the grid. Warriors who had crossed the line and lost their way. They searched out places like this, beyond the reach of civilization or human dignity. Marc met Crowder's gaze and replied, "Shame we're duty-bound and honest. Isn't it, Colonel?"

The mercenary chief gave Marc a deadly grin and eased back into his seat. He flipped on his headset, said something into the microphone that caused both pilots to laugh. Marc understood the man's actions all too well. Crowder wanted nothing more to do with him. Which suited Marc just fine.

When they landed at the Red Cross camp, Crowder's men stationed themselves by the choppers and off-loaded the supplies into a snaking line of arms. The Lebanese traders emerged from their makeshift huts and glowered at the work parties. Crowder's men all wore well-pressed military fatigues and worked like automatons. Crowder stood at parade-ground rest, arms linked behind his back, and surveyed everything from a stern distance.

Marc climbed the nearest rise and stood with his back to the camp. The village where Serge had been taken was a smudge on the horizon. Behind it loomed the pillar of smoke, as though the volcano took pride in the role it had played in Serge's disappearance.

At the sound of footsteps Marc turned to find Kitra climbing up to join him. They stood in silence and studied the terrain, until a shout from below drew them back. As they descended the hill, Kitra said, "You have never lied to me, have you?"

"No, Kitra. Not once."

"No. It is your nature to be honest. Even when it hurts." She moved ahead of him, then said over her shoulder, "Serge often said we were the rarest of breeds, people who feel at home in situations where others fear to enter. I like that about you."

"I wish I could have a chance to know Serge."

"He would call you friend." There was utter certainty in

her voice. They walked back to the thrumming helicopters. As she started to climb in, she looked at him, the tragic green gaze reaching deep. "You have a good heart."

Marc followed her into the chopper and settled in the seat beside Crowder. He was immune to the mercenary chief's hostile silence, encased as he was now in the comfort of Kitra's words.

Chapter Twelve

When the choppers landed at the Nairobi airport, Kitra and Charles thanked the Lodestone crew and headed for the taxi stand. Marc followed Crowder and his men to the four vehicles lined up by the hangars. The armored Tahoes were black with black windows and black leather interior, the favorite color scheme for mercs around the globe. Crowder pointed Marc into the last vehicle and joined his aide in the first SUV. Two of Crowder's men took the front seats, turned on a rock CD, cranked up the volume, and shut him out. Marc observed the city beyond the fortified glass and marveled at how it felt as though he had been up-country for years, rather than only five days.

Every place of value in Nairobi—homes and offices and factories and warehouses—was situated inside compounds. The wealthy and the powerful moved from one guarded enclave to another. If someone walked the city's streets, it meant they were either poor or tourists. Or they were looking for trouble. And usually found it. The Lodestone compound was in the city section between the airport and the Wildlife Park. The offices were located in a home dating from the colonial era, with stinkwood floors, high ceilings, and a broad front veranda. A more modern building contained the living quarters and was situated along a path that wound through the thorn trees and carefully tended gardens. The Lodestone residence contained some two dozen bedrooms, dining hall, lounge, cinema, and gym. It was an idyllic setting, intended to soothe nerves frayed by up-country stress and bad food and constant danger.

Marc dumped his gear in his assigned room, took a long shower, then headed downstairs for a meal. The kitchen was on duty twenty-four-seven, and the food was both fresh and well made. Marc ate surrounded by men who pretended he did not exist. Their exclusion did not bother him. He was well accustomed to the military mind-set, where trust was something earned in the heat of battle.

As he ate, he mentally reviewed what he knew of the Lodestone operation. Besides the newer emergency-supplies division, Lodestone managed security and armed transport for a number of the crisis groups and international camps. They also supplied short-term security for overstretched UN details. A second contingent was hired out as instructors to the local police and Kenyan army. The only point at which these divisions converged was at the top. Boyd Crowder.

Marc was pondering whether he should report back to Walton when his new satellite phone rang.

"This is Marc."

Charles said, "We need to talk."

"When and where?"

"We're outside the Lodestone main gates."

The prospect of seeing Kitra again quickened his pulse. "I'm on my way."

As Marc followed the path around the older house, he sensed trouble brewing up ahead. Voices from the front lawn carried a carnal edge, like a pack of hunting dogs braying the alert.

The first thing he saw were four men, who stood by the veranda railing, their card game forgotten. Squat clay pots smoldered to either side of the group. Smoke intended to keep mosquitoes at bay drifted about the four men in angry tendrils. The men laughed and pointed with their beer bottles at the drama on the front lawn.

A blond giant stood in the center of the lawn. He grinned at his mates and dangled Kitra from one outstretched arm. His two buddies added to the banter while one pinned Charles to the earth with his boot. Kitra saw Marc's appearance and struggled harder. She might as well have been beating her fists against a mountain.

Marc understood instantly what had happened. The giant and his two buddies had returned from the street market, where the men liked to eat impala steaks. These three were clearly too big and too dangerous for even the jaded Nairobi bandits to take on. The men liked to swagger through the streets, showing one and all who was the baddest cat in Kenya. They were also bored. They had been up-country. They had lived for days or weeks on adrenaline and gunpowder. They came back and they slept and they ate, and as soon as the batteries were charged, they were hungry for action. They laughed about being addicted to the rush of incoming fire. As though they could walk away from it at any time. But they all knew. There was no other high on earth to compare.

The giant had obviously caught sight of Kitra and Charles waiting outside the front gates. He probably said something, and Kitra had cut him down. A beautiful white woman in Nairobi learned to do this swiftly and without compromise. But this particular man did not take the dismissal well.

The giant dangled Kitra by her backpack, lifting her just high enough so that her toes drifted for a hold. Charles struggled against the boot clamping him to the grass, one hand reaching out in protest. The native guard on gate duty watched it all with fearful eyes. He looked like a miniature stick figure beside the three men on the front lawn. The guard pleaded for the giant to release her. The colonel's aide, Karl Rigby, emerged from the main house and barked an order. The giant pretended not to hear. Crowder could probably have stopped this before it got worse, but he was nowhere to be seen.

Marc stepped onto the lawn. "Let the woman go."

The giant must have weighed in at three hundred pounds. He had the ruddy confidence of a man who was never challenged. Marc knew the kind. In-country, the man wielded a fifteen-inch carbon blade and draped his upper body with gun belts and carried a fifty-caliber monster like it was a pistol.

"Hey, if it isn't the bookkeeper!" The giant looked genuinely happy. "Lookee what we got here, boys! Lunch!"

Karl Rigby's voice was the only soft thing about him. "Dirk, do us all a favor. Let's head to the bar and—"

"You boys head on back. I'll join you directly." Dirk jiggled Kitra like she was a sack in pastel fabric. She swatted at his arm, swung a kick, but his reach was so long she could not connect. Her face was red since her breathing was partially cut off. "The lady and I have a date. Don't we, bookkeeper?"

The best method of attack was straight ahead and without warning. But first Marc needed to have the giant release Kitra.

He couldn't risk having the man punish Kitra when Marc proved more than expected. Which meant showing his hand. At least partly.

Marc closed the distance, putting himself inside the man's range of fire. "Don't make me tell you again."

The giant took Marc's lack of fear as a direct challenge. He used his free hand to launch a massive haymaker that Marc easily ducked. He watched as Kitra's struggling weight and the man's own swing took the bully off-balance. Then Marc struck.

He slipped down to two hands and used his entire body as a fulcrum, swinging both legs in an arc so smooth the violent speed was almost invisible. He hammered the giant's knee with two blows so swift they probably felt like one.

Dirk's eyes widened in genuine shock as his leg buckled.

He fell on his injured knee and grunted with a fighter's mixture of rage and pain. But the assault had its intended effect, and Dirk was forced to release Kitra in order to take his weight on his hands. Kitra bounced hard and rolled away to safety.

Karl Rigby darted forward and dragged Kitra farther out of range. When one of the other soldiers started toward Marc, the colonel's aide barked, "Stay out of this."

Dirk was an angry bull now, rising to full height and punching out his chest by drawing back his arms, the two ends of a human bow. "You heard the man. This is my song. Come on, bookkeeper. You asked for it. Let's dance."

But Marc was already moving.

He knew the giant was still coming to terms with the fact that this lesser mortal would take him on. A man of Dirk's size attacked the world on his terms. Which was why Marc did not wait. Speed was his only chance.

He darted in and planted two blows, one to the heart and the other to the neck. There was a nerve ganglion just beneath the jaw, and striking it sent an electric current through the brain and upper body. The effect did not last long, there and gone in the space of half a heartbeat. Which made the electric flash all the more stunning. Experiencing the uncontrolled current race through the body and disappear caused most attackers to turn and run. Instead, Dirk grunted a second time and shook it off.

Dirk was faster than a big man should have been, but Marc had been expecting this. Colonel Crowder might be many things, but he was undoubtedly a good judge of men. And Lodestone paid enough to let him choose the best. Dirk almost caught Marc's cheekbone with a powerful left jab. Marc ducked again and weaved back inside, the last thing the giant expected. Marc hit the heart again and the neck. Then slipped down to the ground.

American training stressed the need to remain upright and in control. Eastern combat taught that any position was favorable, so long as the balance was tilted away from the opponent. And the bigger the enemy, the more every possible avenue had to be utilized.

Marc balanced his weight on his shoulder blades and kicked up, two stabs as fast as his hands, both blows aimed at Dirk's heart. The ribs gave somewhat—not even muscles hard as Dirk's could shrug off two direct kicks. Dirk gave out a drumbeat of sound, a lion's rugged cough. He tried to stomp down on Marc, but Marc was already scuttling away, crablike and fast.

Dirk roared with genuine fury and leaped.

Marc knew the man expected him to run. But there was another tactic in Eastern disciplines where a rise from the floor is turned into an offensive rebalance. The body ripples, like wind ruffling a sail, and whips the individual back to his feet. The movement unfolds from that into a full-body strike, like an uncoiling snake, leaping up and into the blow with impossible grace. Marc trained for three years before he could attain the smoothness required to go from prone to strike without pause.

Dirk saw the hands moving toward him and tried to backpedal. His unconscious response was drawn from a newfound respect and the way his heart now beat out of sync. But Marc was already closing. Two more strikes to the neck and the heart. Then dancing back out of range.

This time Dirk slowed. He gasped for air and weaved, trying to shake off the constriction to his breathing and how his heart no longer obeyed his need for power.

Marc struck again. Two more blows. Then a swinging kick that had him leaping up so far he kicked down upon the man's head.

Dirk fell and did not move.

"Hold!"

Marc swung about, only to find the four men on the veranda frozen in place midway between their table and the front stairs. The colonel's aide had one fist planted in the chest of the third man, while his other hand took aim at the two men on the front lawn. Karl Rigby snarled, "This is not your fight. And this *is a direct command*. Retreat in good order."

Marc nodded his thanks to the aide and turned to Kitra. "Are you all right?"

"I think so, yes." Her gaze darted between Dirk on the ground and Marc. "That was—"

"You and Charles get out of here. Now. Call me tomorrow."

"But—"

"Go."

Chapter Thirteen

Marc climbed the veranda stairs and took aim for the front door. He did not even glance at the men standing to either side. He slipped past them and entered the house, offering them no challenge.

He crossed the main foyer as voices rose behind him. He walked the long central hallway and took the stairs into the main cellar. The storerooms had been rebuilt as a pair of highly secure safes. The one to his left held the company finances, backup electronic files, and lockboxes for each Lodestone employee. The gun room opened to his right. Marc knew the code to the gun room's steel door because he had hunted it down. He keyed in the ten digits and slipped inside.

Marc did not have any particular weapon in mind. He had never been in here before. There had been no reason. What did a bookkeeper need in the way of serious weapons?

The rifles were arranged along the far wall, glowing dark and malevolent in the yellow lighting. Marc selected a military-grade carbine with black stock and carbon grip. The clips were full and stacked neatly beneath the guns. He fed six into a web belt, slung it over his shoulder, and then added three compression grenades. He spotted a beautiful pistol, a Remington .45

with gleaming chrome finish and genuine pearl handles. Marc plucked it from the walnut case and slipped it into his belt, then pocketed a box of hollow points.

He relocked the gun room and mounted the stairs. He went out the front door, toward the voices. He wanted them to see, to know.

The four cardplayers were now clustered on the front lawn with Dirk's two mates, helping the giant rise from the ground. Karl Rigby and the African sentry stood two paces back and were the first to notice him. Then all heads turned Marc's way and the conversation immediately stilled.

Marc stood on the top step and let them see. Even Dirk stopped his groaning and grousing when he noticed how Marc was armed. Officially, only the colonel had access to the gun-room codes.

Once Marc was certain they understood the message, he turned and headed back for the rear house.

When they came for him, he would be ready.

Marc barricaded his door with the room's meager furniture. He opened his window ten inches, using a rubber doorstop to wedge it into position. He closed and latched the wooden shutters and pulled the shades, so no attacker could see where he was. He then took up station beneath the bathroom sink, where all the surrounding walls were concrete and the line of attack was limited to the narrow doorway.

Marc cushioned his post with blankets and pillows, and dozed on and off. He knew he was leaving with the dawn, but his departure needed to be on his own terms. Marc was determined to remain in Kenya and hunt down the reasons behind Serge's disappearance.

The Lodestone compound was just over a mile from the entrance to the Wildlife Park, the only one of its kind in the world. Nairobi bordered the nation's richest farmland, which had grown up around a rail station used for carting produce. The region also bordered one of the world's richest game areas. The modern city had fenced in the game park on three sides, but left it open to the west for animals to come and go. The country's four-year drought, however, had interrupted the wildlife's natural migration patterns. Many animals remained year-round even when food was scarce, because the park's deep-bore wells supplied the region's only steady source of water.

Marc sat on the tiled floor and listened to the lions roar from inside the preserve. A lion's call could be heard five miles away at night, when the dry and cold air best carried sound. The beasts sounded so close, they might as well have been prowling about the front lawn. Marc smiled grimly. It sounded to him as though the city resonated with the compound's menace.

The last thing he expected was a polite knock on his door. Again. Then the colonel's aide called softly, "Royce?"

"I'm here."

Karl Rigby said, "Will you let me in?"

Marc checked his watch. It read ten past midnight. "Who else is out there?"

"I'm alone," Rigby answered. "We need to talk."

Marc found it difficult to release himself from imminent threat mode. "What about?"

"Taking the next step," Rigby replied. "And keeping you alive."

The only weapon Marc carried with him was the pearl-handled pistol. If they were out to ambush him, another gun wouldn't help. But he didn't think that would happen. He had a warrior's instinct for dangers ahead. And his gut told him the night was clear. Which astonished him almost as much as Rigby saying, "Thanks."

"Excuse me?"

"For coming out. And not shooting me through the door."

"Where are we headed?"

"The mess hall. The colonel wants to have a word." Rigby carried a manila folder in one hand as he took the stairs two at a time. When he arrived at the doors leading to the lounge and mess hall, Rigby stopped and said, "If it had been me, you wouldn't have gotten off so easy."

"But it wasn't you," Marc replied. "And this isn't about who'd come out on top of a fight that won't happen."

Rigby smirked, as close to approval as the man had ever shown Marc. The aide pushed through the doors, crossed the room, and slipped onto the bench next to the colonel.

Crowder waited until Marc was seated opposite him to say, "That's my weapon you've got tucked in your belt."

Marc pulled the pistol free and set in on the table in front of Crowder.

"You like a beer?"

"No, thanks. Don't drink."

"That a fact. Karl, go get the man a cuppa joe. You take coffee, don't you, Royce?"

"Coffee's fine. Black."

Crowder waited in easy silence until his aide returned. They were surrounded by Lodestone security forces, who pretended not to be watching and smoldering. Dirk was nowhere to be seen. But two of the men who had watched from the porch were stationed by the bar. Another shot eight-ball. They never looked Marc's way.

Marc assumed the colonel was going to discuss his terms of departure. Marc had no idea how he was going to respond. Or how he might find what he needed to do his assignment if he was barred from the compound. Or where he was going to go.

"I am going to lay it on the line, Royce."

Marc sipped at his mug. The coffee was fresh and strong. The Kenyan bean carried a subtle earthiness, a hint of the land from which it sprung. He took small pleasure in what was at hand. A cup of excellent coffee. A safe breath.

"I need to find a way for you to trust me."

Marc set down the mug, eyebrows raised, and stared across the table at Crowder.

"We're sitting in the canteen for a purpose," Crowder said, voice low. "Me and my aide, we're showing you respect in public for a reason. Most of the men you see here are headed out tomorrow. I want them to take this image with them. So when they return home, they carry this instead of how you wiped the lawn with one of my best men. I want them to remember the three of us are sitting here, talking ops. They need to understand you're remaining here with my direct approval."

Marc took his time responding. "So I'm staying. Here. With Lodestone. In Nairobi."

"Unless you've got other plans."

His surprise must have shown, because suddenly Crowder and Rigby were both grinning. The men at the bar and the pool table caught that as well, as the room's forced banter gradually faded away.

Crowder said, "Rigby, show the man your chart."

The colonel's aide opened a file he'd been carrying and extracted a well-worn map. He unfolded it on the table between them.

Boyd Crowder poked at a spot north of Kitale with a stubby finger. The position was marked in yellow. "Recognize this position?"

"The refugee camp."

"Roger that. These blue dots signify points where I've got men on semipermanent station. Watching main arteries, guarding depots, securing valuables."

"Our conversation on the chopper." Marc had realized something. "Your telling me about the chance to rob the towns beyond Kitale. It was all a test."

The colonel and his aide showed Marc genuine approval. It must have been a rare sight, for a murmur of surprise rose from the other men around them.

Boyd Crowder stabbed the map. "This point here. We lost three men. They had time to radio in that they were taking incoming fire. From pros. All African, far as they could tell. Dressed in jungle fatigues. And all wearing the blue armbands."

Soldiers in uniform meant a trained operation force. The blue armbands meant they were a UN contingent. "I'm sorry for your loss, sir."

"Only there's a problem," Rigby said. "There aren't any UN forces operating in that area."

"So they were brought in from another operation," Marc suggested. "Or security forces on temporary assignment."

"I repeat, there were no UN forces within a hundred miles. We checked, Royce. Hard."

"And Lodestone is the only outside group permitted to operate security forces in Kenya," Crowder said. "But you already know that. Don't you, Royce?"

He avoided that one by asking, "What about bandits masquerading as UN troops?"

Rigby answered, "Bandits wouldn't hit an armed band of highly trained mercs. Where's the profit in that?"

Crowder added, "Bandits wouldn't stand a chance against my men. Much less wipe them out."

"Besides which, our guys were playing traffic cops on the juncture between the Trans-African Highway and the north-south artery to Eldoret," Rigby said. "There were a couple warehouses there, both almost empty. Which they burned to the ground."

Marc heard the brassy sorrow to both men's voices, and liked them for the loss they felt. "Why are we discussing this?"

"Because yesterday it got a whole lot worse." Crowder leaned across the table. "I've been ordered off the case."

"Sorry, I don't follow."

"Two days ago I traveled up-country with Rigby and my best trackers. Found the path the attackers took, both inbound and heading back into the bush. Nothing else. No bodies, no spent shells. Like they had just up and vanished into the African dust." Crowder's voice was a feral growl. "Before leaving for your camp, I reported back to HQ. Soon as I returned to Nairobi with you and your pals, HQ ordered me to cease and desist."

"Why would Lodestone in Washington seek to override you on an in-country investigation?"

"They claim the Kenya-based contracts are too rich to risk by riling the natives with questions they won't answer anyway." His hands bunched into fists. "Do you have *any* idea how that makes me feel?"

"Furious," Marc said. "You've spent your life never leaving a man behind."

"These were *good* men. These were my *friends*. And some empty suit back in Potomac-land wants me to *walk away*?"

"It's not happening," Rigby said, grim as his chief. "Not now. Not ever."

Crowder said, "Give the man his ammo."

Rigby slid the file across the table. "Lock and load, Royce."

Crowder went on, "Inside are confidential data on my missing men. I'm asking for your help. Be careful who you tell. If word gets out we've discussed this matter, my career is nothing but dust. And I couldn't guess what'll happen to you."

Marc made no move to touch the file. "I'm not clear on what I'm supposed to do with this."

"So you and your secret allies can help us gain some answers." The coppery glaze returned to the colonel's eyes. Like an armored lid slipped back into place. Boyd Crowder rose from the table. His aide stood with him. Crowder looked down at Marc and said, "Sooner or later, you're going to have to give trust for trust, Royce. It's the only way either of us is going to survive whatever it is we're up against."

Chapter Fourteen

Marc phoned Ambassador Walton from the garden's rear corner. It was the first time they had spoken since Marc had arrived at the refugee camp. Updating his former boss and head of State Department Intel took over an hour. The local security guard patrolling the compound's interior made three full rotations before he was done. Marc finished just as the first faint trace of sunrise dusted the eastern sky. His voice sounded slurred with fatigue to his own ears.

Though it was approaching midnight in Washington, D.C., Walton sounded as alert as ever. Neither retirement nor age nor the hour could touch him. "I don't like the idea of you trusting this Crowder," he said "I don't like it at all."

"I'm working from as isolated and exposed a position as I've ever known," Marc replied. "I'm still trying to get a handle on who can help us move forward. And my gut tells me . . ."

Walton gave him a moment, then prodded, "Finish your thought, son."

"I think Crowder is on our side. I agree it's a risk. But I think we should trust the man."

"Our intel specifically details Boyd Crowder as working for the opposition."

"We don't even know who this opposition is, sir. Much less who their boots on the ground are."

"Crowder had one point right. There are no other mercenaries operating under contract in Kenya."

"That we know about," Marc corrected. "Why couldn't a group have slipped in from somewhere else?"

"Because to do so would violate international law and render both the soldiers and their parent group criminals."

Marc rubbed his face, trying to scrub off the exhaustion and think clearly. "I'm awaiting your orders, sir."

"I can't tell you what to do from here," Walton said sourly. "You're out there because I trust your judgment."

"In that case, I'd like a look at Crowder's file. And Karl Rigby's as well."

"You'll have them both tomorrow. Anything else?"

Marc shifted the bulky phone to his other hand. The signal was so weak he needed to mash it to his ear, hard enough to bruise. "Any word on Serge Korban?"

"Nothing at all. Our contact at UN Security says it can only be so quiet because someone is intentionally squelching all available intel."

"I'll be in touch tomorrow afternoon your time. Royce out."

Marc returned to his room, straightened his bed, showered, and was out before his head hit the pillow. The sat phone's jangling ringtone woke him. It sounded intentionally harsh, as though the apparatus was meant to draw attention from miles away. He fumbled for the button, then croaked, "Royce here."

"It's Charles. Are you safe?"

"Yes. Hold a sec." Marc set down the phone, walked to the

bathroom, and washed his face. As he seated himself and picked up the phone, he glanced at his watch. To his astonishment, it was four in the afternoon. He had slept all day. "How is Kitra?"

"Fine, thanks to you. We need to meet."

"When and where?"

"The Sheraton Hotel in two hours. There are people who very much want to speak with you. Will you come?"

Marc stopped by the front gate and asked the guard to book him a taxi. He then returned to the mess hall and ordered a huge breakfast. Marc was surrounded by a new contingent of security forces, recently arrived from the field. Their hunger and their thirst and their raucous laughter were fueled by the cordite and danger they had just left behind. They crowded the bar and the pool tables and the massive entertainment area. Rock music and frenetic chatter filled the room. Marc ate his meal and did his best to tune it all out.

Ten minutes later, the colonel's aide entered the mess hall and winced at the racket. He flashed a hand at his neck and the rock music vanished. Rigby stopped by the chef's counter for a coffee, then sauntered over and settled onto the bench opposite Marc. "You sleep like a soldier."

Marc understood what he meant. A frontline trooper learned to eat whatever was on offer, whenever it was available. Ditto for bunk time. "Where's the colonel?"

"He's traveled out to the front. Settle in the new men, make sure they're on full alert. Stop any more mysterious vanishings before they happen. He left me as duty officer." Rigby sipped from his mug. "The colonel has named you as one of the team. He ordered me to stay behind and make sure it sticks."

"I appreciate the gesture."

Rigby stood and snagged Marc's empty coffee mug. "You like pie, Royce? They make good pie here."

"Sure."

The entire room watched the colonel's aide cross to the chef's station and return with a slice of pie and Marc's recharged mug. "So why don't you tell me what it is you're really doing here?"

Marc took his time. Walton's concerns and distrust rang in his head. But the ambassador was in Washington and this was Nairobi. And Marc's gut told him he needed to take a risk. So he gave Rigby what he was waiting for. "Let me start with a couple of observations. Feel free to jump in at any time if I get something wrong."

"I'm good at that," Rigby replied. "Telling recruits when they take a false step."

"You and Crowder are proud of your operation here in Kenya. You do your job and you bring your men back alive. But there's a problem. You and Crowder keep catching wind of things not being right at Lodestone HQ in Washington. You're used to dealing with bureaucrats and top brass. You focus on your job and you protect your men, same as always. Only the signals you're picking up keep getting worse."

Rigby's face might as well have been made of stone. He sipped from his mug, said, "Go on."

"Recently you discovered you can't protect your men anymore. Not only that, but you have no idea whom to trust. Or who is behind the unseen threat."

Karl Rigby's features were marred by two small scars, one beneath his left ear and another that started above his left eyebrow and disappeared into his hairline. "And then you arrive."

"Here I am, a guy out of nowhere, turning up at your doorstep," Marc agreed. "Crowder didn't buy how I was assigned by a top supplier. The question for you is, am I more of the problem, or something different?"

"So Crowder ordered you dropped into a hot spot." Rigby smirked. "We both figured you'd last about forty-eight hours."

Marc pushed his plate aside and started on the pie. The colonel's aide was correct. It was excellent.

"I told the colonel that trusting you was a mistake. Crowder said he didn't have any problem putting his rep or his life on the line. But when it came to his men, he runs on a different set of rules. And with three men down, he has to find new allies or pack up his tent and move on."

Marc didn't say anything more until he finished the pie. He knew the next step was his. And it was time to take it. "My primary problem at this point is the missing medic."

"Serge Korban."

"My superiors think he's the trail we should be following. A link to something bigger."

"What is the bigger issue?"

Marc put down his fork. "Corruption in your HQ."

Rigby mulled that one over. "Interesting how you're sent down to check on the same thing we're worried about."

"My superiors back in Washington are concerned that you're not to be trusted."

"Are you comfortable with that uncertainty?"

"My superiors have decided to trust my judgment. And I'm thinking you and Crowder are on our side. So the answer is yes. For the moment." Marc gave that a beat, then asked, "You're sure there aren't other mercs operating inside Kenya?"

"That was the first thing we checked. Crowder used his old contacts and searched the dark places where the hard cases lurk. I can confirm to you that we're the only game in town. And to answer your next question, we checked with the Kenyan forces and the UN. We asked our closest allies to give us the straight and dirty. We checked with units operating in the vicinity of the firefight, and here in Nairobi. At the time of the attack, there were no ops within a hundred klicks of our guys."

"Tell me about the UN forces."

"There are two brigades working in refugee camps on the Somali border, almost a thousand klicks from where our guys went down. Another two working with natives impacted by the recent civil unrest, getting them resettled and keeping them safe from tribal conflict. That's it."

"Then we're missing something," Marc said. "Something crucial."

"You could've taken the words right out of Crowder's mouth. Between us, Crowder and I have served in Panama, Bahrain, Iraq, the big dance in Afghanistan. We bring our men home. Crowder's got the words carved into his heart. You understand what I'm saying?"

"Finding out what happened to his men and making sure it doesn't happen again is priority one," Marc said.

"Roger that." Rigby reached across the table. "Glad to have you on the team, Royce."

Chapter Fifteen

Marc's taxi crawled through rush-hour traffic. Nairobi's official population was two and a half million. Experts with the international aid groups placed it closer to five million. But these numbers were just estimates. There had never been a decent census, and even this would not have solved the riddle.

Because of the drought, thousands poured into Nairobi from all over the nation. They entered the slums where their tribal groups were concentrated. They built hovels of plastic wrapping and corrugated iron and wire and concrete and wood. Billboards and fencing never lasted long in and around the city's poorer districts. They were torn down and turned into homes.

As a result, Nairobi had outgrown its road network, its power grid, its water system. Traffic jams were the stuff of legends. One could wait at the same stoplight for half a day.

The city had not had a real water supply for two years. Tankers served the wealthier neighborhoods each week, refilling the cisterns that topped every building. The city had become carved into a series of districts, each dominated by a tanker company who paid kickbacks to city officials so that the water system was not repaired. But slum dwellers depended on bore-hole pumps. Most walked miles every day for fresh water.

Marc arrived at the Sheraton compound to find Charles standing on the sidewalk in front of the hotel's guard station. Marc paid off the taxi and walked over. Charles offered a solemn greeting and a native's loose handshake. "Kitra and I owe you our lives."

"Where is she?"

"Come." He led Marc around the corner to an ancient Mercedes parked beneath the shade of a blooming tree. The car had once been either white or beige. Charles directed Marc into the front passenger seat, slipped behind the wheel, and asked Kitra in the back seat, "Have you spotted anyone?"

"No. Let's go. We've been here too long already."

Marc turned to look at her. Kitra's features were a taut mask. He thought of all she had endured, and simply said, "I'm sorry about what happened last night."

She glanced at him, her eyes hidden behind dark glasses, and said, "Thank you, Marc."

Charles ground the starter, slipped from the curb, and joined the sluggish stream. Marc asked, "Where are we headed?"

"We have friends who wish to meet you. It is important that they decide how much to tell you about what we are facing." Charles sounded apologetic. "Long before Serge was taken, we have heard rumors that your company is fronting for, well . . ."

"The bad guys. I know." Marc leaned against the side door so as to be able to look at both Charles and the lady in the back seat. Seen in profile, Kitra's nose was arrow-sharp, her cheekbones slanted. Marc thought she had never looked more appealing. "Do you have any word on who these bad guys are?"

Charles glanced again in the rearview mirror before answering, "Sorry. No."

"I don't think the rumors about Lodestone are correct."

Kitra said, "After what happened last night, you still think this?"

"One bad man does not mean the entire Lodestone team works for the dark side. Don't forget, the other men didn't join in."

Kitra inspected him from behind the shield of her sunglasses and did not reply.

Charles broke the car's silence. "We are taking you to Kibera, the largest slum in Africa. I spent my early years here. How many exactly, I cannot say. Just as I do not know where I was born, or when."

All the car's windows were cracked open half a hand's width. The A/C did not work and the heat was fierce, but Marc did not lower his window any further. Young children were trained to approach as beggars, then reach into open windows with lightning speed and grab valuables, using knives or razors to slash away purses and backpacks and even watches.

Charles went on, "My earliest memory was of living in a drainage pipe with my sister. She was older and she looked after me. She taught me to hide in the pipe's shadows when she went looking for food. I do not know how old I was, perhaps three or four. My clearest memory of that time is her voice. Sometimes I still hear her in my dreams, telling me to never leave the shadows."

They became locked in a jam encircling a massive round-about. Charles turned to look at Marc, but it was unlikely the pastor saw anything of the car's interior. "Then one night my sister did not return. I remained where I was. I don't know how long. Days. I knew I was dying. Even so, I obeyed my sister and remained hidden inside the pipe where she had left me."

Marc studied the world beyond the car's safety through the lens of Charles's words. A boy and a girl approached Marc's window, little stick figures with solemn eyes. Their skinny arms were rimmed with gaudy plastic bracelets, which they offered to him without hope. Marc pulled a bill from his pocket and passed it through his window. The boy took it and murmured what might have been a blessing, or a condemnation. The pair shuffled away.

Charles continued, "And then a new shadow fell upon my hiding place. A tall shadow, with a kind voice. I was too weak to see this person clearly. I felt hands reach in and take hold of me. Even in my weakened state, I knew I could trust these hands. Even though my sister had told me to trust no one. Even though I could not understand the words this tall white man or the woman who accompanied him were speaking."

Kitra asked, "Why are you telling him this?"

Since they remained stuck in traffic, Charles was able to turn fully around and look at her. "You know as well as I do that a person who is ruled by fear does not last long in Nairobi."

Kitra's mouth opened, but no sound came out.

The traffic started moving again. But Charles remained where he was until a truck beeped its horn. Charles resettled himself behind the wheel and started off.

Marc asked, "What happened then?"

"I was taken into an orphanage operated by World Vision. I was taught in their school. The missionary pastor and his wife, the couple who had rescued me, took me back to America with them. I could have remained over there, in safety and peace. My new family wanted me to stay. But I knew that God had rescued me for a purpose. My mission in life was to return and help others like myself. Young ones huddled in fear and hopelessness. With no strong arms reaching down to them." Charles glanced in the rearview mirror and directed his words at Kitra. "That is why I speak to this man as I do. Because he has proven himself to be our ally, and he needs to know who we are."

They turned off the main road and left the asphalt behind. The lane was deeply rutted, so much that their car swayed and rolled and groaned as they entered Kibera. Most of the people who surrounded the car were walking. A few rode bicycles, all of which were laden with goods or passengers or both. The number of children was astonishing. Many wore precise school uniforms of navy tops and khaki short pants or skirts. Those who did not, the young ones in rags, stared sullenly at the uniformed children. The uniforms were neat, but faded and threadbare from multiple washings. The people they passed gravely examined the car for danger, then lost interest. The car rolled on, accompanying the afternoon tide of humanity entering Kibera.

Charles glanced over and warned sternly, "Do not look at these people with pity. It puts you up and puts them down."

Marc acknowledged the truth of his instruction, but did not take his eyes off the vista beyond his window.

"The adults are returning home after twelve hours' work," Charles explained. "The fortunate children come from school. You cannot fathom the sacrifice their families make so their children can enter a school and gain a ticket out of Kibera."

The ramshackle houses were rammed up as close together as the refugee camp huts. The older ones were built of concrete siding with corrugated steel sheets for roofs. The newer ones were built from anything and everything.

"They walk three miles out at sunrise, catch buses into Nairobi, and work or study all day long," Charles told him. "Now they walk back home from the bus stop. Their journey can take two hours each way. Now they will do errands. They must be inside before dark. That is when the gangs come out and take over the streets of Kibera." Charles glanced over. "You have never experienced darkness like the night in a Nairobi slum."

They passed a line a quarter mile long, people of all ages waiting at a public faucet. Their buckets and plastic jerry cans formed a colorful punctuation to the poverty.

They passed hundreds of storefronts, more people standing patiently in lines. All business was done through wire-mesh openings. No one went inside or touched the merchandise until first the money was handed over.

Ladies on the side of the roadway fried fish in rusty woks over open gas flames. Others sold items from filthy burlap sacks—onions, sweet potatoes, turnip greens, single cigarettes. Open-sided coffee shops played reruns of soccer matches on decrepit televisions bolted to pillars. The drinking houses were filthy and dingy and dark. Women leaned in their doorways and watched the car's passage, their eyes smoldering like their cigarettes.

Charles and his passengers slowly bounced into a dusty square. Surrounding them were what at first glance appeared to be just another dozen or so storefronts. They all sported the same rusting hand-painted signs as the shops they had passed. Only here the names were different. Red Cross. World Vision. Catholic Relief Services. Southern Baptist Mission Board.

Charles said, "These mission groups used to be located separately around Kibera. It has a nice sound to the people back home, how they are lonely islands in the sea of Kibera. But the gangs began attacking the mission workers. Some were kidnapped. So the groups decided they could better protect everyone if they gathered together. Now there are eight of these clusters. They have become centers of sanity. People pay double the rent to be close to these squares."

Before Charles cut the motor, their car became surrounded with children. They besieged Charles with desperate joy. Marc had seen this scene any number of times back at the camp. Still, it amazed him, how the children responded to the pastor. They sang and danced and reached out to touch him, grip his arm, the tail end of his shirt, anything.

Marc and Kitra followed Charles and his children through an orphanage's open doorway and into a dusty compound. More children poured out of various doors. Charles squatted on the concrete stoop and allowed himself to be swallowed up by the kids. Marc climbed a set of steps so as to better watch how Charles sang and laughed and joked and listened, seemingly able to take in a hundred different voices at once. His dark eyes were filled with love.

Kitra climbed the stairs to stand beside Marc. "I have seen this happen many times, and still it astonishes me how the young ones respond to Charles."

Marc observed, "He has heard his calling. He has obeyed his Lord. He is in his place, using his gift."

Kitra removed her sunglasses and turned to face him. "You know your place, Marc Royce. But you fear yourself. As you should."

"Why do you say that?"

"It is every soldier's burden. To have such power and remain human, you must temper it with the knowledge of all you have done. And will do tomorrow." Her gaze was turned translucent by the sunlight. "You face the trial of David. How to hold fast to your faith when the power courses through your veins. When everything is within your grasp, even the power of life or death."

Marc stood and sweltered on the courtyard steps, stunned by her ability to touch his very core.

Kitra nodded acceptance to his silence. "I am glad not to be you, Marc Royce. And Charles is right. I am glad you are here with us."

Chapter Sixteen

Finally Charles extricated himself from the children and led Marc and Kitra back across the square. They tramped down a dusty lane and entered a whitewashed church. Inside they found a group of elders similar to those at the refugee camp. These sat on the traditional carved stools in a semicircle to the right of the dais. Before them stood a trio of young women.

The church pews were full. Marc and Kitra were the only white faces. The congregation followed the proceedings with intense fascination. They glanced over when Marc and Kitra entered, then resumed their observation of the elders.

Charles led them to a pew at the back and directed their attention to the proceeding. Each time the elders spoke the people before them hummed a response, an almost musical choir to the elders' words.

When Marc had settled into the seat beside Charles, he quietly asked, "Tell me what I'm seeing."

Charles smiled at him, vestiges of the previous joy from the children still there in his gaze. "The answer to your question is this. You are seeing a miracle." He pointed to the man at the center of the semicircle, a true ancient who wore a multicolored robe draped over a black suit jacket. "That is Philip's uncle."

"Philip, the chief at the refugee camp?"

"Yes, the same. Only it is not truly his uncle." The time in the courtyard had sharpened his accent. "But the relation is very complicated. So 'uncle' will do. His name is Oyango. Philip brought his uncle to faith in Jesus. This is a true miracle, but not the one I speak of now. The telling of two such miracles would take too long. So I will tell you only that for a young man to change the course of an elder's life is so rare that all the Luo tribe speak of it. They say it was not Philip, but Jesus working through the young man. They say this because Philip and the uncle, they both speak the same words. That Jesus reached through the voice of Philip and turned Oyango to the light."

Charles crossed his legs and laced his hands over one knee. "The Luo tribe are Nilotic. Just like the Masaii—you have heard of them, yes? The Luo migrated down the Nile from the north. The first migration took place around a thousand years ago. There have been several more, the last during the Victorian era."

"Philip spoke about it as though it was yesterday," Marc recalled.

"Yes, that is how it is with people who remember through story. The children memorize the tale from the voice of an elder, who is chosen to be the memory of their village and their tribe. Each teller speaks the words in simple fashion, always in the present. Making the tribe's history live today. Even when the lessons are taught in a refugee camp. Even when their village is no more."

Marc listened and studied his surroundings. On his other side, Kitra had gone utterly quiet. Overhead, a battery of ceiling fans turned in lazy circles, flicking the hot air around. The people seated before the elders rose up and bowed and said their thanks. As the group moved away, Philip's uncle raised one scrawny arm and gestured to the next group.

Charles went on, "When Christ comes to the Luo, the effect is *very* strong. Many Luo are Muslim; others still hold to the animism they carried with them down the Nile. Among many Luo Muslims there is still much witchcraft and superstition. When I tell you that Philip's uncle says he turned away, the words must be shouted to reveal the truth. He rejected everything from his past. He was stripped bare. He was brought to a newness that reaches back and changes not just him but his history. The change is . . ."

"Seismic," Kitra whispered.

The unexpected word caused Marc to shift around, only to discover that a tear trickled down Kitra's cheek. He had the urge to lean over and brush it away.

Charles said, "The Luo believers are known throughout Kenya. They are very fervent, very evangelical. And something more."

Marc forced himself to turn back. "More?"

"They are open to mysticism. Some say that God speaks to them. Directly."

"Like the dream Philip told us about," Marc said.

"Just so. Philip dreamed that his uncle would become an instrument of Jesus. A beacon to the world. But only if Philip shared his faith with Oyango. Normally such a thing would never happen, for a young man to speak with a clan elder about such matters. But he followed this dream or vision or calling and shared his faith with Oyango. The conversation lasted three days. At sunrise on the fourth day, Oyango asked Philip to walk with him down to the river and baptise him."

Charles began rocking in place. "One month later, Oyango's village was suddenly evacuated. They were bused into Kibera. Dumped here. Promised a new village. Soon, the bureaucrats said. Very soon. That was eighteen months ago. In the Luo's tradition, the chief should be held responsible for not protecting the village. For Philip to claim that God had spoken through a dream and told him that the uncle would become a leader of all Luos and more besides, this was . . ."

"Absurd," Marc offered. "Impossible."

Kitra leaned forward so as to glare at Charles and demanded, "Why am I hearing this for the first time?"

In response, Charles held Marc with his gaze. Unblinking. Waiting.

Marc asked, "Philip has had a dream about me?"

On his other side, Kitra's breath was a swift blade of surprise.

Then a sound from the front of the room drew them around.

Philip's uncle reached out a clawlike hand and gestured them forward.

Marc was directed into a chair drawn up before the semi-circle. Charles started to sit down beside him, then seemed to think better of it and stood at his right. Kitra did not come forward at all but remained seated at the back of the room. Philip's uncle glanced back and nodded, as though finding her decision correct.

Marc felt his pulse racing. Not out of fear. More like the way it seemed when he was being dropped into action. Supposedly landing in safety, there just to get his feet solid on the ground before moving into the free-fire zone. But adrenaline-amped with the uncertainty of what was soon to come.

Charles addressed the elders, his tone respectful. Silence followed, as if the elders needed time to digest what they had heard. Then one of the others, not Philip's uncle, spoke at length. Philip's uncle directed Charles to seat himself beside Marc. The elders talked among themselves, a low murmur with long and frequent pauses. As though the silence was as important as the words.

Charles said softly, "I have told them of Philip's dream. And of the message he gave before sending me on the helicopter with you. That we are to entrust you with the secret if you gave me the sign."

The unusual words jarred uncomfortably in Marc's head. *Dream* and *message* and *secret* and *sign*. He settled on what was probably the most important question of that moment. "Secret?"

"That is for the elders to say," Charles replied.

"Sign?"

"When you saved Kitra at the compound. That fits with Philip's dream."

"Will you tell me what Philip dreamed?"

"That you were to become a hero for his people and bring them home."

"Back to their village?"

"No, Marc Royce." The black eyes glittered with an otherworldly light. "Back to *all* their villages."

The uncle looked at Marc and spoke. Charles listened for a moment, then translated, "Oyango welcomes the man whom Philip has seen in his journey to the True World. He wishes

139

to know who you are, and why God has spoken through his nephew, naming you as the bringer of miracles."

Marc had faced a White House hearing. He had spoken to a battery of generals. He had made presentations to professional intelligence agents. He had briefed the most powerful men in the most powerful nation. But never had he felt so exposed, so *visible*, as now. Beneath an array of creaking fans, in a whitewashed church, in the center of the world's largest slum.

He told them precisely how he had come to be here. Who he answered to. And what he sought. Charles's translation formed a murmuring backdrop to his tale.

The elders listened with the unblinking severity of hanging judges. When he was finished, the silence clung to them with the heat until Philip's uncle said, "You search for answers."

Until that moment, Marc had no idea any of them spoke English. "I do."

One of the other elders said, "We must know whether his questions are ours."

"No," another said. "His questions are fashioned by Western minds for Western problems. Ours are Kikuyu and Luo and Masaii and Nubian. What we must know is, will his answers become our answers as well."

The discussion reverted back to Swahili. Marc gave it time, then asked, "May I pose a question of my own?"

If the elders were offended by his interruption, they did not show it. Philip's uncle said, "You may speak."

"Charles called this gathering a miracle. Will you tell me why?"

"It is a good question," a rotund elder said.

Oyango shifted his colorful robes. "You know my tribe?"

"You are Luo."

"It is so." He reverted back to Swahili. Charles translated, "The blood enemies of my people are the Kikuyu. And the Nubian. All of the clans represented here are bound by tribal loyalty. The enemies of my great-grandfathers are my enemies, as they will be the enemies of my children's children. These things do not change. You in the West make alliances and you make marriages and you break them all. This is not the Luo way."

"Or the Kikuyu," one of the others said in English. "The first president of Kenya after liberation was from the Kikuyu clan. The vice president was Luo. These two tribes formed the largest voting blocs. They had an agreement. After two years the Luo was to become president. But what happened, after one year and eleven months, the president fires the vice president and all the Luos on his cabinet. He says they were incompetent and could not do their jobs."

Another of the elders said, "And all the Kikuyu, they cheer. They say, this is very smart. Because they know, the Luo are not to be trusted."

Oyango went on, "And the Luo, they vowed revenge. Just as they have for a thousand years."

"This is not just politics, and it is not just in the past," the rotund elder said. "A hundred and fifty years ago, the British colonial government brought in Nubians from Egypt. They gave these Muslims from the north this land here, Kibera, as their own. At the time it was an outpost far from the colonial capital of Nairobi. Now the Nubians are our landlords. So those Luos who are Muslim formed alliances with the Nubians. The Luo gangs and the Nubian gangs, they prey on the Kikuyu and the Kisii."

"Yet look now at what you see." Philip's uncle pointed to each of the others in his circle. "Nubian. Kikuyu. Luo. Luhya. Kalenjin. Kisii. All of us sworn enemies. Yet here we sit in peace. How is this possible?"

Marc answered, "Because of Jesus."

"You are a follower of the risen one?"

"I am."

The chief turned one way, then the other. "I accept my nephew's direction now as I did before. At the turning. At the new beginning of my life. I say we should trust this man."

After a time of silence, the elder at the far end said, "Tell him."

One spoke, then another, then a third and so on. Back and forth the exchange went, almost as though they intended to add force to their words by weaving the sentences together jointly. Those who were not speaking hummed a single note of emphasis, a soft sound from the savannah, from the African night, from the vast seas of grass and beasts and days without end.

Charles translated, "The land of our fathers is not just for growing crops and hunting game and building our homes. It is our heart. It is our blood. It is our fathers and our mothers."

Marc said, "It always comes back to the land."

They responded with a unified drumbeat of sound, a deep resonant force. One of the Kikuyu reached down and grabbed a fistful of dust from the floor. He held it out and spoke. "This earth is dead. It is infected with all the city's ills."

His words were taken up by another. "This earth is infecting our children."

And another. "It is for the children that we speak with you. It is why we ask for your help."

Marc said, "Tell me what I can do."

Charles bound the voices together into one continuous dialogue. "With all the villages represented here, the process was the same. A bureaucrat they had never seen before arrived. He walked the village. He smiled at the elders. He spoke kind words.

"A few days came another man. And another. And a third. This last man, he came with papers and with trucks and with guns. He told the elders that the land was not theirs and never had been. The men with guns herded them into the trucks. The man gave the elders the papers that promised new villages. And payment for the land that was not theirs. Enough money to build new villages and plant new crops."

Marc guessed, "The money never arrived. Or the land."

"Soon, we are told. Tomorrow. Next week. After the rains. But the rains do not come. Or the land. Or the money."

Philip's uncle said, "We can wait no longer. Our children hear the city's call. Do you hear what I am saying, Marc Royce? Our children, they are forgetting their name."

Chapter Seventeen

The next morning Marc departed Nairobi on a Lodestone helicopter. A pair of sharpshooters armed with automatic rifles and RPGs leaned out the open rear door. Boyd Crowder and Marc and Karl Rigby joined the two pilots up front. With all three jump seats occupied, the cockpit was cramped. No one complained, for their view of Kenya was spectacular.

The chopper left the Nairobi sprawl behind in a matter of minutes. Once the air cleared of city smog, the Rift swooped open below them and a hundred lakes flashed and glistened. The vista was immense. The air rushing in the open doors was filled with all the flavors of Africa.

Marc studied a map supplied by the Kibera elders. Its surface was stained by a thousand hands. On it were noted all the known villages that had been erased by some bureaucrat's uncaring hand. Crowder and Rigby checked it carefully and declared that none of the evictions had used Lodestone forces. Marc knew Walton would be skeptical, but he was glad he had decided to trust these men.

They headed east, aiming for Oyango's home village. A half hour later, Lake Victoria emerged from the blue-gray horizon. The lake spanned over ten thousand square miles, the world's second largest freshwater sea. From their height, Marc could see smoke rising from three neighboring hamlets. Marc asked the pilots to survey them before landing and then slipped into the chopper's rear compartment. Children raced out and waved and danced as they passed. Men and women straightened from their stations in the fields. Cattle and goats scattered. Through the open doorway Marc smelled woodsmoke and earthy fragrances.

But the village cleared of people was something else entirely. There was no sign that Oyango's village had ever existed.

Instead, they descended on the outskirts of a modern factory farm. A neat rectangle of perhaps three square miles was planted and watered and sheltered beneath plastic ribbons. A pair of tractors dragged massive rotor blades and raised flocks of screeching birds. The dust was terrible.

As the rotors slowed, Crowder slipped off the headphones and said to Marc, "This is your show. When Lodestone HQ asks what went down, I'm telling them I was here as your official escort."

"Got it." Marc exited the chopper and walked toward a team of workers uncoiling irrigation piping and settling it into shallow grooves. But before he arrived, two men rushed over. They wore pale blue coveralls without insignia and waved angrily at his approach.

"No, no, you are not being here! This is a most private place!" The taller of the pair was not African at all, but Indian. Glistening black hair was slicked across a head large as a pumpkin. Angry eyes glinted from within deep folds. "You must leave now."

"I'm here representing—"

"I am not caring for anything you say. This is private land,

and you are a trespasser!" He waved his hands in Marc's face, as though trying to block his vision. "You are going now!"

"I need to ask what happened to the villagers."

"You are illegal! You think I am caring what questions you bring? No, I am not caring! You are trespassing! I shall call the army and report you!" He whipped about and said to his associate, "You are making careful note of this helicopter's tail number?"

"It is done, sir."

"Now you are taking photographs of this man."

Marc protested, "I just want—"

"Go, go now! You will see much trouble, oh yes!"

Marc allowed himself to be turned around and shoved back toward the chopper. It was either that or fight the man. And nothing was going to be gained through violence. The Indian showed no fear of the armed men, who watched through the chopper's open door. Marc clambered aboard and the helicopter rose into the sky. The Indian administrator watched them depart with fists planted on his hips while the African continued to shoot photographs.

Marc slipped past Rigby and pointed out the windshield. "Set us down on that rise over there."

Between the factory farm and the nearest village was a lonely hillock. The chopper's arrival flattened the grass and sent monkeys shrieking from a pair of thorn trees. This time when Marc hopped down, Crowder and Rigby joined him.

The factory farm was a fragment of Western-style order in the midst of the Kenyan landscape. Five long whitewashed buildings stood at its center. Marc assumed they contained admin and lodging and storage and barns. The workers operated in tight coordination. The fields and their plastic covers were neat and orderly.

Crowder demanded, "This make any sense to you?"

Marc did not respond. He watched as four trucks rumbled into the central compound and backed up to loading bays by the largest of the whitewashed buildings. Crowder walked back to the chopper and returned with binoculars. He watched them for a time, then announced, "They're loading up bundles of flowers and what looks like turnips."

Marc said, "Why would they evacuate one village and leave those others right where they are?"

Crowder tapped the binoculars on his thigh. "If they're setting up factory farms, why scatter them around the region? Transport alone would eat up their profits. You want as much land all together as you can get. It's the only way these things work. My family's farmed for ten generations. I might have chosen the military over black Arkansas earth, but I know a mistake when I see one."

Marc replied, "They wouldn't have kidnapped Serge over some experiment in modern farming techniques. We're asking the wrong questions."

Rigby added, "Serge Korban was taken from an area blanketed by ash. You couldn't grow stones in that place."

The colonel growled toward the factory farm, "What is going on down there?"

Marc turned back to the chopper. "We won't find the answers out here."

They followed the elders' map to two other displaced communities and found identical situations. The surrounding villages remained untouched. They landed at one occupied village, where the lone headman who spoke English related how their village had been warned to keep all animals away from the factory farm. The elder complained about cattle that had been shot for straying too close, and said their wells were going dry. As to the displaced villagers, the elder shrugged his lack of information. The government, he replied. Men in suits came with papers and armies and trucks. The villagers were forced to leave. It is the way of this age.

When they took off, Crowder ordered the chopper to the south and east. The pilots did not need to check their maps for this final destination. As they descended, Crowder told everyone on board, "We are not here."

He received a series of grim nods in reply.

They landed at a major intersection. The two roads were both well paved. Connected to them were a series of small feeder trails, surrounded by the inevitable trading shanties. Pie dogs sniffed and snarled. Goats bleated and pulled at their ropes as the chopper's engine wound down.

Accompanied by an armed escort, they left the chopper and crossed the Trans-African Highway between crawling trucks. Crowder led Marc to a broad expanse of burned earth.

"This was just another regional supply depot," he said. "Used by a dozen different aid groups operating in this district. At least, that was the plan. But when the attack happened, my men were standing guard detail for empty godowns."

"The traffic jam at the Mombasa port," Marc recalled.

"The goods being off-loaded from the ships were sent straight to the camps. Until the attack, this duty defined boring. They are in the middle of nowhere, bothering nobody."

Marc surveyed the terrain. A series of drainage ditches bordered the supply center. Stone pillars stood like blackened teeth in the western sun. "Tell me what happened."

"Just before midnight they radioed in that choppers were inbound. They said the choppers weren't responding to their radio queries, but when they landed they saw the soldiers on board were wearing blue UN armbands. You follow?"

"Your men assumed they were all on the same side."

"Roger that. Then we got one alert, a thirty-second burst of panic. They were under attack. We didn't believe them. We thought it was some kind of practical joke born out of tedium. But then we heard the gunfire. And the shouts. Then the line went dead."

"Did you record the conversation?"

"Of course. I'll play it for you when we get back." Crowder stomped forward, kicking up plumes of ashes as he led Marc to the nearest clump of trading shacks.

Only then did Marc realize the shanties were empty. All of them.

A crone bent almost double with age and infirmity emerged from a shack by a goats' pen. She shuffled toward them, leaning on a stick as warped as her back. Her outstretched hand was held in an arthritic curl as she whined an appeal.

"Last time in, I brought an interpreter," Crowder said, handing the woman a bill. "There are six people left from a community of maybe thirty Indian and African traders. All those who remain are too old and too sick to leave. The rest were ordered away by the soldiers. And now you know what I know."

"You've spoken with the UN?"

"They claim it's all a myth. They grew angry when I insisted this had happened the way I described. Like I was insulting them, instead of just hunting answers."

"I'll talk with the Kibera elders and Uhuru, see if they can tell us anything." When Crowder responded by kicking the burned earth, Marc said, "If I can help you, I will, Colonel. I'm certain your mystery is tied to my own."

They returned to Nairobi well after dark. Streaks the color of blood filtered across the western horizon. Otherwise the world was intensely black. On the approach to the airport they passed a few islands of lights, small townships that served as feeders to the mammoth silver-white creature on the horizon. The connecting roads became veins illuminated by crawling headlights. Other than that, the land was invisible. The air through the chopper's open door was filled with alien spices, the wind warm as a caress. The dark landscape seemed to mask a million dangers.

Marc ate, showered, and called Ambassador Walton from the front lawn of the Lodestone compound. He had to assume his office and room were bugged. It wasn't Crowder or Rigby who concerned him. It was the unseen threat, the unnamed foe, the beast that lurked beyond the shadows.

Walton heard him out in silence, then declared, "These evacuations are not happening for the sake of experimental farms."

"I agree one hundred percent."

"It doesn't matter how fertile the soil. I don't care if they're raising a new breed of living gemstones. This is not the reason."

"The authorities are masking something," Marc agreed.

"I'm still not in agreement with your decision to bring in

Lodestone's military arm. They could be showing you a friendly face just to determine your primary objective."

Marc held his ground. "You said it yourself, sir. I'm the operative in the field. I need to follow my hunches on this one. From what I've seen, Crowder is on our side."

Walton chewed on that for a time. "We've run into a surprise on Crowder's file. Our operatives discovered an electronic guard dog. Our guys think they slipped away before they were discovered. But there is definitely someone keeping a tight watch."

"Lodestone could suspect Crowder of switching allegiances. Now they want to know who else is interested."

"I'm still not convinced," Walton growled. "I will see if there is anything listed on new experimental farms. In the meanwhile, you watch your back."

Chapter Eighteen

The next morning Marc attended another gathering of the Kibera elders. When he climbed from the taxi, Charles stood alone in front of the church. Marc shook the offered hand and asked, "Where is Kitra?"

"She returned yesterday to the refugee camp. A French convoy made it through from Mombasa, and she is riding back with them." Charles must have seen Marc's disappointment, for as they entered the church Charles patted his shoulder and said, "She likes you very much. This much I know. And I suspect it is why she left no word."

Marc stopped midway down the aisle. "I don't understand."

"She is conflicted. Over what, I do not know."

"Another man?"

"No one here in Africa. Of that I am certain. One comes to know people very well in the camps. Back in Israel?" Charles shrugged and motioned them forward. "Come. It is not correct to keep the elders waiting."

As in the previous session, Philip's uncle held the central position. Marc accepted a tin mug of black tea sweetened by coarse raw sugar. He turned his mind away from the absent woman, thanked the elders for seeing him, and related the previous day's journey.

As he talked and Charles translated, two of the elders lit up misshapen cigars, like lengths of knotted rope. The smell reminded Marc of the flavors drifting through the chopper's doorway, a heady draught of tobacco and earth. He described the factory farms, the hostile reception, the threats, and their visit to the highway juncture.

When he was done, the Kikuyu said, "We have heard of these farms. We have also faced this mystery. We all say our land is the finest in our regions."

"There is more at work here than experimental farms. My superiors in Washington agree."

"Then what?"

"That is the question we need to focus on," Marc replied. "We must seek a single factor that links all the villages together." Marc let them talk among themselves for a while, then asked, "Could you tell me what led up to the day you were expelled? I'm looking for anything out of the ordinary. Because I've got to tell you, I'm stumped. This is not adding up."

The elders discussed this for a long time. Marc did not mind the wait, his thoughts drifting to Kitra. He wondered what might have created her internal conflict. He did not believe it was due to his assignment with Lodestone. Something else was behind this, of that he was increasingly certain.

Eventually Charles drew him back by translating a summary of the elders' discussions. They spoke of the drought and failed crops. They recalled a sudden rainfall. The birth of a lame calf. Clearly they thought Marc had asked about signs. Marc did not correct them. He had sifted through disconnected fragments before and been rewarded with the unexpected diamond.

When they finally went silent, Marc asked them to repeat their description of the government man's arrival. They showed no irritation over his request, and once more described the bureaucrat's sudden appearance, his smiling face, his official forms, his lies. Soon, they all said, the chorus turning their expressions bitter. They had come to loathe that word *soon*.

Marc asked, "Tell me again about the yellow men who came with the government official."

Marc listened to the elders describe the small slender men in suits and how they grubbed at the earth. "Did they carry any electronic apparatus? It could have been something as small as a cellphone."

"No, just the shovels. They dig tiny holes. They move like beetles, like ants when the nest is disturbed. They go here, there, they say nothing, they see no one. Just the earth. When they are gone, they leave tiny holes, like where night creatures have searched for grubs. After the first wind, the holes are gone."

"Tell me about their shovels."

"Very small. The size of your hand. Smaller. Shaped like a spear with the edges beaten so they curve."

When Marc started to rise, the Luo chief spoke. Charles's forehead creased with evident surprise. He motioned Marc to remain where he was. "They wish to tell you a secret."

The senior Kikuyu spoke, and he was followed by others. As though all wanted to participate in this revelation. Charles's concern radiated through his translation, "After the miracle of Jesus worked in our hearts, and this gathering began, we came together and chose twenty of our best young people. We sent them to the university. You understand?"

"Their fees are being paid by the collective."

Philip's uncle elaborated, "Not by *one* tribe. By *all* our tribes."

The Kikuyu added, "These young men and women carry a great responsibility. In earlier days, they would have been trained as warriors and healers and leaders, all in the tribal manner. Now we arm them with the ways of this modern land, the same knowledge used by others to force us from our home."

"I am amazed," Marc said, "by your wisdom."

Oyango went on, "We sent two who study the law out to see if they could learn something of value about these displaced villages, and why we have not been given new lands."

"What did they discover?"

There followed another deep chorus, splinters of each sentence supplied by one and then another. Charles translated, "They returned with a man. He was not Kenyan."

"He was white?"

"Black. Perhaps Angolan, or Ghanaian, but not of any tribe you see here. He spoke Swahili with difficulty. He was . . ."

Marc read the word imprinted on the elders' faces. "Dangerous."

"He does not care for life. You understand?"

"A hired killer."

"He tells us, we have two choices. We can continue to ask questions through these two we have sent. And if they do, people will die. Starting with these two students. Then their families. Then their friends. Anyone who has even spoken with these two, even shaken their hands, they too will leave this earth."

Marc felt a taut electric chill; then a thrill ran through him. The prey was glimpsed for the very first time. "Describe everything about this man."

"Very tall. Not like the Masaii are tall. Like a warrior who has feasted on the cattle of his enemies. The nose of a hawk. And eyes with no bottom."

"I know these eyes," Marc assured them. "Any tribal scars, tattoos, anything that might help me identify him?"

Charles listened, then touched his earlobe. "He is missing the bottom of one ear."

"Right or left?"

There was a discussion, then, "The right one."

"How was he dressed?"

Two of the elders smiled at this, but there was no humor. Only grim recollection. Charles translated, "There are visitors to our land. Singers of the Western music who incite the young ones to hate and fight and lust after bad women. And the famous players of sport. They come dressed like this. The man's shirt was of silk and open to his chest. Gold chains about his neck. A gun on his waist. Another under his pant leg bound to his ankle. A watch that was too big, so that it rattled like a woman's bracelet on his wrist. He was driven here in a very large black vehicle, as big as a truck, with black windows."

Marc asked, "Has he returned?"

"We have given him no reason to come back," Oyango replied. "We ordered our treasured young ones to stop their questions."

"Who have you told of this?"

"I have spoken of this to my nephew and now to you. No one else."

The Kikuyu said through Charles, "He offered jobs. If we behaved, he said we could send our young ones to work on these new farms. But we do not seek their money. We want our land, our earth."

Oyango began a deep rocking motion with his body. His words were a chant of mourning and loss. "We have watered their earth with our blood. Our ancestors lie beneath the blades of their tractors. We beseech you, Marc Royce. Give us back our earth."

Chapter Nineteen

Marc returned to the Lodestone HQ and struggled to focus on all the paper work generated by his newfound success—updated lists of approved suppliers, procurement documents, payment schedules, and delivery modules. Finally at midafternoon he phoned the French refugee camp. The new camp director was mildly irritated over being drawn from a crisis meeting, but remained polite just the same. Marc was, after all, slated to deliver them crucial supplies and do so under the UN budget. The director told Marc to wait, then walked the satellite phone across the compound. The silence was filled by an electric crackling, the signal passing from Marc's sweaty palm up to an unseen satellite, then back to the verge of a smoldering volcano.

Then he heard her voice. "Hello?"

"Kitra, it's me."

"Marc?"

"You left, and—"

"Wait a moment."

He could picture her footsteps, passing by beds where children whimpered. A door creaked and slammed shut. Then, "Why are you calling me like this?"

"I missed saying good-bye."

"Oh, Marc."

"Did I do something to upset you?"

"No, Marc. You were . . . just right."

He could no longer remain in his seat. He sprang from the chair and moved catlike about the office, pacing out his territory. "Why didn't you say something, Kitra?"

"I am complicated." Each word was a struggle for her to form. "My life is complicated. You should not . . . It isn't wise . . ."

"Kitra, I haven't needed anyone for so long, I thought it was never going to happen again. Now . . ."

He wondered if she would shoot him down, hang up on him and extinguish his hopes, his heart. But she came back with a small, "Yes? Now . . . ?"

"I just wish you'd give us a chance."

"This isn't supposed to happen."

"Why not?"

"Because."

"That's not much of a reason."

"I need to focus on one thing right now. You understand?"

"No, Kitra, I don't. I am here for you and for Serge. The two do not negate each other."

"You are here to do a job."

"That's right. And you are part of it. Soon enough the job will be over. And I want us to begin." He had no idea whether he was making any sense at all. But the words had to be spoken. Marc didn't have a choice in the matter.

"I have to go. The director is waving for his phone." She hesitated, then added, "I'll try and call you later. If I can. If I—"

The line went dead.

Marc entered the mess hall to find Dirk, the giant who had assaulted Kitra, standing at the lunch counter. The satellite phone Marc carried in his hand suddenly felt wrong, as though he had no business bringing this connection to someone who had just given him a tiny measure of hope into this man's presence.

"Marc, hey, I was just coming up to see you." Karl Rigby, the colonel's aide, pitched his voice so it would carry. "Grab a place. I'll be right with you."

The other men who had returned from in-country with Dirk gave Marc the blank stare of combatants taking aim. But no one made a move toward him or spoke a single word. Even so, Marc felt the laser targets on his back throughout ordering his meal and finding a table.

If Karl noticed the hostility, he gave no sign. Instead, he settled onto the bench beside Marc and spread out a map on the table. "The colonel called in a couple of favors before he left with the next in-country contingent. Our tame techies did some checking. There is no geological formation that connects the dots."

All the villages Marc had heard about from the elders were marked with bright red points. The map was far newer than the one the elders had given Marc. The lost villages were scattered like blemishes around the border of Lake Victoria. Marc pointed to the northern shoreline and said, "This is where Serge was taken. About twenty-five klicks from the French camp. Maybe six from the Red Cross camp's main gates."

"That doesn't make any sense at all." Rigby planted his elbows on the table and frowned over the map. "I thought, you know, they were after gold or oil or diamonds."

"So did I."

"The hunt for minerals fuels more than half of Africa's civil wars. But the techies tell me nobody could go in and scrape up a little dirt and learn anything."

"The elders were definite," Marc confirmed. "The yellow men scrape up surface samples and disappear."

"Yellow men," Rigby repeated.

"Small and precise and totally silent," Marc said.

"There was this thing last year," Rigby spoke to the map on the table. "The largest company in Korea leased one third of all the arable land in Mauritius. They were going to set up the world's largest factory farm, ship the produce back home. They were set to evacuate almost half the population living outside the capital city. But two church groups operating in the region took legal action and had it stopped."

"I've been through this with the colonel," Marc said. "Factory farming requires huge stretches of land. Why take one village and leave the ones to either side in place? Plus . . ."

Ribgy's attention was drawn up from the map by Marc's hesitation. The colonel's aide held him with a steady gaze.

Marc nodded slowly. Either he trusted these men totally or it was all a waste of time. "My superiors in Washington would have no interest in land grabs for factory farms. It wouldn't register on their radar."

"You're sure about that?"

"Positive."

"You ready to tell us who they are?"

Marc took a breath. "I'm ready to ask them for permission. Yes."

Ribgy did not actually smile. It was more a tightening of

his features, a rearranging of the tension, a silent approval. "Well, all right."

"So what . . ." Marc stopped because his satellite phone started buzzing. He swiveled around, shielding himself and the woman whose voice he hoped to hear. "This is Marc."

A rich African voice boomed, "Frederick Uhuru, Mr. Royce. I've just arrived in Nairobi. We need to meet. Now. Immediately."

He turned back and gestured for a pen and paper. Rigby slipped both from his shirt pocket. Marc said, "Give me the address, sir."

"The New Stanley Hotel. Every taxi driver in Nairobi will know its location."

"I'm on my way."

"Your company will thank you for hurrying. Uhuru out."

Marc cut the connection, and sat there, cradling the phone with both hands. Thinking hard.

Rigby asked, "What is it?"

An idea gradually took form. "Do you have a camera with a telephoto lens?"

"There's one up in the office, sure. We use it to document hostile terrain from the air."

"Could you maybe shoot a photo for me without being seen?"

"Don't see why not."

"If you're caught, it could mean serious trouble."

"No problem." Rigby's smile was tight. "Be like setting up a sniper shot, only without the cordite."

When Marc entered the hotel's main courtyard, Frederick Uhuru rose from a table beneath the patio's canopy. The UN official was in an expansive mood. "By Nairobi standards, Mr. Royce, you are almost on time."

"Sorry it took so long." Marc settled into the chair, then spoke to a waiter in starched whites hovering at his elbow. "Just coffee, thanks."

"Oh, bring the man something to eat. The food here really is quite good. You can't be so full as to decline an excellent meal." Uhuru spoke to the waiter in Swahili, then turned back. "You have some documents for me to see?"

"Yes, sir." Marc had borrowed a briefcase from the compound, a cheap plastic Samsonite. He spun the dials and pulled out the new procurement agreements from beneath the satellite phone.

Uhuru settled a pair of ridiculously small reading glasses on his nose. His massive hands flipped through the pages with a fluid ease. He did not look up until the waiter returned and deposited a steaming plate in front of Marc. "Lake trout, caught just this morning," the large man said. "The fish of Lake Victoria are said to be the sweetest in the world. Tell me what you think."

Marc tasted a meal he did not want, and had to agree, "It's fabulous."

Uhuru beamed as though the compliment was meant for him personally. He spent a few more minutes on the pages, then tossed them on the table. "You have performed well, Mr. Royce. But I do not see a notation for your own recompense."

"I receive my salary from Lodestone."

"Come, come, Mr. Royce. You are being taken on as a fixer. A fixer always receives a personal contribution from every transaction. I am not doing business with Lodestone. I am doing business with *you*." Uhuru fished a cellphone from his pocket and set it on top of the documents. "Call your directors in Washington and see if I am not right in this matter."

"I'll do that," Marc promised. "Soon as—"

His words were cut off by the sight of a tall man emerging from behind the patio's furthest pillar. He wore a dark suit, tailored to fit his very broad shoulders and narrow waist. He was obsidian black, with a bald head that gleamed in the sunlight. But what caught Marc's attention was how the lower half of his right ear was missing. The man's eyes, hidden behind wraparound shades, swept over the gathering, ever restless, a professional doing his job. Then he vanished back behind the pillar. Facing outward, toward a potential incoming threat.

"Yes, Mr. Royce? You were saying?"

Marc forced his attention back to Uhuru. "I'd prefer to call them from my office."

"Most unwise. You must assume everything you say indoors is heard by a multitude of others. Which is why I always carry two phones. An official one for all the conversations that need to be heard by the unseen listeners. And another that I change every week." Uhuru beamed proudly at his own acumen. "And also why we are seated on the patio of this fine establishment. Do you know this place, Mr. Royce?"

"My first visit."

"The New Stanley Hotel was once the epicenter of safari high life. The Thorn Tree Café received its name from a tree that has been cut down, just like so much of the former colonial culture. I hope you understand what pleasure it gives me to sit here and regale you with such facts."

"You are Kenyan?"

"I am African, Mr. Royce. And I am happy to inform you that this is our time, and our land. You are most fortunate to be seated here at this juncture."

Marc supplied the response the man was clearly expecting. "And even more fortunate to have you as my sponsor."

Uhuru beamed. "You are indeed a fast learner. And here is one final tidbit for you to carry with you back to your office. Are you listening, Mr. Royce?"

"Sure thing."

Every vestige of Uhuru's good humor vanished, replaced by a brooding menace. "Do not waste your hours on the mutterings of old men inside a shantytown church. Their time is gone. Ours has arrived. Yours and mine. But only if you have the good sense to remember whose side you are on. Africa does not offer second chances, Mr. Royce. Only shallow graves await those who refuse to listen to the wisdom of their betters."

Chapter Twenty

Marc and Karl Rigby returned to the Lodestone compound to find Boyd Crowder waiting for them. Soon as Marc detailed the meeting with Uhuru and described what he had in mind, the colonel insisted upon joining him.

As Marc printed out the best of Rigby's photographs, shot from a shadowed corner of the Stanley Hotel's courtyard, he recalled the African guard's restless scanning of the perimeter. Marc was certain the man could sense a sniper taking aim.

Rigby drove them in one of the armored Tahoes. As promised, Charles awaited them at the turnoff into Kibera. As they entered the slum, the colonel grew increasingly grim. "I've been on duty here for almost three years and never had a reason to make this journey."

Rigby said worriedly, "No amount of armor will guarantee our security, Colonel. Maybe we should return to the highway and request backup."

"We are among friends." Crowder glanced at Marc. "Isn't that correct, Royce?"

"Long as we're gone by sundown."

Crowder gave Marc a tight smile. "That was good thinking, having Rigby shoot the man's picture."

"It may be nothing."

"Eliminating possibilities is still further along than I've gotten. And Uhuru definitely warned you off."

"He couldn't have made it clearer with a gun in his hand."

Ahead of them, Charles parked his decrepit Mercedes in the square. Marc directed Rigby to pull up behind him. As they emerged from the vehicle, Marc told him, "You need to stay with the car."

"That's a negative."

"Trust for trust, that's what the colonel told me," Marc replied. "We need these people to treat us as allies."

"Stand down, soldier," Crowder said, but his tone was a gentle growl.

Rigby glowered but remained behind the wheel. Marc led Boyd Crowder to where Charles stood in the alley's entryway. When Marc introduced them, Crowder said, "I owe you an apology, Reverend Matinde. One of my men assaulted you and your female companion. That is totally unacceptable. On behalf of my entire squad, I apologize."

Charles nodded nervously. "Thank you, Colonel."

Marc asked, "Are the elders willing to see us?"

"They'll see you. I didn't say anything about the colonel coming with us."

Crowder offered, "I can stay out here."

"No. This meeting is vital," Marc said, then to Charles, "There is a chance that I won't be around later. The elders need to know this man and hear that I trust him. Face-to-face."

In response, Charles turned and led them into the church. He motioned for them to stand at the back, then hurried up the front aisle.

Crowder studied the elders gathered on the church's dais. "That man in the center, he's Luo?"

"A chief," Marc confirmed. "And relative of the camp's leader."

"The guys to either side look like they're Kikuyu."

"They are."

"The Kikuyu and the Luo are sworn enemies."

"I know." Marc gave him a swift summary of what he had experienced thus far. By the time he finished talking, Crowder was watching the group in front intently.

"Miracle," the colonel repeated.

"That was their word, not mine," Marc replied.

Crowder shook his head. "A lot of people in power are going to see this as a serious threat."

Marc was about to ask the colonel what he meant when Charles called back, "The elders will speak with you now."

The elders shook hands in the African manner, limp and soft, the gesture of warriors trained to show no strength or aggression. Marc set his briefcase on the chair, shifted the satellite phone, and took out the envelope holding the photographs taken by Rigby. They first passed the UN administrator's picture from hand to hand. The image showed Frederick Uhuru at his most unflattering, a predatory gleam in his eye as he ordered Marc to keep away from this place and these people.

Finally the elder handed it back and said through Charles, "This one we do not know."

"None of you have seen him?"

They were definite. "The man whose name changed from village to village was another."

He passed over the second photograph, of the man with the mutilated ear. "What about this one?"

This time, the response was instantaneous. Every one of them reacted the same way. Their nostrils flared, and one finger tapped the face in the photo. Over and over. Passed to the next man, who tapped it again. Staining the face with their anger and their sweat.

"He is the one who came and threatened," Charles confirmed.

Crowder's face tightened in a warrior's grin, all anticipation and hunger. "I'll show this around, see what I can dig up."

"Quietly," Marc warned.

"Off the grid," Crowder assured him. "I've got my career and my men to think of."

Charles softly translated everything they said. Marc turned back to the elders and said, "I came to Kenya thinking Boyd Crowder was the enemy. I assumed he was behind Serge's disappearance. Now I am certain I was wrong. I trust him. I think you should do the same."

The men's gazes flickered back and forth between them. The silence lengthened. Marc waited them out. Beside him, Crowder might as well have turned to stone.

Finally the Luo said in English, "We would speak to you, Marc Royce. Alone."

Crowder said, "I'll be in the car."

When the officer started down the aisle, Oyango spoke with Charles. The pastor's eyes widened. Charles glanced at Marc, then rose from his chair and followed Crowder from the church.

When the church was empty, Oyango motioned to the

Kikuyu beside him. The elder's accent was very strong, but his English was precise. "The missing man."

"Serge Korban."

"And his sister."

"Kitra."

The Kikuyu elder nodded. "What do you know of these two?"

"I . . . Serge was a medic." Marc corrected himself. "Is a medic. He and Kitra are Israeli. Their mother is French. They were both born in Tel Aviv."

The elders all shared a somber frown, as though they found something distasteful in what he said. The Kikuyu's voice was surprisingly light. He repeated, "What do you *know*?"

"I-I'm sorry. I don't . . ."

"Why are they in Kenya? Have you asked this question of them?"

Marc looked from one face to the next.

The Luo chief spoke then. "Sometimes we see what we want. Not what is."

"It is the warrior's first lesson," the Kikuyu agreed. "To find the lion hiding in the grass."

Oyango flicked his fingers in front of Marc's face. "To survive, a hunter must detect the slightest motion."

"The flicker of color that does not belong," the Kikuyu confirmed. "This is the difference between life and death."

"I'm sorry," Marc said, "but I—"

His satellite phone rang.

Marc pulled the bulky apparatus from his briefcase. He hesitated, his mind buzzing louder than the phone. "I must take this."

The elders nodded. Marc wanted to rise. He disliked having all the eyes on him as he spoke with Kitra. Their questions were framed in their dark gazes. He punched the button and remained where he was. "This is Royce."

"Oh, Marc." Kitra's voice was as terrified as it was soft. "They are *here*."

Chapter Twenty-One

They rushed straight from the slum chapel to the Nairobi airport. The snarled traffic became just another enemy they had to fight. Marc called Kitra back twice, checking in, gaining new details. The UN contingent had arrived at the camp in two SUVs and two battle vans. They presented the camp elders with eviction notices. The evacuation was to begin in thirty-six hours. The officials ignored the director's protests and the elders' pleas as they had in previous evictions. Marc fed the status updates to Boyd Crowder, who in turn made plans with Karl Rigby.

The third time Marc phoned, Kitra did not respond.

They were met at the Lodestone hangar by six more security personnel. They loaded their gear into the chopper and headed into the sun, now low on the horizon. Crowder passed around the photograph of Frederick Uhuru and the man who had threatened the elder. "We don't know if either of these men will be among the attackers. But if they are, do not, repeat, do not put either man down."

"Say again, Colonel."

"They may have our first lead regarding our missing personnel. Disable them as required. But it is essential that we question them."

When Crowder settled into the cockpit's other jump seat, Marc said, "I've just realized something. Uhuru offered me that contract because he wanted to distract me."

"You're assuming the UN guy is part of the problem."

"The man who threatened the elders was there with him."

"Correction. He was on the same porch of a hotel café." Boyd Crowder waved his own statement aside. "You know what I hear most clearly in your words? Trust. Far as I'm concerned, there's nothing finer, especially when we're heading into action."

Marc did not reply. It seemed so clear to him now. Uhuru's intention all along had been to remove a potential obstacle from the grid. And Uhuru had almost succeeded. Marc's thoughts swirled, as malevolent as the volcano plume looming on the horizon. He recalled the warning embedded in the elders' questions. And wondered what else he had gotten totally wrong.

They landed almost a mile away from the gates of the camp. The sunset was a ruddy glow as they loaded up their gear and set off. The volcano's plume glowed like a fiery pillar, a huge tent of ash and smoke that covered the western sky. But the wind was away from them and the air was clear.

The dust thrown up by the men's passage held a bitter taste, like a fire that threatened to engulf them all. They joined the road leading to the camp but held to the verge so as not to be slowed by the exhausted refugees. Boyd's men held to a pace one step below a full run. The adults they passed glanced over, saw there was no threat, and looked away.

When the main gates came into view, Crowder directed his men into the same copse of trees where Marc had defended the women. He took the satellite phone from Marc's pack and said, "Make the call."

This time it was the director who answered. His French accent was made far heavier by the tension. "Kitra, she is in the clinic. Where are you, please?"

"Just outside." Marc used Crowder's binoculars to scan the front gates, which appeared to be unmanned. "Where are Sergeant Kamal and his men?"

"The trucks, they came for all the soldiers two hours ago."

"The camp's been left with no security?"

"The official from Nairobi, he said the camp is to close; there is no need for guards."

"We're coming in. Royce out." Marc stowed the phone and asked, "Who would have the clout to order a contingent of UN soldiers away from their assigned station?"

"Someone so far up the food chain he could roast us both for dinner," Crowder replied. "Okay. On my signal. Let's move out."

But the enemy was no longer in the camp.

Marc and the arriving Lodestone operatives were met at the gates by his young contingent. They split into three groups and wound through hovels veiled by shadows and woodsmoke. Children watched them pass with round solemn gazes. Chickens and pie dogs scattered before them as they hurried into place. The intent was to spring on them from all sides. Just appear from nowhere, round up the intruders, and interrogate them while surprise left them vulnerable.

But as they approached the central compound, Marc heard trucks come to life and rumble down the main road. From behind him, Crowder said, "We can still stop them."

Marc shook his head. "Not without firing."

The soldier behind Crowder huffed, "That's how we get things done, bro."

Marc said, "As far as we know, this is a contingent of UN troops. Even if their purpose is bogus, attacking them would land us in a world of trouble."

Crowder hesitated, then said into the body mike attached to his wrist, "Do not attack. Repeat. Hold your fire."

The trucks raced past unseen. Marc heard the roaring motors and surmised, "They knew we were coming."

The soldier behind Crowder said, "Well, duh."

Crowder said, "That's enough, mister."

"Come on, sir. We gear up, we flush the quarry, and we let them go?"

"I said, that's enough."

Marc decided the best thing he could do was ignore the exchange. "They posted a watcher outside the gates."

"Probably in the woods we passed through," Crowder agreed.

"So what does that tell you?"

Crowder was silent.

"Whatever it is they're really doing here," Marc said, "they intend for it to remain secret."

Crowder mulled that over. "You got those photographs with you?"

"In my pack."

"Let's go see if anyone spotted them hereabouts."

The photographs that Rigby took meant nothing to Philip or the other camp leaders. The pictures were passed from hand to hand, then given back. The old men and Philip were almost apologetic. Crowder stood in the shade of the hut's overhanging roof as Marc seated himself beside Kitra, who tried to serve as translator in Charles's absence. But her Swahili was not nearly up to the challenge. Finally Philip began translating for the other elders. His deep voice carried a strong accent, but his English was surprisingly good.

The camp elders described how the UN official had been accompanied by six African soldiers and four of the yellow men. Marc asked, "The Africans were not Kenyan?"

The elders discussed this at length. Philip finally said, "We are trying to decide their tribe. We think it was Somali. These people are everywhere. They did not speak or show any ID. They could also have been Angolan, or Ethiopian. There is no way to tell for certain. But we all agree the soldiers wore the blue armbands."

"We are going to try and stop the eviction from happening."

Philip responded with a slow nod. But the colonel interrupted his response by jerking in surprise, touching his earpiece and speaking into his body mike, "This is Colonel Crowder. Are you certain this is genuine?" He glared at Marc as he listened. "Roger. Crowder out." The colonel rose from his chair and said to Marc, "I need a word."

Marc excused himself and followed Crowder from the yard. The colonel walked to the center of the central compound and signaled for his guard to join them. The trooper was short and slight in the manner of a hidden dagger. He had dark hair and even features and languid eyes. He cradled a semiautomatic Remington, wore a pistol and a brace of carbon-bladed knives on his belt.

Crowder said, "Nairobi reports we've got incoming VIPs from D.C. We're ordered to return immediately."

"We log out of the compound, we talk with the elders, we fly out here, and suddenly we learn that a group of Lodestone top brass are leaving on a private jet from Washington?"

"You were included in this direct order," Crowder said. "We are to return to base immediately."

"What's crucial is *how they responded*."

Crowder shrugged. "Somebody in my operation is feeding them intel. I've assumed that all along."

"You're missing the big issue. Something about our being in Kibera and then out here has them so worried they'd jump on a plane. We need to find out why."

Crowder squinted at the horizon. Marc felt a faint southerly breeze on his face, dry as old bones. He tasted the day's fragrances, the woodsmoke and the packed humanity and the animals. A faint hint of volcanic sculpture drifted with the wind. The colonel conceded, "Hunting for answers will be tougher with the Washington bureaucrats crowding our moves."

"There's something else. When the Kibera elders asked to see me alone, they questioned Kitra's motives. I've been going over what I remember about her and Serge's files. There are some issues I should have red-flagged long before now."

Crowder focused on him. "You want to tell me who generated those files you're not sharing?"

Marc met his gaze. "Soon as we're back, I'm making an official request to my superiors. I think they should set aside their reservations and let me share everything with you."

"Including who they are, and what is behind their concerns?"

"Everything," Marc replied.

"Okay, I'll ride the bird back to town, then order it to return for you tomorrow midmorning."

"Thanks, Colonel."

Crowder tapped the face of his watch. "Just you keep listening to the drumbeat. We're facing opposition that doesn't want the questions asked, much less the answers found. And they're closing in."

Kitra was bedded down in the women's dorm by the time Marc returned to the central compound. Marc waited until chapel was over the next morning, then led her into the shade of the neighboring baobab tree. Ever since seeing Crowder off, Marc had debated what to say and how to shape the words. But standing there in front of her, he knew he had no choice but to tell her, "I need to be straight with you. We don't have much time. Why are you really here?"

The instant she hesitated, the moment she jerked her gaze from his, Marc knew he had finally asked the right question. He went on, "Your brother trained as a medic during his service in the Israeli Defense Force. I always assumed you two were down here fighting the good fight. Which meant I ignored a vital bit of information. You told me Serge was now an electronic engineer. Does that have anything to do with why you came to Kenya?"

Kitra's gaze rested on her hands clasped in front of her and did not respond.

"What was Serge doing before you came to Kenya?"

Kitra remained silent.

"And you. What is your background?"

Kitra did not answer.

"You also trained as a nurse with the IDF. But your file says you took your university degree in business administration. Since then, what have you done?"

No response.

"Why didn't you request the help of the Israeli embassy when your brother went missing?"

"I went to them," she said softly. "They told me to file a notice. Which I did. Since then I've heard nothing."

"Why did Serge go into that village? He was looking for something, wasn't he, Kitra?" Marc had nothing to go on except hunches. Until Kitra's silence offered definite confirmation. He felt a hand squeeze his heart until his voice was robbed of strength. "Why haven't you been honest with me?"

"Everything I have told you is the truth."

"But it's never been the whole truth, has it? What—?"

Kitra bounded to her feet. "I have to make a phone call."

"What? No, Kitra, wait—"

"You want answers? All right. I need to speak with someone first." She tried for scorn, but the shakiness to her voice belied her deeper emotions. "If you are really that concerned with the truth, then you can wait another few minutes."

Marc watched her leave. He wished he had a reason strong enough to bring her back. He sat there for a long time, feeling the heat gather.

Philip found him there, still seated beneath the baobab, vainly searching his surroundings for answers. The young chief said in English, "You will walk with me, Marc Royce?"

"I'm waiting for Kitra."

"She has spoken on the phone. Now she paces with the apparatus held in both hands. She waits as you are waiting." Philip gestured into the sunlight. "Come."

When Marc rose to his feet, the chief took his arm and

guided him around the admin building. Once they were out of the central compound, Philip said, "My friend, you are troubled."

The simple way Philip spoke, without any question, released the torrent. Marc spoke softly, but the heat released with his words was as strong as the sunlight.

As they crossed the compound, Marc spoke of his late wife. Their love. Her illness and her passage. And the dark days that followed. Then the trip to Iraq, he mentioned that as well, for the travel ignited what he was feeling now, a need to move on.

Philip led them through the first rim of hovels, then took a winding trail away from the main road. As they traversed the camp, people emerged from the huts. They murmured a low greeting to Philip, eyeing Marc with solemn awareness. Marc was aware of them as well. He had no idea how much of what he said Philip actually understood. But he was not sure that the chief's understanding was nearly as important as the fact that he spoke at all.

By the time Marc went silent, a collection of children and young teens formed a motley retinue. The youngsters spoke quietly among themselves. When Marc was finished, one of the teens had the temerity to speak with Philip. Behind the boy, a woman from a neighboring hut came into view. Two more stepped forward, and an elderly man. All waiting their turn. Philip used his fly whisk to point them all back in the direction from which he and Marc had come, clearly telling them to bring their concerns to the elders' hut. They dropped their gazes and moved away.

Philip took hold of Marc's hand and steered him on. He said, "You loved your wife long and well. It is a good thing, this love. Even when you must bury your heart with your love when she departs." He pointed them down an even narrower trail. His words were far clearer than before and carried the easy resonance of an educated man. "But now the Lord Jesus, he has performed the miracle. Your heart is called from the cave of death. And you are afraid of the light." He used his whisk to offer a greeting to an ancient crone, who appeared from within her hut's shadows. "Will you accept advice?"

"Absolutely."

"There are two issues you face. Not one. The first has little to do with the woman Kitra. She lit the lamp, yes. But she and the lamp are not one and the same. Do you understand?"

"Yes," Marc replied, thinking how fortunate the tribe was to be led by this man.

"Now there is the second issue. And this is not your decision at all. It is Kitra who must choose." Philip stopped and faced him. "But whatever the woman decides, the lamp has now been lit."

Here the man's true stature was revealed, Marc decided. Along a snakelike trail, followed by the ragged teens, the true man shone clear.

Philip was a king.

Not because he commanded armies or held conquered people beneath his sandal. Rather because he saw their needs with unearthly wisdom, and called their concerns his own. Because his people loved him.

Philip was the servant who led, the leader who served. The impossible combination made real.

Marc cleared his throat and said, "Charles mentioned that you had a dream about me."

A glimmer surfaced in the dark gaze, a faint smile. Enough to suggest Philip had been hoping Marc might speak of this. "I dreamed of a hero," he corrected. "I still wait to know whether you are that man."

Marc did not know how to respond.

Philip's gaze fastened upon him. "I suspect we are both waiting for this answer together."

Marc took in a deep breath of the hot, dry air. "If the dream is prophecy, isn't that a vision of what will happen?"

Philip's response was as instantaneous as it was grave. "God's greatest gift was the salvation that came through his Son. Bonded to this is God's gift of *choice*. Mankind's freedom to choose their life's course is mostly spoken of in terms of sins. And this is true. But the choices do not end there, Marc Royce. They *begin*. We are saved from sin, yes. But to what end? Do we choose rightly and grow to God's purpose? That is the question I wait for you to answer. Because you are the one called. Oh yes. I do believe this. Now you must decide if you are *ready*."

Marc felt the words strike him with such resonance his entire being seemed to vibrate.

Philip stepped in so close, his handsome features and his intensity filled Marc's vision. "There is an expression among my people, *bado kidogo*. It means, not just yet. It is an expression of great sadness, an end to hope. So much in our land remains just beyond the horizon. Our people are told to wait, and wait, and wait some more. Do not force my people to wait upon you, Marc Royce. Do not disappoint us, or our God. Yours and mine."

Chapter Twenty-Two

Marc crossed the central compound to be met by the camp director, who handed him another list of urgently needed supplies. Kitra emerged from the medical facility and waited until the director thanked him and departed. She then walked ahead of Marc to the baobab tree where she stood in its shade. Waiting.

Marc stepped up beside her. He saw the tense way she gripped her arms across her middle, and hated that he was the cause for such tension. Especially now. "There's no room in my day for arguments. I've just come from witnessing miracles. And I can't help but hope there is room for one more."

A long breath slipped out, exposing the weary strain in her features. But she still would not look at him.

So he said it again. "I think it's time that you trust me. I want to make your objectives my own. I see the pain of your brother's disappearance. I see how you help these people. I have to trust that whatever secrets you carry are good ones. I want to help you make them—"

"You must go and speak with my father."

He stopped. "What?"

"You won't understand anything until you see it for yourself."

"Your father," he repeated.

"Yes."

"In Israel."

"He will meet you at the Tel Aviv airport."

"You've spoken with him?"

"That was who I had to call."

"About me. Coming to Israel."

"Will you go?"

"Kitra . . . Yes, I will."

She looked at him then. A faint disquiet tainted her voice and her gaze. "Will you? Really?"

"Of course I'll go. I thought . . ."

"You thought I would shut you out." She sighed once more. "Perhaps I should. But I can't."

Marc could not stop his grin from surfacing. "You can't?"

"This isn't funny."

"No. Well, yes. In a way it is. But I'm smiling because I'm happy."

"I have never lied to you. Do you believe that?"

"I don't just believe it, Kitra. I feel it in my heart. It's the only way I can be standing here, talking with you like this. Because you have always told me the truth. Just, well, maybe not as much of the truth as I might have liked."

"I've told you all I can."

"All right. Sure. I can accept that." The blood zinged through his veins. "You're a good person in an impossible situation. I wish you would tell me what I don't know, but if I have to go hear it from your father, fine."

She started to reach for him. Her hand touched an invisible barrier between them, and stopped. Marc felt the sparks fly between her fingertips and him. Kitra murmured, "How is it you always know the right thing to say?"

He wanted to close the distance between them. But something inside said the first move had to be hers. "I'll leave tomorrow."

The chopper sounded on the horizon, a vague drumming that grew steadily louder. Calling him away. Kitra tried to smile, but her mouth could not seem to find the proper shape. "I hear your ride."

He wished for nothing more than to stand there for hours, feeling the barriers between them crumble. "Why don't you come with me? To Israel, I mean."

Pain bloomed on her features. "I can't. Don't ask why. Please. It would tear me apart to explain."

He swallowed his protest, and nodded.

Kitra signaled to five young boys hovering by the admin building. They smiled and held out a dirty backpack. Kitra motioned to Marc and said, "This is for you. I asked them to secretly follow the Asian visitors and note everywhere they took a sample of the earth. They went back and dug in the same places."

Marc thanked the youths, who beamed proudly and ducked their heads in unison. He unzipped the pack and found himself staring at several dozen plastic baggies stamped with the words *Medical Samples.* "This is great. I can't tell you—"

"Give them to my father," she said. "He will know what to do."

Marc closed the pack and set it on the ground by his feet. "Serge didn't go into that village looking for the missing people."

She spoke to the youths, who smiled once more and drifted away. "I never said he did, Marc."

Marc tried to recall her exact words, but could not. He decided it really did not matter. "He went to take samples of the earth. This is why you came to Kenya, isn't it? For whatever is here in these samples."

"What we suspect. No, more than that. What we hope."

From beyond the camp's borders came the sound of rotors winding down. Marc's satellite phone rang in his pack. "I have to go."

"If there is anything there of importance, my father will know. And tell him . . ."

"Yes?"

Her voice broke under the strain of forming those words. "Tell him I'm sorry."

Ten minutes into the flight back to Nairobi, Marc's sat phone rang. The chinless bureaucrat, the one who had interviewed him in Washington and now served as Marc's boss at Lodestone headquarters, was definitely not happy to have his team arrive in Nairobi and not have Marc there to greet him. His bad attitude was made worse by having to shout to be heard. "Where have you *been*?"

"Back at the French camp, sir. They have a new director in place. I needed to liaise. The camp director has given me a massive new order for urgent supplies." Marc fished the list from his pack. "These include—"

"Never mind that. You're being reassigned. To Manila."

Marc stared at the chopper's sun-splashed windscreen. "Say again."

"We have an urgent situation developing out there, and the current administrator is not up to the job. You leave immediately. Your replacement is already on the ground in Nairobi, and my deputy is prepping him."

"Sir, in the past week I've gained new orders for our company, orders worth at least a half-million dollars."

"Your replacement will take over, Royce. The situation in Manila is critical and growing worse. We like how you handle emergencies. We're giving you a substantial bonus for your good work."

"Sir, the UN administrator made it clear this was a personal connection."

"We are aware of your relationship with Frederick Uhuru, so we cleared this with him first." When Marc did not respond, the bureaucrat said, "You should thank me, Royce. You're jumping three pay grades with this relocation."

"I am grateful, sir." Marc thought fast. "But before I head over, I am putting in for a week of leave."

"Denied. We need you there *now*."

"That was not a request, sir. I've been under enormous pressure here. I need some down time in order to perform at peak—"

"You can't stay in Kenya. I won't have you second-guessing your replacement."

"Actually, sir, I was thinking about taking a break on the Med."

The silence was not due to a bad connection. "Seventy-two hours and not a minute more," the Lodestone executive agreed with bad grace. "Then you will report to your new post or you will be posting your résumé."

Marc needed to report in to Washington. Walton needed to be updated. But his first call was to Boyd Crowder. "I'm being reassigned to the other side of the globe."

When he related his conversation, the colonel said, "Their move is a smart one. Manila is one of Lodestone's biggest operations. If anybody questions their actions, they can call it a promotion."

"You don't sound surprised."

"I'm not," Crowder replied. "Since the same thing has also just happened to me and Rigby. We're ordered back to Washington. We ship out tonight."

"They know."

"They suspect," Crowder corrected. "If they knew, we'd be destined for a shallow grave next to my fallen men. Speaking of which, don't under any circumstances go back to Lodestone-Nairobi. They have promoted Dirk to my old job. His first command as the new CO was for the gate to flag him the instant you show up."

Marc knew he should be worried. But all he could think of then was the evidence trail. "Lodestone is behind this. The evacuation of villages, the appropriation of land, the killing of your men. They're in it up to their eyeballs."

"I hate to say it, but I'm growing ever more certain by the minute that you're right."

"But you're not part of this. Which means Lodestone has another group operating inside Kenya."

"There isn't. I've checked. Then I had my buddies at HQ check. Lodestone has no other operation in the country."

Marc listened to the static for a time, but could come up with no alternative answer. "I've been granted seventy-two hours' leave, long as I take it outside Kenya."

"They're not taking any chances, are they?"

Marc related the gist of his conversation with Kitra. He

finished by saying, "I've got the sack of samples at my feet. Kitra told me to deliver them to her father. Why, I have no idea. But I'm going to do it."

Marc sat and listened to the rotors hum. Nairobi was not yet visible, but the city's smog stained the porcelain blue sky. When Crowder finally replied, his voice had lost its edge. "I appreciate the trust, bro. Will you let me know if you discover anything further?"

"The very instant."

Crowder read him off a number. "That's my personal sat phone. I got a new one and I carry it everywhere. You find yourself needing a band of trusted men, you give me a shout. I'll be there. Wherever, whenever. Crowder out."

The conversation with Walton was shortest of all. When Marc completed his summary, Walton said, "An embassy official will meet you at the Nairobi airport."

"I don't have a flight yet."

"That will be taken care of. If anyone asks, you have hitched a ride on a plane owned by your new friend."

"What's the friend's name?"

"Smith."

"I thought you might have objections over my taking off for Israel."

"On the contrary. Our opposition is worried enough about you to post you to Manila, five thousand miles in the wrong direction. You have effectively been barred from Kenya. Crowder has been relieved of duty and returned to Washington, where they can best keep a close watch over him and his man. You have the samples of earth?"

Marc watched the gloom of Nairobi rise in the distance. "Here at my feet."

"When you get to the airport, you will supply portions of each sample to the contact. You will then travel on to Tel Aviv, meet this father of the missing young man, and report back immediately."

"Roger that. Can you have your embassy guy swing by Lodestone HQ first and pack up all my gear? I've been warned off the place."

"Consider it done."

Marc started to cut the connection, but Walton said, "I've heard back from the security chief about your friend Uhuru. He has asked that we not include Frederick Uhuru in our investigation."

Which could only mean one thing. "They have him under surveillance and they don't want us to tip their hand."

"I agree with your assessment." Walton hesitated, then added, "Watch your back."

Despite the static and the chopper's noise, Marc heard genuine concern in the ambassador's tone. "Roger that, sir."

"The stakes are rising," Walton went on. "You've just been given the only warning they are likely to offer. Next time, you won't see them coming until it's too late."

Chapter Twenty-Three

When the chopper landed in front of the Lodestone hangar, Marc was met by a stocky young woman wearing a dark suit with low-heeled pumps. Her hair was cut short and framed her head like a cap of brown straw. She stood before a dusty Toyota Land Cruiser and chatted with a rail-thin African whose dark curls were frosted by age. Her voice was as crisp and professional as her features. "Marc Royce?"

"That's me."

"Deb Orlando, Mr. Royce. I'm with State and serve as deputy intel officer for the Nairobi embassy. I've been sent to advise you that your jet is inbound." She checked her watch. "ETA just under two hours."

"Did you bring my personal things?"

"In the rear of our SUV." She eyed the dirty backpack. "I was instructed to obtain samples that are to be sent by diplomatic bag to Washington."

Deb Orlando appeared extremely competent and very alert. The women Marc knew who had made it up the intel ladder trained twice as hard as most men. He handed over the pack and said, "Leave me at least half of each baggie."

"Is any of this material hazardous, sir?"

"Not as far as I'm aware." Marc followed her to the Land Cruiser and retrieved his case. "I'm going to go clean up."

At the rear of the Lodestone hangar, Marc found a well-equipped ready room. Marc stayed in the shower long enough to wash off at least some of his fatigue. He shaved and dressed in fresh clothes, then entered a bare-bones mess hall stocked with instant meals and a microwave. The coffee smelled as though it had been cooking for years.

Marc ate standing up. A few Lodestone personnel came and went. Nothing was said. But Marc had the distinct impression that things had changed, and not for the better. He had been in the field enough to know that word spread fast out here. People's survival depended on their being up to the minute with any threat assessment. He had been allied to the colonel, who was now gone. Marc was therefore contaminated by whatever it was that had gotten their boss kicked out of there. No one spoke or even met his eye. Marc dumped the rest of his meal in the garbage. He would eat on the plane.

As he left the hangar's shadows, Deb Orlando said, "Sir, your pack keeps ringing." An irritating buzz emerged from the Land Cruiser's tailgate. "There it goes again."

Marc unzipped his dusty pack and retrieved the sat phone. "This is Royce."

"Mr. Royce, this is Lodestone-Nairobi. I've got an urgent inbound for you."

"Who is this?"

"Simpkins, sir. Temporary comm officer. Everybody else is getting prepped by the new admin chiefs and the suits over from D.C."

Marc could not fit a face to the name. "Go ahead."

"Your presence is requested in Kibera. They claim it's urgent."

Marc squinted into the sun. "Say again."

The man's voice was flat and toneless, a soldier assigned duty in the comm room, just fighting the clock. "A call came in forty-seven minutes ago, sir. You are requested to return to Kibera. ASAP."

Marc asked, "Who passed on the message?"

"Sir, I asked the guy four times and couldn't understand the name. It was African, I can confirm that much. He said you're to go back to the church. I asked which one, and he said where you met the elders. He said you'd know."

"Did they leave a number?"

"I asked for that too, sir. They just said you had to come. Now." He hesitated, then added, "They said it was life or death."

Marc thanked him and cut the connection. He turned to where the embassy staffer was peeling off plastic gloves and stowing them in a briefcase with her set of the sample bags. Marc asked, "Are you in contact with the jet?"

"I can be."

"Call and tell them to wait for me. I've received an urgent request. Can you give me a ride?"

"Where to?"

"Kibera."

The driver turned and stared at him but did not speak. Deb Orlando said, "Sir, the Nairobi slums are officially off-limits to all embassy personnel. I'll have to call that in."

Marc watched the heat shimmering off the empty tarmac and felt a subtle gnawing at his gut. Like rats of the slum had emerged to feast upon his day. "Do it."

It took them almost an hour to cover the eight miles to Kibera. Marc tried to reach Charles twice. But the number the pastor had left with him just rang and rang.

The embassy driver's name was Joseph. He listened to Marc's description of the square rimmed by relief agencies and said dourly, "I know this place."

Deb Orlando occupied the rear seat beside Marc. She cradled the phone she had used to call the embassy in her lap. "Is it safe?"

The driver's shoulders bounced in a humorless laugh. "Safe is not a word that belongs in Kibera."

Marc said, "Our destination is a church."

The driver's shoulders jerked a second time, but he did not speak.

Deb Orlando eyes grew steadily larger as they turned off the highway and bounced their way into the slum. Marc asked, "How long have you been in Kenya?"

"Nine months." She met the gaze of a woman lounging in the doorway of a wretched bar. "I was raised in Boston. I thought I'd seen some rough places. But this is something else."

Marc felt the gnawing in his midsection grow stronger. He studied the world beyond the tinted windows and tried to tell himself that it was just the woman's nerves he felt. But something about this situation did not sit right. "Do you carry arms?"

Joseph glanced at him in the rearview mirror.

"Small arms only," Deb Orlando replied. "And body armor. All in a coded compartment next to the wheel well."

The driver asked Marc, "You feel it too?"

That was all the impetus Marc required. "We need to gear up."

Deb stared at him a moment, then swiveled around and reached into the rear hold. Marc shoved himself between the two front seats, gripped the padded rail over the passenger-side window, and pulled himself over. Marc asked the driver, "How far out are we?"

"Another mile, perhaps. It has been some time since I was here."

"Okay, Joseph. You've been trained in defensive tactics?"

"Every year I am training."

"Great." Marc accepted a Kevlar vest and pistol and three clips from Deb. The Smith & Wesson was matte black and reassuringly familiar. The grip was already damp with her perspiration. He worked his arms into the vest and fastened the Velcro straps across his chest. He slapped a clip into place and worked the lever. "You want a gun, Joseph?"

"I am a driver. Not a shooter."

"Okay, pull up here so you can slip on your vest." Marc pretended not to notice the palsied jerks to Joseph's hands. "Here's how it's going to play. You will enter the square and make a circle, pointing back out the way we came in. Slow and steady. We'll check things out. If there is any indication of threat, we leave. If everything looks quiet, I will enter the chapel alone. Ms. Orlando, you are backup. If you hear gunfire, even if you see me fall, you are ordered to get out. You will not wait; you will not come in after me. Clear?"

It was Joseph who replied, "Clear."

"Is this vehicle armored?"

Joseph's forehead bore a faint sheen that defied the car's A/C. "Against small arms. No protection from heavy fire."

"That's fine. Everybody ready? Okay, Joseph. Let's go."

As they approached the point where the lane entered the dusty square, Deb asked, "Who *are* you?"

"I've been sent up-country to assess a series of events that may be tied to national security. My principal contacts in Nairobi are elders who operate out of our destination. I received a call from—"

That was when they struck.

Chapter Twenty-Four

The attackers had chosen their strike point with deadly care. The alleys from which the two pickups emerged were extremely narrow and flanked by cement block houses with overhanging roofs. The corrugated sheets hid the trucks until the very last moment.

Marc's only warning was a sudden glint of sun off their windscreens and the roar of motors. Then they were struck.

The normal response to incoming threat was to *brake*. But Joseph's training worked now, even when he was only granted a hair's breadth of time. Joseph slammed down on the gas pedal. The car lurched forward. Not far, just a couple of feet. But far enough so that the two trucks collided just behind the rear doors.

The right-hand truck hit first, then the left. Marc and the others were tossed like puppets in a steel box. The side windows over the rear compartment splintered but did not give. He heard a sharp *bang* and assumed a rear tire had exploded. It did not matter. The impact had been strong enough to crumple the axle. They were going nowhere.

Deb Orlando screamed, "What is *happening?*"

"Gangs!" Joseph yelled.

Marc saw the left truck pull back a pace, and knew the attackers were readying for another assault. They would slam and slam and slam until the windows shattered and the doors buckled and the people inside were left unable to resist whatever came next. Marc took the only option available to him.

"Stay in the truck!"

The first rule of defense was to do the unexpected. Unbalance the enemy. Leave their plans in disarray. If possible, inject an element of uncertainty. Uncertainty led to fear, and fear to mistakes.

Marc punched open his door and leaped out. He knew they expected him to run for cover.

Instead, he ran straight at the left-hand truck.

He could feel the attackers in the other truck taking aim. Yet he hoped they would hesitate before shooting at their allies.

He mounted the truck's front bumper, firing as he ran. His first bullet was through the truck's hood. And the second. Hoping to disable the motor. Then one more through the filthy windscreen. Dirt obscured his view. But Marc had a fleeting glimpse of a huge astonished man, who struggled to raise his automatic rifle. Marc jumped onto the roof, firing down into the cab. He knew he had seen that man before. But it was not until he bounded across the rear hold, leaped the tailgate, and rolled in the dust that he remembered. The attacker was one of the men Marc and Kamal's soldiers had expelled from the camp. It seemed like years ago, that dawn raid in the ash-covered forest. Marc's heart was pumping so fast, the adrenaline so charging his brains and sinew, he could splice every second into billionths and recall all this while scrambling through the dust, shooting out the truck's rear tires and planting a final bullet through the rear window before fleeing.

Behind him was bedlam.

Gunfire fashioned a cordite thunderstorm. Marc sprinted down the alley, took a three-point turn to the right. As he rounded the second corner he ejected the empty clip and slapped in another. He turned the final corner and emerged from the shadows into the road the embassy vehicle had just traveled.

Soon as the attack point came into view, he accelerated and took aim.

Three attackers stood by the embassy vehicle and fired rounds at the windows. The glass appeared to be holding. Two more ran down the alley where Marc had vanished. Another waved his gun and shouted orders. Marc thought he recognized all but one of the men. He roared a ferocious greeting to get their attention away from the Land Cruiser and fired.

The scene before him would have been comic had it not been so deadly. They gaped at him in openmouthed astonishment.

Marc ran straight at them, firing his weapon and shouting at the top of his voice. Not caring whether he hit anyone, not even bothering to take aim. He wasn't after strikes. He was after clearing the area of hostiles.

Deb Orlando emerged from the SUV's far side and screamed at Marc, *"Down! Get down!"*

Marc tumbled into the dusty road and rolled toward the concrete steps fronting the nearest hovel. Deb planted her arm on the SUV's roof and fired over him. Taking on assailants that had tracked him from behind. The closeness of the assault left him fighting hard for air. As though the bullets had taken him out. As though breathing was no longer an option.

Their attackers bolted. All but one. The man with the tribal scars who had led the attack into the forest was wounded in his left thigh. He crawled across the road, leaving a stain behind him. He did not look so fierce now.

Marc halted the man from crawling further by taking aim with his pistol. When the man froze, he said to Deb, "You all right?"

"Yes. Our ride's totaled."

"Joseph!"

The driver's door cracked open. Joseph gave him a frightened gaze. "Sir?"

"You okay?"

"Shook is all."

"Check out that truck to your left, see if it still works." As the driver ran over, Marc said, "Deb, seal the armaments locker, grab your samples and my pack."

Joseph called, "This truck appears to function, sir."

"Deb, come give me a hand with this man. Let's get out of here!"

Chapter Twenty-Five

They dumped the injured attacker in the rear of the pickup. Marc used Joseph's tie to lash his hands together and bind them to the truck. Marc rode in the middle position. Every time Joseph changed gears, Marc had to press his legs over tight against Deb. The tires shimmied and a hissing rattle filled the Nissan's cab. Its front end was badly damaged. But no one complained.

When her breathing had steadied, Deb asked, "What are we going to do with him?"

Marc opened his pack and pulled out the sat phone. It was covered with dirt, as the attack had split a number of the sample bags. Marc wiped the phone with his shirt, taking small comfort from how his hands did not tremble. It did not mean he wasn't scared, only that he managed not to show it. He dialed Charles's number from memory. This time the pastor answered. Marc asked, "Where have you been?"

"Searching out information," he replied. "Why?"

"We've been attacked." Marc described the call and the assault and finished with, "We have one of the wounded men with us."

"I am certain the elders were not behind the message."

"I agree."

"They will want to question this man."

"I won't be party to any rough stuff."

"Nor will they," Charles agreed firmly. "They will offer him two choices. Give them answers and be permitted to remain and be granted medical treatment. Else he will be cast out."

Marc assumed Joseph would have no interest in driving back into Kibera. So he made arrangements for Charles to meet them at the point where the slum's entry road joined the highway. He then signed off and called the colonel.

Boyd Crowder's voice mail kicked in automatically, which Marc assumed meant the man was already in transit. He gave a quick summary of events and hung up. Deb said, "I have to check in. My cellphone is shot."

Marc handed her the sat phone. "Blame everything on me." He watched her take a two-fisted grip on the bulky phone. Saw the white knuckles and the tremors that ran all the way from her hands to her chin. "You were great back there."

"I've never been in a live-fire action before. It all happened so fast."

"I know." He waited while she talked with her superior, liking the terse way she dissected the action.

Deb handed him the phone. "My boss wants a word."

"This is Royce."

"Your associate in Washington said nothing about jeopardizing the safety of my personnel." The man's voice was one notch below a full whine. Marc could picture him instantly. The pencil neck, the tendency to duck his head whenever trouble erupted, the well-honed ability to climb the diplomatic ladder on the backs of his subordinates. "I am lodging an official protest over this entire incident."

"Do what you have to do," Marc replied.

"I don't like your tone, mister."

"Roger that." Marc cut the connection and said to Deb, "How often does he let you out of the embassy compound?"

"Basically, never. He detailed me to meet you because he assumed it was just grunt work." Deb offered him a shaky smile. "I'd love to have seen him with those hostiles in Kibera."

The driver laughed out loud.

Marc said, "There's a man in Washington I want you to contact. His name is Walton. Ambassador Walton. He used to be head of State Department Intel; now he serves as an unofficial consultant to the White House."

"He's the man who spoke with my superior?"

"Yes."

"No wonder my boss okayed the trip to Kibera."

"Walton probably ordered him to do whatever I requested."

"*Ordered* him." She smiled, liking the sound of that.

"Phone Walton. Tell him I said he needs to help you move into ops. Ask him to call me for details."

Her eyes shone. "You'd do that for me?"

"You saved my life back there," Marc replied. "That carries serious juice in my book."

They dropped Marc off at the airport entrance for private planes. The building was fronted by limp palm trees and sported a newly renovated interior. Marc's arrival caused quite a stir. Several African businessmen paused to gape as he passed. Ditto for the staff behind the counter and the passengers waiting inside the café. His pants were ripped so badly, one strip of cloth flapped against his right thigh with every step. Most of the buttons of his shirt were gone. His elbow was bleeding, as was a scratch on his neck which he had not noticed before. Marc debated cleaning himself in the washroom, then decided it wasn't worth the bother.

The customs officer did not want to let him pass. But a man in a white shirt with pilot's epaulets said, "Marc Royce?" And there was Carter Dawes, grinning at him.

Marc couldn't believe it, and they were soon laughing and slapping each other's backs.

"Heard about the party over here and talked the brass into letting me in on a bit of it." Carter Dawes had been a vital member of the rescue mission back in Baghdad.

"Hey, man, I can't tell you how glad—"

Dawes held up a palm and smiled at Marc's tattered appearance, then said to the customs agent, "This gentleman is the passenger we've been waiting for."

The officer sniffed. "This is no gentleman." But he stamped Marc's passport and waved him through.

Carter said, "You want to wash up?"

"I'll do it on the plane. Let me just stop by the gift shop, see if they have any clothes my size."

"What's in your pack?"

"Mostly dirt."

Carter's grin broadened. "You ask me, I'd say you're wearing enough already. You can tell me about it after we're in the air."

Chapter Twenty-Six

The jet was a needle-shaped Lear that swiftly wound up its engines and launched off the runway. The rear bathroom was so tight that Marc left the door ajar so as to have enough room to swing around. He cleaned up as best as he could, then dressed in gift-shop shorts and T-shirt. He wolfed down one of the jet's ready meals, then a second. The two pilots looked at him through the open cockpit door and chuckled. Carter Dawes joined him after a while and heard as much as Marc was free to tell him about the operation to date.

Marc eventually lowered two seats facing each other into a camp bed and conked out.

He awoke when the copilot shook his shoulder and announced they were descending into Ben Gurion Airport. As the plane touched down, Marc was filled with a sudden regret for having made the trip at all. No matter that Walton had agreed the trip could be vital. All he could think of was how vulnerable Kitra was back in Kenya. How isolated. How alone.

When they finished taxiing, Marc thanked the pilots and said good-bye to Carter Dawes, descended the stairs, and joined the crush through customs. Several tourist flights had all landed at the same time, and he found himself surrounded by a multi-tongued babble.

A wall clock behind the customs officer told him the flight from Nairobi had taken three and a half hours. The main terminal was an astonishment of architectural design, so lovely it slowed every arriving passenger. The domed hall was built as a series of concentric circles, formed into a sculpture that seemed to embrace and welcome all who passed. Sunlight poured through an opening at the very crest, bathing a fountain that splashed scented water in a constant musical rush.

After passing through customs, Marc was approached by a tall man with the leathery features of a desert dweller. "Mr. Royce, I am Levi Korban."

Marc accepted the handshake, which felt like flesh-covered stone. "How did you identify me?"

"Kitra emailed your photograph." The man wore a skullcap, and traditional fringes emerged from his shirt to dangle over his belt. He gave Marc's disheveled appearance an unsmiling inspection. "Did you have a rough flight?"

Kitra's mother was a French rendition of the daughter, petite and lovely and very refined. She smiled over her shoulder from the driver's position as Marc bundled into the car's back seat. "Good evening, Mr. Royce. How is my daughter?"

He wanted to lie. The woman's smile was that sweet. But he could not. "Very sad, I'm afraid."

She said, "Call me Sandrine, please," as she put the car into gear. "She blames herself for Serge."

"Yes."

Levi Korban slammed his door as his wife pulled from the curb. "She should."

"Levi. Stop. We have been through this a thousand times. It serves no purpose. Do you carry no luggage, Mr. Royce?"

"I have asked this already," her husband replied. "He was attacked. His luggage was lost."

"Attacked where?"

"A slum in Nairobi," Marc said. "On the way to the airport."

"Why were you in a slum?" When he hesitated, Kitra's mother read him correctly. "It had to do with our daughter, didn't it?"

"In a way." Marc then asked, "Why should Kitra blame herself for Serge's disappearance?"

"Because all this was her idea." Levi Korban pointed into the sunset. "We want this exit."

"Am I the newcomer? Have I never driven you to this airport? Answer our guest's question. Tell him why our innocent daughter should blame herself for anything except being her father's child."

And just like that, Marc was in. He had no idea how it happened. One moment he was just another arriving guest. The next, he was swept up in a family's ongoing drama. The Mitsubishi pickup had an extended cab with a full back seat. Marc stretched out his legs and rubbed the bruise developing on his thigh. "Kitra wanted them both to go to Africa?"

"Kitra wanted to make her father's lifelong dream come true. Isn't that correct, Levi? Tell the man how your daughter loved you so much she dreamed of nothing else."

The man was lean and hard and silent. From Marc's position in the middle of the back seat, he could observe half of both faces. Sandrine Korban spoke with a delicious accent. Her features were an older rendition of Kitra's, not so much softened as distilled. Where her husband was lean and taut, she was gentle. But Marc could not have said which of Kitra's parents possessed the tougher core.

He asked, "Where are we going?"

"My husband, Mr. Royce, he is a dreamer. He has been a dreamer all his life long. It is what I loved first about him. It is what I love most about him now."

"Please, call me Marc."

"I am Sandrine, as I told you, and this is Levi. Tell our guest hello, my husband."

"We've moved beyond hellos," he said. But the anger was gone now. Passing headlights illuminated a man who appeared hollowed by grief. Marc wondered when the man had last smiled.

Sandrine changed gears, then reached over to settle her hand on her husband's thigh. She went on, "My husband founded a kibbutz in the plains southwest of Jerusalem, Marc. I met him in Lyon, where he was raising funds. I fell in love with his vision and his heart and his ability to dream big dreams. Kitra shares my husband's gift. Does she not, my dear?"

"Gift," he muttered. "I lose a son because—"

"Let us wait for word about Serge," she said quietly. Her voice cracked over the name, revealing a mother's heart. "It is not yet time to say the Kaddish."

He sighed, but did not respond.

"Gift," she said, forming the word on an indrawn breath, rebuilding her composure and her world. "Gift I said, gift I mean. Kitra has always searched for dreams as great as her father's. Serge is more like me. The gentle, beautiful boy who gives strength and legs and arms to my daughter's vision."

Marc nodded slowly. The passing headlights coalesced into a deeper understanding. "Their work as medics was a cover. They went to Kenya searching for . . . what?"

"Answers, Marc. Answers that would give wings to my husband's dream." She shook her head decisively. "And everything else can wait until tomorrow."

"I brought samples of earth," Marc said. He saw the two in the front seat exchange glances. He lifted his sack and handed it forward. "From where the strangers were digging. The bags got damaged in the attack, so they're all mixed together."

Sandrine watched her husband accept the pack and stow it at his feet, then repeated, "Tomorrow."

They pulled off the main highway onto a long dusty drive running straight into the middle of nowhere. After a few miles the road ended in a parking area that fronted a compound of low-slung buildings. The lighting was too dim for Marc to make out much beyond the first row of white prefab structures. Sandrine saw how he eased himself from the car and asked, "You are injured?"

"A little bruised is all."

"We have reserved you a room in the bachelors' quarters. Come."

As he followed them down the graveled walk, he said, "Excuse my question, but why aren't you there with her?"

Sandrine replied, "Levi wanted to go immediately to Kenya and help Kitra search for our son. But our community ordered him to stay here. We are unfortunately facing a crisis of our own. Kitra said it was right for him to stay. What could he possibly do, not ever having been to Africa before?"

"But she refused to return home," Levi said. "At the time I did not have the heart to argue. Perhaps I should—"

"You were not wrong, husband."

"But the danger hasn't simply vanished because our son has vanished."

"You were not wrong."

Levi sighed to the night sky overhead and went silent.

Sandrine pointed Marc toward the building ahead of them and said, "Now you will clean yourself and rest. Do you need food?"

"I ate on the plane, thanks."

"I will leave clothes for you in the hallway tomorrow. Good night, Marc. All else can wait until the sunrise."

Marc awoke to the sound of a metallic hammering. Not bells. Like someone was banging a length of steel. He assumed it was some form of alarm and rose from his bed. When he opened the door to his tiny room, he discovered that Sandrine had left him a set of clothes, along with a razor, shampoo, and toothbrush. He washed and dressed hurriedly, trying to ignore his stiffening bruises. The clothes were one size too large, but the pants had a drawstring and the shirt was fine. Marc wondered if they belonged to Serge.

The morning sun was as hot as Nairobi, but very different. The air was dry here, but with no sense of drought. Here, the dryness was permanent. The brown hills rising to the east were painted by centuries without rain. The earth surrounding the shiny new buildings was the color of broken clay, a hundred hues, all of them rust brown.

He joined the flow of people moving toward a central

building. They made way for him, but offered no welcome. They spoke in soft voices, either Hebrew or Yiddish, and pretended not to observe him as he crossed a desert plaza and entered the dining hall.

The first woman to speak to him was behind the counter. "What you want, hey? There are eggs and there is toast. But there is no ham or, what you call, bacon. This is kosher kitchen."

Marc thought back to the ritual fringes dangling from beneath Levi Korban's shirt. "Kosher."

"Yeah, sure. All is kosher. Look there, you want cheese, salads? We eat good here. You take. Eat. You like."

Neither Sandrine nor Levi was visible. He finished his breakfast and left the dining hall with the others. There was a gradual drift toward a building at the plaza's far side. Marc joined them. He entered a meeting hall. He watched men draw small books and prayer shawls from pockets and fanny packs. Women covered their heads with scarves and moved to a different section behind a cream-colored screen as translucent as a bridal veil. Marc wondered if he should leave. People glanced at him, but there was no sense of hostility to their gaze.

Then he saw the cross.

It was very small, less than two feet high. It was carved into stone behind the dais. Easy to miss. But it was there.

So too were the red velvet drapes covering the alcove just below the cross. He took a seat on the rear pew as a bearded ancient pulled back the drapes and extracted a scroll. He kissed the border of the velvet cover and set it on the table by the dais. He then read from a book open on the dais. The other men and women joined in. Some swayed. Others covered their heads with the shawls and moved rapidly back and forth.

Sandrine came in first and slipped behind the screen. Levi arrived a few minutes later. He stepped into the pew beside Marc, opened his prayer book, adjusted his shawl, and began chanting with the others.

Marc sat and listened and wondered.

Both Sandrine and Levi departed before the service ended. They gave no signal for Marc to follow them. Marc wandered around the community. There was a quiet intensity here that matched what he had seen in his hosts. As though all of them shared some secret bond, something they were reluctant to reveal to any outsider. He was neither welcomed nor shunned. The few times he actually spotted people looking his way, he thought he detected anxiety.

The kibbutz was actually three unique segments. By far the largest was the farm. Neat plastic-covered rows blanketed a flat area of perhaps thirty acres. He had heard of this practice, where the plants were trickle-fed water from underground pipes and plastic sheets were used to keep water from evaporating. Some people were harvesting at a far corner of the fields, sun-browned limbs dumping armloads of leafy greens into a truck. The heat was fierce. Marc thought he heard singing.

A second section was made up of a dozen low-slung buildings. At first Marc thought they were related to the farm, until he followed a humming noise around a corner and confronted a series of industrial-grade air-conditioners and generators and what appeared to be air compressors. He spotted a trio of white-uniformed people walking from one building to the next, and hurried over. As he approached, he realized they were not uniforms at all, but disposable body suits like might be found in surgical wards. The two women and a man all had face masks dangling from strings around their necks, and their hair was tucked into matching white caps.

Marc caught up with them as they approached the entrance to one of the central buildings. They coded in numbers to a pad placed by the door. Marc heard the doors sigh open. The men glanced back, then hurried inside. The woman stood where she blocked his passage and demanded, "You are wanting something?"

"I'm just interested to know what is going on here."

"Yes? You are interested? Why is this interesting to you?"

"I just—"

"I am not in the answer business. And I am not knowing who it is that is interested. You understand?"

"What you do in here is confidential?"

"If it is secret, why would I be discussing it with you?" She shooed him away with her hands. "Go, and take your questions with you. Good-bye."

Marc watched her shield the keypad with her body before coding in the numbers. She kept glancing back at him as she entered. Then she passed through a set of interior doors and vanished.

Marc stood there, thinking about what had just happened. When the doors had opened, he felt a slight puff on his face. Meaning the air inside the building was kept at a slightly higher density than the outside. Which explained the compressors. But not what the people were doing inside.

Marc returned to his room. He took his time stretching his sore limbs, then sat at the narrow desk. The most obvious answer was, they worked inside clean rooms. Here. In a desert kibbutz. They did something that required an environment free of dust and all contaminants. He said to the window, "What are they doing in Africa?"

But the sunlight on his window did not offer any answers.

Chapter Twenty-Seven

Marc was still staring out his window at the blank sun-lit landscape twenty minutes later when the sat phone buzzed. "This is Royce."

"Charles here. You are in Israel?"

Marc debated going outside, in case his room was bugged. Then he decided there was nothing he intended to keep from these people. And every passing minute was one more lost opportunity. Let them listen. "Somewhere south of Tel Aviv."

"How is it?"

"So far, pretty confusing. What do you have?"

"I remained with the elders while they spoke with your wounded attacker. He was sent by the head of his gang. They were all newcomers. He and his men were told this was a test. You understand?"

"They had to earn the right to belong."

"Yes, it is so. He has no idea who might have arranged this ambush through the gang. To have even asked such a question would get him killed."

Marc heard the man's tension magnify his accent. "Is something the matter?"

"Kitra, she has not taken the news of your attack well."

"Tell her I am fine."

"She will not listen. She feels responsible for Serge. And now she has led you into peril."

Marc recalled what her mother had said the previous night. "She didn't send me into the slums, Charles."

"But you are looking for her answers. Just like Serge. She asks . . ."

"Yes?"

"She asks me to tell you that she prays for your safe return."

"Tell her I'm with her parents now, and I'll be back as soon as I'm done here. I promise." Marc thanked the pastor and signed off.

He sat cradling the phone for a time, listening to his heart and the A/C's hushed breath. Wishing she was there to share with him this new world.

Marc phoned Walton. It was before dawn in Washington, but the ambassador answered with the same swift precision as always. Marc remained seated at his narrow desk while he dissected the previous few days, starting with the trip by chopper to the farms. He knew he was repeating himself. But the ambassador never gave a hint that he minded. Walton understood that sometimes the repetition was necessary to achieve clarity. Marc related the events in temporal order. Not trying to connect the dots. Just laying it out.

When he was done, Walton asked, "Do you have a contact number for Crowder?"

Marc read out the number for the colonel's new sat phone. "Maybe I should alert him that you intend to get in touch."

"No need. I'm not after a debriefing. I just want him to know he's got an ally at this end."

"You've decided to trust him, then."

Walton changed the subject. "We've got some preliminary lab results on your samples."

Marc felt the news press him back in his seat. For Marc's samples to have already been tested meant a second jet must have been standing by in Nairobi, ready to transport the bags to the nearest available lab technicians with security clearance.

Walton demanded, "Are you there?"

"Yes." All this could only mean one thing. "You knew the significance of what I was bringing before you got the samples."

To his credit, Walton did not play coy. "We suspected."

"This is why the intel alert went all the way up to the White House," Marc said. "You knew all along what the yellow men are after."

"They are Chinese," Walton replied. "Your samples confirmed a number of things we have been very worried about."

"I'm listening."

"The samples contain elements that fall under the heading of rare earth. Our technicians say the samples were clearly corrupted, as several of the elements are never found together."

"Some of the sample bags were destroyed in the attack."

"We assumed as much. All right. We are talking about five different chemical elements." There was the sound of rustling pages. "Neodymium, a core material for permanent magnets used in mobile phones, computer memory, and lasers. Lanthanum, used in catalytic converters and electric car batteries. Terbium, essential for modern sonar systems. Dysprosium, used in hybrid car motors and nuclear reactors. And Europium, crucial for the production of LCD and LED screens. Okay so far?"

"Yes."

"The largest sources of all these materials are in northeastern China. For years, the prices have remained at a very steady level, basically twenty percent above cost. According to my in-house experts, extraction and refinement of these materials are not particularly tough. The extraction process can be very polluting. This is not necessarily the case, as new technologies can provide a purification system that creates virtually no toxic waste. But so long as the cost of the refined materials remained low, no one invested in new plants. You follow me?"

Marc said, "The Chinese factories are old and polluting."

"Extremely so. Back to the raw materials. A few other potential sources have been identified. Some of the five elements have been found in the central Australian desert. Others are in North Dakota. One mine recently opened in the Congo, but the UN issued an embargo because the minerals were fueling the civil war. No one bothered to develop these other areas because the Chinese prices were low and the world got all they needed. You see where this is headed?"

"China decided to up the ante," Marc surmised.

"Precisely. Last year, China entered into a diplomatic dispute with Japan over ownership of several islands which rest above major oil deposits. In retaliation China cut off all shipments of rare earth. Japan is the largest user of rare earths after the U.S. Suddenly the world woke up to the fact that China has a virtual monopoly. Now here's the interesting thing. The pointy heads around here aren't sure if China ever understood just what a bonanza they had in their backyard. Maybe they did, and used Japan as a test case. Most of our analysts think China was as surprised as the rest of us by what happened next."

"The markets erupted," Marc said.

"In the past six months, prices of those elements I mentioned have skyrocketed. Three of the elements are now selling for *twenty-five times* what they brought two years ago."

Beyond Marc's window, the acres of plastic sheeting glinted hard as metal in the sunlight. Farther away rose desert hills, tan earth and rocks and stunted desert scrub. Long ocher strips ran about midway up the slopes, like a giant's finger painting. "Why wasn't I told about this before being inserted?"

"Because we were certain about none of this. There had never been any indication that the minerals were available in Kenya. Then eight months ago we began receiving reports from African operatives. But these reports did not add up. An increase in the numbers of Chinese scientists visiting Nairobi? So what? China visits African nations for any number of reasons. But the rumors persisted. Finally we put two and two together. Then the UN security chief came by, requesting help with Lodestone, whose name has come up a number of times. We decided it was our best chance to see if our fears were real."

"China is trying to establish a worldwide monopoly," Marc guessed. "They want to grab hold of this new source, and keep prices artificially high."

"That is our assessment."

Marc stared out the window at the clean-room facility. Just another featureless structure, put together like Lego blocks. "So what does this have to do with a kibbutz in the middle of the Judean desert?"

"That is what you need to determine. And without delay. Walton out."

Chapter Twenty-Eight

Marc left his quarters and headed for the exit. The empty hallway echoed with his footsteps and the A/C's hum. He pushed through the door and entered the sunlight. The heat was a dry weight that turned the sidewalk and the rocks and the windows into fierce mirrors. He took a deep breath of desert fragrances, sorrel and pine and raw earth. There was no wind.

Marc took his time and walked around the entire compound. Everything was pristine and orderly. The few people who emerged from the featureless buildings scurried through the heat and entered another building, then the doors shut and the silence returned. There was nothing out of the ordinary. No reason for him to feel as he did. That this place was a repository for secrets. That this supposed normality was nothing more than a mask.

The question was, a mask for what?

A bearded man emerged from the mess hall's rear door. He walked to a pair of metal pipes hanging from a wooden arc and hefted a crowbar. He drummed the two pipes, making them ring like gongs. An electronic chime rose from the loudspeakers planted throughout the compound. Doors sighed open and people began heading for the mess hall. Marc stood where he was and let the people move around him. No one met his gaze. He remained standing in the blistering sun long after the others were safely inside. If necessary, he would stay there all day.

His shirt was dark with sweat by the time the mess hall doors opened and Kitra's father emerged. He had a furtive look to his features as he approached. Marc waited until Levi Korban stopped.

Then Marc said, "I know."

Levi Korban gestured toward the mess hall. "You are wanting to perish? You stay out here too long, the heat will melt your bones."

"Rare earth minerals. I know about them."

Levi gripped his arm and pulled. "So you are knowing. Now come."

"The problem is, I don't know anything at all. I don't know why you are here. I don't know why Kitra is there. Alone."

"She wasn't alone. Serge was there with her."

"You sent your two offspring to Africa. Against the Chinese."

"Sent? You think I *wanted* her to go? I did not. I begged her not to go. I *ordered* her. You see what difference it made, all my words?" He fingered the skullcap, as though the sun made the black silk uncomfortable. "Someday when you have children you will see just how much your words can mean. And now here I stand, waiting for the word to come, and my wife and I will be forced to say Kaddish for my son."

Marc let Levi take a grip on his arm and pull him forward. The man radiated such strength that he could manage to compress his grief into a small private space, then go on with his duties here. Function almost normally. Marc asked, "What is so important that your daughter would go against her father's express orders? Kitra is not impulsive. Everything about her is deliberate."

Levi stopped just outside the mess hall doors. The glass reflected the two of them, the iron-hard older man and the taller American. Marc kept talking. It was the only way he could make sense of these half-seen shards of a hidden truth, all of them carrying a force more potent than the heat. "She went down to Africa to search out something that is bigger than any of you. It wasn't the rising value of these minerals. I have never met anyone less interested in money. She was after something bigger. Bigger than her brother's life, even though she feels ravaged by his absence." Marc stopped talking, though his mind kept moving forward. *Bigger than any relationship she might want to have with me.*

Levi Korban began rocking slowly, as though he was back in the chapel with the secret cross. Covered by his prayer shawl. Praying unseen to the invisible God.

Secrets.

He tugged once more on Marc's arm. "Come."

The cafeteria tables fashioned a broad U around the service counter. The noise was like the constant rush of water in a stream. No one looked at them as they crossed the room. But Marc knew they were all watching. Talking. Wondering. Worrying if he was a foe. Afraid he might be there to take away something else. While they remained trapped by forces he did not comprehend.

The room's chilled air held a biting quality. His drying sweat turned his skin cold. He followed Levi to the far corner, where two tables were isolated from the main room. This side held no windows. The pair of tables offered the cafeteria's only isolation. Kitra's mother sat alone at the table by the wall. She cradled a cup of tea in her hands. She tried to smile as Marc approached. But he could see the worry in her gaze. And the sorrow. And the calm. An impossible mix. As impossible as sterile clean rooms planted in the middle of the Judean wasteland.

Marc seated himself and said once more, "I know about the minerals."

"You must be hungry. Go. We can wait—"

"Neodymium," Marc said. "Lanthanum, terbium, dysprosium, and Europium."

Kitra's parents exchanged a long look. Levi said, "There is a sixth element. Tantalum. It is a crucial component in the manufacture of semiconductors."

"Tantalum was actually the element that started us down this path," Sandrine told him. "It was the first rare earth discovered in Africa, in the Congo. The only other mine is in Mongolia. You know about China's near monopoly?"

"A little," Marc replied. "Not enough."

"Recently the U.S. Congress passed a law forbidding the use of tantalum from Congo. The tantalum mine, like the diamonds, have become fuel for the civil war. Most other nations have followed America's lead, including Israel. You know what happened next, yes?"

"The price skyrocketed."

"Ten thousand percent in five months," Levi confirmed. "Then we heard a rumor. The bearded man over by the window, Moshe. See him there?"

Almost all the men seated beneath the windows wore beards. Most were dressed in disposable lab whites. A few still had their hair covered by the gauze nets. Only one man wore a business suit. He was barrel-chested and gesticulated intensely as he talked.

"Moshe is our salesman. He travels the world, bringing us business."

Kitra's mother said, "Tell the gentleman what we make."

"Anything," Levi Korban replied. "Anything and everything. We specialize in taking technology and building innovative products that are ready for the market. Many of the designs brought to us by Moshe reflect brand-new concepts, but for some reason they do not work as they should. Or they have potential, but are too large. Or they have only been made for a different purpose. We redesign. We shrink. We adapt them to meet emerging needs and markets."

"All this from nothing," Sandrine said. "This my husband has built. From the desert. A haven in the wasteland. You understand?"

"Not yet," Marc replied. "But I'm trying."

"Moshe there was head of sales for the largest electronics conglomerate in Israel. My husband was vice president of our country's largest maker of defense systems. There at the table in the corner, see those three women? All university professors. Beside them is the head of our farm unit; before now he was also a teacher. In high school. With them, the two men, they were rabbis."

"We are not all so educated," Levi inserted.

"Never such a thing did I say, my husband. I was just telling our guest that we are from many different places and many different lives. Levi took these people and gave them a *new* life."

The shards swirled in the over-cooled air, a great mass of brilliant images and thoughts and emotions. Rushing together. Needing just a few more words to bring them into cohesion and clarity. "You were telling me about Moshe."

"You are listening. Good. Very good." Sandrine glanced across the room. "Moshe traveled somewhere, looking for his next deal."

"Switzerland," Levi said. "That was where he heard it first. Then Egypt. The University of Cairo."

"Wherever. Moshe heard that a new source of tantalum had been discovered. At levels of purity far greater than either of the two mines in operation."

"Kenya," Marc said. "Below the lake. Where the first villages were pushed off their land."

"And then came more rumors. Of different elements. And suddenly we realized that there had to be a reality behind these rumors. Not all of them could be false."

"But why Kitra and Serge? Why *you*?"

Both of them sighed together. Levi studied the white linoleum tabletop. "A question I have asked myself a thousand times. A million."

The cafeteria emptied out in a quiet rush of footfalls and conversation. Kitchen staff emerged and began clearing away. The bearded man who had banged the pipes started washing down the floor with a long-handled mop. He sang softly as he worked. Marc thought he recognized the tune as a hymn, but the words were in Hebrew. The smell was not unpleasant, an astringent cleanser that fit with the harsh light spilling through the eastern windows.

Kitra's mother said, "All over Israel there is a secret phenomenon. People are discovering the love of Jesus."

Marc felt a shiver course through his frame. The softly spoken name became the cohesive force. The means through which all these broken shards began pulling together into a mosaic.

"You cannot imagine the response. You would have to be Israeli to understand what is happening. Families who learn one of their own has accepted Jesus as the Messiah are saying Kaddish for their own living relatives. Such is the hold of the Jewish tradition. Can you possibly understand this? No. It is not feasible. You have no idea what power the family has in this land."

"We have returned to this land because of family," Levi said. "As a nation we are determined to provide our families a haven. A place to grow in safety and worship our Lord God."

"And yet these same families are casting out their own loved ones," Sandrine said. "Can you imagine what that means? Listen carefully to what I am saying. If the family does this, if they are so violently opposed to this idea that Jesus is the *chosen one*, what do you think is the response from their friends? From the place where they work? From their own country?"

"They are cast out," Marc said, watching everything come into blinding clarity. "They are banned."

"They have nowhere and they have nothing," Levi said, the recollected sorrow etched deep into his weathered features. "They have lost everything."

"For Jesus," Marc said. Now he was nodding, then rocking. It was not a conscious response. The gathering comprehension pushed him to move. It was either rock, or shout or leap up and race about the room.

"For the Messiah. The risen Lord. They name him, and they pay the price. They become outcast within their own clans. They are the banished ones, even here in their homeland. They are persecuted for accepting the power of eternal love."

Sandrine did not weep; she simply shed tears. They came in a soft stream. They were not wiped away. She gave a physical sign of the sacrifice her own life contained. "And then my husband had his brilliant idea."

"There are other kibbutzim for Messianic believers," he said quietly.

"But they merely survive. This one, Marc, do you see now? Yes, you understand. My husband was not satisfied with surviving. We have incredible minds here, and great passion. We must find a way to do *more* than survive. We must fulfill our roles. Build a place for us within the society that seeks to exclude us. We must find our own path. A new path. One that allows us to grow and build a future for our children and give us hope. Here. In the land that is determined to cast us out."

The passion was there, even with the tears, even whispered. And the answers Marc had come to find. They were there as well. "Kitra went to Kenya for the same reason your husband started this kibbutz."

"She is her father's daughter," Sandrine confirmed. "How could she not hope? How could she not want to build upon what he has started? My brilliant and headstrong child did not go to Africa just to find these elements. She went because she wanted to transform our haven into something so vital, so important to Israeli life, that they would be *forced* to make room for us. To fashion a new and secure place in our society."

"To make them accept you for what you are," Marc said.

"She wanted a technology so powerful, so rich in potential, that the entire nation would accept your role in the nation's future. And Serge went—"

"Serge," the father moaned. "My Serge. He went because he had to. Kitra needed him. She could not do this alone."

Marc said, "Kitra blames herself. For everything."

Sandrine reached across the table and gripped his arm. "You must tell my beautiful and headstrong daughter, such guilt is not hers to bear. She cannot take responsibility for a dream that has propelled us for two generations. This dream has given us *life*."

"She did what she felt was right," Levi agreed. "Serge has a mind. He made his own decision. Not her."

"My son went with her because he chose to do so," Sandrine said. "Kitra argued against it. For days they argued. Serge would not let her do this thing alone."

"Kitra went because she felt she had to," Levi said. "It was her decision, made against my will. Just as Serge went against *her* will."

"Tell her that," Sandrine begged. "Maybe you can make her accept what we cannot."

Marc rose to his feet. He was done here. And there was a woman and a cause that needed him. He said to the father, "Kitra needs to hear this from you. And so do some others."

Levi lifted his gaze. "You want me to travel to Kenya?"

"It's either that or let the Asians take it all," Marc replied. "Go pack a bag. We need to leave immediately."

Chapter Twenty-Nine

B ut things did not move forward according to Marc's plan. Several times over the course of the afternoon and evening, members of the community noted his impatience and told him the same thing. Nothing ever happens swiftly at a kibbutz. Levi and Sandrine Korban were meeting with the collective, he was told. When he tried to press for details, he was met with shrugs and the repeated words, "It is what it is." The kibbutz operates on its own timepiece.

At Levi's request, and probably to keep Marc occupied, two staffers showed him around, one from the farm and another from the labs. He listened to their explanations and heard the quiet pride. He felt the eyes on him still, but they no longer excluded or isolated. And yet another sound was overlaid on everything he saw and heard. The minutes of Serge's life kept ticking down . . . if the clock had not already stopped.

When at sunset the community gathered once more at the chapel, Marc reluctantly forced his impatience aside. The prayer service resonated with all that remained unspoken. They assembled and prayed as Jews. The cross shone with a soft luster. The dais again held the unrolled scrolls. The prayer shawls and the swaying forms and the chanted words and the women clustered behind the beige screen all formed part of the greater mystery. Marc found an English book of Psalms at the back of the chapel. He opened and he read and he prayed his own petition.

After the evening meal, Levi ushered him into a room behind the chapel. The building also housed the administrative and accounting offices, he informed Marc. They entered a conference room as simple and unadorned as the rest of the kibbutz. Sandrine sat midway down the left-hand side. When Marc was seated, Levi went over and joined her. A gray-bearded elder at the head of the table asked Marc about his time in Nairobi. The woman who had refused him entry to the clean rooms that morning demanded to know what good it would do to have Levi accompany him back to Kenya. She did not give him a chance to finish, cutting him off in mid-sentence and declaring it was all a mistake. The enemy had already taken Serge. Why give them the kibbutz's leader as well, the man they could least afford to lose? Marc did not respond. He let the discussion sweep over and around him. He was asked a few more questions and then the elder thanked him. He felt the woman's hostility follow him from the room.

He was crossing the star-lit courtyard when his sat phone buzzed. Charles said, "I hope I am not disturbing."

"It's good to hear from you."

"I have some information." The pastor sounded very tired. "What good it can do you, I cannot say."

"Tell me."

"I have been working through friends in the faith community. I have had to go slowly, because there are people who do not want these questions asked, much less to reveal the answers. I am protecting more lives than my own. So one person has asked this part of the question, and another ally has asked a second part."

"It sounds a lot like what I've been doing," Marc said. "Breaking down the questions into manageable fragments, then trying to fit the puzzle together."

"Yes, it is so. I do not bring answers, I'm afraid. Only more fragments. The places in the south where the villages were first taken, they are now officially registered with the Land Office as experimental farms."

Marc started to tell him about the minerals, then decided that could wait. "It's a cover."

"Of course it is a cover. What is important is that someone considers this important enough to *make* a cover."

"Someone high up the political food chain," Marc said, nodding again with his entire body. Seeing another shard fall into place. "So intent on masking their trail that they use fake IDs when they go into the different villages. So if the elders complain, the bureaucrats can say that person doesn't exist."

"And if the elders who protest have their enemy's name wrong, the bureaucrats can assume the elders have much else incorrect as well," Charles agreed.

"Including the villages' claims of having been deeded this land to begin with," Marc said.

"Our opponents are taking the long view. And I fear they are winning." Charles sounded one step from sheer exhaustion. "Three or four years from now, everyone will have forgotten about the displaced villages."

"Except the villagers themselves," Marc added. An idea came to him then. A tiny flicker of hope, a candle's flame threatened by the winds that swirled around him. So small a light, it was impossible to believe it could actually defy the dark. But an idea just the same, so clear and precise he had an instant's knowledge that it came from somewhere beyond himself. And felt the shivers rock his frame.

Charles went on, "Before long, the village elders will become just more voices crying from the slums. Their claims will be empty, their complaints go unheard. Everyone will forget how that patch of earth once supported a clan and a heritage that stretched back to the borders of mankind's time on earth. The new owners will shut down the farm. They will claim it failed. Africa is full of many such failed dreams."

"We're not there yet," Marc said, thinking about the sorrow etched in the faces of those exiled from their homes. "I have an idea."

Marc hurried back to the administrative building. He entered the conference room just as the meeting was breaking up. "I need a minute."

The woman from the labs demanded, "Who are you to enter this chamber without our permission?"

"Rivka, shah. Manners, please."

"I ask an improper question? This man, he is one of us?" She made a shooing motion at Marc. "Go. Leave. We are tired, and this meeting is done."

"Five minutes," Marc said. "Three."

The gray-bearded gentleman settled back in his seat. "Young man, we will give you two."

A few of the others resumed their seats. Most remained

standing. Watching. The woman snorted, crossed her arms, and stood glowering at him.

Marc laid out his idea. Feeling it take shape as he spoke. Grow from a candle into something more. A bit brighter. More real. The shivers returned, making it hard to shape a few of the more important words.

When he finished he was met with silence and thoughtful gazes. Even the woman scientist's hostility had slid from her like a forgotten shroud.

Finally the elder said, "Your name, young man, what is it again?"

From her place by the side wall, Kitra's mother said, "Royce. Marc Royce."

"You are CIA, Mr. Royce?"

"I was formerly an agent with State Department Intelligence. We focus on security of all nonmilitary establishments outside the nation's borders."

"And now?"

"Officially, I'm nothing. A bookkeeper. Unofficially I'm working for an advisor to the White House."

"And these people, they will support you in this idea?"

"Crazy, is what this idea is," the woman scientist said. But her words lacked antagonism. As though she spoke in order to deny herself the threat of hope. "Insane."

"I will ask them," Marc said. "Tonight."

The elder looked around the room and clearly found what he was after in their silence. "*Nu.* Go and ask your superiors, Mr. Royce. And tomorrow we will meet again, yes? Tomorrow we will hear what your allies have to say. And if this answer is yes, then how can we say anything else?"

Chapter Thirty

The next morning after the dawn service, Sandrine approached as Marc was finishing breakfast. She greeted the people at tables to either side and seated herself beside him. Sandrine kept her voice low enough that it would not carry. "Levi should be able to travel this evening."

Marc stifled his impatience as best he could. "No earlier?"

"He could leave immediately, but only if he resigned from his position as head of the collective. Which he wanted to do. I urged him not to."

Marc could not help but glance at his watch. That morning he had awakened filled with a burning concern for Kitra's safety. Almost as though he had been infected with the worry her parents must be carrying. She was still exposed, still visible to the unseen enemy, still seeking the answers their foes wanted to keep hidden. Marc hated being so far away. No matter how vital the reason. "Maybe he should just go ahead—"

"No, he shouldn't."

"You sound just like Kitra. Totally definite. No chance of changing your mind with argument."

"Because it is correct, what I say. And you know I'm right."

"Kitra again."

She studied him a long moment. Then, "I like the way you speak my daughter's name."

Marc was still trying to find a possible response when Sandrine asked, "You have been to Israel before?"

"Never."

She rose from her place at the table. "Come, Marc Royce. There is something I want you to see."

They took the same dusty pickup that had brought Marc from the airport. Marc drove because Sandrine had asked him to. They pulled down the long graveled road to the main highway, where she directed him north, back toward Tel Aviv. Marc caught glimpses of the Mediterranean Sea to his left, brief tantalizing hints of its cool waters beyond the dry ocher hills. They passed exits with names from his Bible study, before taking the main highway headed inland. As they climbed into the central highlands, Sandrine said, "Tell me about my daughter."

His answer came unbidden. "Kitra has brought back to life a spark of hope I thought was gone for good."

Sandrine wore clothing that suited the surrounding landscape, loose fitting cotton pants and a linen top striped in hues of beige and tan and copper. As though the designers had extracted a sample of desert shades and printed them onto the fabric. "Tell me why you think this."

"Her love for family, for Serge, for you, is a fire as fierce as anything I have ever known. Even when she's smothered in grief for her brother, she lives and breathes a determination to help you out. To secure her father's dream for another generation. This defines her. And now, when I'm three thousand miles away from her, I feel like I can more fully understand her."

"Can you give me a specific, please?"

"She has never lied to me. Even when I knew she wasn't telling me everything I needed to know, I trusted her." Marc struggled to fit his tumbling thoughts into words. "Even when I ordered her to tell me everything, I could sense in my gut that she had reasons for holding back. Good ones. Even when I forced her to talk, I wanted to wait. For her. I'm sorry. I'm not saying this at all well."

"No, you are saying it perfectly." Sandrine pulled a clump of napkins from her pocket. She unrolled one and dabbed at her eyes. "Please continue."

Only then did Marc realize why the woman had asked him to drive. He described the first time he saw Kitra, watching him with blank hostility through the medical unit's screen walls. The volcano's eruption, his deposit in the thick of a camp in severe crisis, the pastor. By the time he began describing their journey to the Swiss camp, and her pointing out where Serge had been abducted, Marc had become more focused on what was going on behind his eyes than the vista beyond the windscreen.

He knew where he was, of course. He had seen enough photos of Israel to recognize the deep cut holding the highway, the series of linked crevasses that formed a natural incline up into the Judean highlands. He knew King David had fought his way up this same slope, as had the freedom fighters in the wars leading to Israel's independence. He spotted the burned-out hulks of tanks left as solemn testimony to the Jewish lives sacrificed to restore their nation. He caught a glimpse of why Kitra was so bound to this place and her father's dream, and wished she was here with them, sharing this first unfolding of an ancient city to him. Jerusalem.

Marc followed Sandrine's directions to a parking area in the shadow of modern high-rises. The old city's walls stood in rose-colored splendor upon those early hills, a crown of stone and saga. Marc and Sandrine joined the crowds and entered the gates and walked down lanes old as time, old as the need for a Savior. Sandrine bought him a falafel and a glass of fresh pomegranate juice. They walked on in silence, down lanes that rose and fell and twisted and turned in confusing sequences.

Finally she stopped before a narrow gate and said, "This is my daughter's favorite spot in all Israel. I came with her the morning before her flight left for Kenya."

They entered a forested garden area to the sound of singing. A Filipino choir stood among the trees, singing hymns with upraised arms. The garden was rimmed on two sides by a curving cliff wall. They walked past a trio of nuns kneeling in the dusty path and halted before a hole in the cliff. Just another narrow cave.

A massive stone carved as a rough wheel shape fit into a groove that ran alongside the cave opening. When rolled into place, the wheel was just large enough to cover the cave mouth. Sandrine said, "No one can say for certain whether this is the burial site where Nicodemus laid our Savior's broken body down. For Kitra, it does not matter. She loves the symbolic power of this place. A point where hope is born from death. A promise to all of us who accept the Messiah's presence in our hearts, and make room for his Spirit to dwell among us."

Marc followed her to a stone bench. The garden was shaded by ancient desert pines, whose growth was measured in inches over arid decades. The choir stopped for prayer, then sang again. A siren rose from beyond the park's safe confines, then faded into insignificance. Marc wondered if he was the only person in the park who had heard the siren at all.

He asked, "Why did you not go to her?"

"Because she begged me not to come. Kitra told me that she could not afford to be weak. Not and have any shred of hope in her quest to find Serge. You have seen for yourself how difficult the kibbutz board can be. So when they refused to allow Levi to travel, I said I was coming no matter how Kitra might object. But she begged me to remain here, on the life of my son." Sandrine's sigh went on for a very long time. "I stayed. I regret staying every day. But I had no choice."

"You did the right thing."

"Then last week she called me. Not Levi. Me. She wanted to tell me about this American who had suddenly appeared at the camp. How you had taken hold of a terrible crisis and forged peace. How you had brought hope to everyone. How the elders called you a hero." Sandrine reached over and took hold of Marc's hand. "You do not know. You cannot imagine, what it has meant to hear her speak your name."

A sudden longing clenched his heart. "She says there is no place for me in her life."

The hold on his hand only grew stronger. "Listen very carefully to what I am about to say, Marc. Our Kitra is committed to a cause. You know this, yes?"

"I know," he replied, and felt his entire being resonate to those two words. *Our Kitra.*

"She is destined to take her father's place. She claimed this as her destiny when she was eleven years old. The community of believers is her life's work. All she imagines, plans, does is aimed at building a future for everyone who has come to call it home." She paused a long moment, then asked, "Do you understand what this means?"

Marc took his time responding. When he spoke, each word reverberated through him like the impact of thunder. "If I am to be with her, I must make this my cause as well."

Her only response was to lift his hand and thump it down on his thigh. Once. Twice. Three times.

Levi phoned them as they departed Jerusalem, confirming that he had the council's permission to travel. Marc phoned Walton, who promised a jet would be ready to roll upon their arrival at Ben Gurion Airport.

Marc said, "I need some way to reenter Kenya without raising red flags."

"I'll take care of that." Walton then told him, "Boyd Crowder is off the grid."

"Meaning?"

"My sources are unable to confirm anything other than the fact that he showed up at Lodestone's Washington HQ, got his next assignment, requested seventy-two hours' leave, and vanished. He and his aide both. I have his name somewhere . . ."

"Karl Rigby."

"There's been no word, no sighting, nothing. Their passports do not come up on any border-crossing register." Walton hesitated, then added, "My sources fear the worst."

Marc shook his head. "For one of them to vanish would be a cause for concern. To have them both be taken out is unlikely in the extreme. These men are pros."

"I hope you're right. All I can tell you is, nobody over there at HQ seems to be overly concerned. Which suggests they are either party to the disappearance, or consider it in line with their own plans." Walton pressed on. "Assuming the worst, what next?"

"I need boots on the ground," Marc replied. "Now. Immediately."

"Lodestone controls all mercs in Kenya. Bringing in outsiders would require an official remit from the Kenyan authorities. Which they will not give. Not to mention how it would alert your opponents to your intentions."

"Sergeant Kamal is with the UN forces," Marc said. "He was formerly charged with security at the camp where I was placed. They were ordered away. He and his men would make for solid allies."

"I'll get on it. Walton out."

The world was russet and gold as they approached the Tel Aviv airport. The sun lowering itself to the horizon burnished the road ahead. At the curb outside the departures area, Sandrine hugged her husband for a very long while. She whispered to him, drew back long enough to stare deeply into his eyes, then held him tightly and whispered again. Finally Levi released his tension with a sigh and a nod. Only then did she kiss him, smile sadly, and let him go.

She had to rise up on tiptoes to hug Marc. Her body held a tensile strength. Sandrine drew back and declared, "I am glad to have met you, Marc Royce. Yes. Very glad. And gladder still that my daughter has you with her."

He wanted to say, if only that were true. But the moment of farewell was no time to give in to such frustrations. Even so, she must have seen something of his yearning in his gaze, for she gripped his arms with the same force she had applied to his hand in the garden of death and hope. "When I heard my daughter speak your name, I knew. Even before that. Is this not so, my husband?"

Levi stared at the two of them. His dark gaze was turned copper by sunset hues and the airport lights. He might have nodded. Marc could not be sure.

"How could I know before she told me of this new man in her life? Well you might ask. I knew, young man, because of another word she had not spoken, a word I had not heard her use since our Serge was taken. That word, young man, was *tomorrow*."

She patted his arm and painted her words with a mother's desperate hope. "Now you and my husband go off and do what must be done. May the Lord our God guide your steps and bless your actions. And bring my children *home*."

Chapter Thirty-One

Marc had felt no fatigue until they were in the air. Then it hit him hard, like someone threw a blanket over him and shut out the world.

They flew in the same Lear that had brought him north. The pilots were different, both female this time, but possessing the same crisp military precision. Marc sat across the narrow aisle from Levi Korban. Kitra's father had started talking in the departures lounge, explaining precisely what was behind their quest. He continued as they climbed on board and belted in, answering questions Marc had not even thought to ask. Levi waited impatiently as the copilot announced takeoff, raised his voice to overcome the engines' roar, and even followed Marc into sleep.

When Marc woke, Levi was there waiting for him. "Sorry. I drifted off."

"I noticed."

Marc excused himself and went back to the washroom. His watch said he'd been asleep for almost two hours, though it felt like only a few minutes. He wondered if Levi had sat there watching him the entire time. Waiting to restart their discussion. Marc decided the man had probably endured a lifetime's worth of waiting since his son had vanished and his daughter refused to come home.

Marc washed his face and dried it with a clutch of paper towels. As he stared at his reflection, he thought about the last dream he'd had before waking. He was standing beside Kitra, looking at a featureless two-room cube. The square house was one of many extending like petals around a squat desert bloom. In the dream, Marc had felt Kitra's arm go around his waist, and in that instant he knew he was looking at their home. He would live there, raise his children there, and be planted in this rocky earth. Far from any place he had ever imagined for himself.

Marc stared at his reflection and faced the question that had carried him into wakefulness. Could he live that life? In her world?

The plane's galley was situated up front, beside the door leading to the cockpit. Marc found two thermoses, one holding coffee and the other hot water. He asked Levi what he wanted, and poured the Israeli a mug of tea. Marc knocked on the door and asked if the pilots wanted anything. One took coffee, the other asked for a sandwich from a tray in the refrigerator. Marc carried the sandwiches and mugs into the cockpit, then loaded a plate and mug for himself.

He knew Levi was waiting to get back into his explanation. But Marc did not need to know more. He would never become an expert on rare earths. He knew enough to get the job done. His focus needed to be elsewhere. He could feel the man's stare but kept his attention on his supper.

When he finished eating, Marc pulled out the sat phone and made two calls. The first was to Charles, making arrangements to meet with the Kibera elders and asking him to book them hotel rooms under Levi's name. He cradled the phone for a long moment, then called the camp director and asked to speak to Kitra. Marc could feel Levi's gaze boring into him. He rose from his seat and carried the phone back to where the engines' noise offered a bit of privacy.

At the sound of her hello, all his one-sided conversations crowded in. "I've missed you. Missed hearing from you. Missed talking with you. Being with your family and in your homeland was hard without you. You were everywhere."

She might have sobbed. He wasn't sure. The sat phone was good for communicating, but all emotions were tinged with metallic hissing. When she did not respond, he went on, "You were right to do what you did. To go to Kenya, seek out a future for your people. With Serge."

"If only that were true."

"You are your father's daughter. Even your mother says that. In spite of everything."

"How is she?"

"A strong woman, like her daughter. Desperate to have you safe at home."

This time the sniff was audible. "Wait a moment, please."

He heard the phone settle, and the sound of Kitra blowing her nose, then, "Where are you?"

"Flying back to Nairobi. We should arrive sometime around midnight local time."

"Is Daddy there with you?"

"Yes."

"I miss you, Marc." She almost broke down forming the words, "If only things were different."

He spoke around his longing. "Kitra, your parents don't blame you for Serge's disappearance."

"They don't need to. I blame myself. Guilty on all charges."

"They both knew Serge would never let you go alone."

She needed a long moment to say, "Serge started hunting for answers the moment he arrived. I tried to tell him it was dangerous, that our best hope was to come in and identify the materials and leave unseen. He wouldn't listen. He was certain the Chinese were intent on finding these new sources and claiming them all. That first week he obtained evidence the Chinese were bribing senior government officials to smooth their way. I begged him to go more slowly. But he was convinced if we did not hurry, we would lose our chance. And in order to block them, we needed cold, hard evidence.

"So Serge waited for another village to be evicted, then went on the hunt. Sometimes I thought he *wanted* to be abducted. Only this would gain us the answers. He was obsessed with uncovering the truth." She blew her nose again. "He always said he was here to protect me. I know the truth now. He wanted to protect the entire country. That is who Serge was. Is." She choked on the last word.

Marc listened beyond the words and heard how this beautiful woman was trusting him now. He wished he could reassure her, tell her everything would be fine in the end. But he could not taint this moment with false promises.

"You and Serge are so much alike," she said. "Thank you, Marc. So much. For everything. Most of all, for hoping. For both of us." Her voice sounded as though fear and sorrow had shrunk it down. "Now let me speak with Daddy."

Levi talked with his daughter in Hebrew for a while. Then he switched to French. Marc glanced over at the change in language and saw that Levi was smiling. Marc assumed he was passing on a message from Kitra's mother. Levi switched back to Hebrew, then pressed the end button and handed back the phone. "She will leave the camp tomorrow, she says."

Marc felt a thrill at the prospect of seeing her again. "Why didn't you go to Kenya? I know what the kibbutz council said. But if my son went missing and my daughter refused to come home, I'd still be there today."

Levi nodded, as though he had been expecting the question all along. "Kitra gave me the only argument I could not refute. And then the community elders ordered me to stay. The two coming together like that was more than I could defy."

"What did Kitra say?"

Levi drummed his fingers on the tabletop. "You should first know that I trained as an engineer. But I was a born manager. I never recognized that fact until my wife told me. She said I would never be happy unless I was in control. And she was right. The community had already been started at that point. A farmer and his family came to faith in Jesus. They took in friends, a professor at the Hebrew University who lost his job when he announced Jesus was the Messiah. Then others, and more still. They lived in such poverty, the conditions, the strain on the families . . ." Levi waved that all aside. He said, "My aim has always been the same."

"Not just to survive," Marc said, "but to thrive."

"I want my clan to forge their rightful place in Israeli society. The majority of Israelis may disagree with us, but it is still our land. Our heritage. And faith in our Messiah links us to the ancient past, the present, and Israel's future."

Levi's voice did not raise so much as take on a new timbre.

Marc felt as though he glimpsed the man who had once been, back before tragedy struck. He rephrased his question. "How did Kitra keep you from coming?"

His smile carried the sorrow of a proud father. "She told me this was one place where I would never be in control. And if I tried, I would only make things worse."

"And she was right," Marc said.

Levi swiveled in his seat so as to face across the aisle. His features held the taut leanness of a man who had carried other people's burdens for so long he assumed they were his own. "My wife spoke to me last night. She said you were to be trusted. She said it was not a matter of bringing Kitra home. But bringing her home *whole*." Levi's countenance reflected the light pouring in through the aircraft's windows. "Sandrine made me promise to trust you."

Marc's reply was cut off by the pilot announcing their descent into Nairobi. He stared out a side window at the approaching city, yet all he saw was the squat, white cube of a home planted in an ancient desert, being buried in a land that was not his to claim.

Chapter Thirty-Two

Although it was after midnight when they landed, Deb Orlando awaited them on the tarmac. She sketched a salute and a smile at Marc's appearance. After he had introduced Levi, Deb drew Marc aside and said, "Ambassador Walton said you would be needing some fresh papers."

Marc accepted the new passport, opened it to the first page, and read his new name. "Mark Marcus?"

Her smile was refreshing. "The ambassador said it would be easy to remember."

Charles was there to meet them as they left the terminal. He greeted Levi with solemn dignity, a Kenyan trait Marc was coming to value ever more highly. After witnessing firsthand some of the trials they faced, enduring a hint of the danger they lived with, he could begin to understand what strength of character was required to remain upright and regal.

They walked over to where Joseph stood beside a new armored Tahoe. Marc shook the familiar embassy driver's hand and asked, "Aren't you worried about driving me again?"

"Maybe a little, sir. Maybe even more than a little." But he smiled as he spoke. "Miss Debs, she is a favorite of many at the embassy, sir. So I am here."

They rode in silence and made good time. As they entered Kibera, Marc could almost smell the old cordite. He also noticed many young men on patrol. "Are there more guards than usual?"

"The elders have spoken," Charles replied. "If there is more trouble, they will respond. Troublemakers will be banished. The people, they are determined there will be no trouble."

Levi scrutinized the slum and the road and the people. He did not speak until they emerged from the embassy vehicle, and that was only to thank Joseph. The driver responded with a single nod.

Deb Orlando asked Marc, "Maybe I should stay out here and guard our ride?"

Marc agreed, thinking one strange Anglo face at a time might be best. Together they crossed the square and entered the church.

After Marc's introductions, Levi greeted the elders on the dais with a solemn dignity that matched their own. He accepted their compliments regarding his daughter with grave thanks. And he waited.

By the time the formalities were done, the church was packed. People came and settled in silence. The windows and doorways were all full. The air became clogged with odors, a thoroughly African combination of city and village. The hour of the night meant little. The reason for their gathering was too important to be ruled by the clock.

Finally Philip's uncle turned to him and said through Charles, "You have traveled to the Holy Land on our behalf. Searching for answers to our questions and your own. You have returned with the father of Kitra, a woman we have come to know and respect and trust. So now we ask you to speak, Marc Royce, and tell us what lessons you bring for us."

Marc matched the chief's formal tone. "I thank you for allowing us to meet with you this night. I would ask that you first hear from Levi Korban, the leader of a clan and village in Israel."

Philip's uncle asked, "You share your daughter's faith in Jesus?"

"I and all my clan. It is why we are joined together."

"Speak then, Levi Korban. We would hear what you have to say."

"My community makes high-tech components for the electronics industry. Israel is becoming the Silicon Valley of the Middle East. I tell you this because it is important for you to understand how I know about the problems you face. From Marc Royce we received soil samples taken from the refugee camp where my daughter works, which is now under threat. These samples contain what are known as rare-earth minerals. Most of these are not rare at all. But they are generally not found in high concentrations, and when they were first discovered the scientists assumed they were the rarest of elements. Thus their name."

Charles translated in a continuous monotone. The elders focused intently on Levi and did not speak. Marc had no idea how much they actually understood, for they absorbed the Israeli's words with stonelike expressions. Behind him, the church was utterly still. Somewhere beyond a side window, a baby whimpered and was swiftly silenced. A dog barked. A truck lumbered down the road. Otherwise there was no sound save for Levi's words and Charles's translation.

"Most of the world's current supplies of rare earths come from ion absorption clays found in Inner Mongolia. This is a region in northern China. Earlier there were mines in Brazil and Australia and America's Midwest. But these have largely been tapped out. Other potential sources have been located in the United States, but up to now they have not been developed. Today China controls over ninety percent of the world's total production capacity."

"The yellow men," Philip's uncle stated.

Marc confirmed, "My superiors believe China is intent on gaining control of these elements worldwide in order to maintain their monopoly."

"So we have these elements in the soil of our villages? This is why we have been expelled?"

"There is a type of mineral structure called placer sand deposits," Levi said. "This is the richest potential source of these elements. The samples Marc Royce brought us contain placer sands with extremely high concentrations of the most valuable rare earths. The soil of your villages contains up to five hundred times greater concentration of rare earths than the Mongolian ore deposits, and they lie right on the surface. They would be easy to extract."

For the first time the elders broke off their inspection of Levi. They exchanged glances. Then the Kisii elder spoke a few words. Charles translated, "What does this mean? When will we return to our homes?"

When everyone looked at him, Marc took a long breath. He replied, "I think it is time we confront this issue. I am sorry to tell you, you will never be able to return."

A rush of sound filled the church like a tragic wind. Marc

waited until the current passed before continuing, "I think it is time you all faced the future. I speak what I believe you have long suspected. The forces at work here will never permit you to go back to your traditional way of life. Not at these places."

Levi added, "The latest estimates predict that there will be a shortfall of forty thousand tons of rare earths this year, and sixty thousand tons next year. This shortfall is only met because China has stockpiled the minerals. At current prices their profits will total six billion dollars a year."

"And prices are rising steadily," Marc said. "Do you understand what this means?"

"The entire world will demand our earth," Philip's uncle said.

One of the other elders erupted in an angry tirade. Philip's uncle leaned forward and silenced him with a look. When the elder subsided, the chief nodded at Marc. "You may continue."

"In my opinion the only way for you to take control of your future is to accept this dislocation as permanent. I have brought this man here because I believe he holds an answer for you. You need an ally. Someone you can trust to hold your own interests as important as his own. Someone who will act as a buffer to the outside world."

"This is why Kitra and her brother came to Kenya?"

"To search out these elements," Levi replied. "Yes."

"And we should trust you because of your loss? I do not mean disrespect. But I question whether this alone is reason enough."

"I understand." Levi withdrew a small book from his pocket. "Since Marc told us of his plan, I have been praying for guidance. This is the answer that has come to me. In the thirty-first chapter of Proverbs, we are told this. 'Speak up for those who cannot speak for themselves, for the rights of all who are destitute. Speak up and judge fairly; defend the rights of the poor and needy.'"

Levi settled a hand on the open page as if drawing strength from the words. "This passage first came to me when I arrived at our community of believers in Israel. Followers of Jesus are ostracized in my homeland. Perhaps you have heard this. We suffer for our faith. I will not say we have endured anything like what you have experienced. But I will tell you that we have lost families and jobs and homes. I feel for you. I want to help. Is this why I came? No. It was tragedy that brought me here. I have lost contact with my son. . . ."

For the first time since the journey in from the Tel Aviv airport, Marc saw the man almost break down. Only then did he realize that total silence had captured the whole group. The entire church seemed to hold its breath. No one rushed him. No one moved.

Finally Levi managed to say, "I will be completely honest. My children came here searching for a way to create a firm hold for our own community. Right now we exist from one contract to the next. It is not hand-to-mouth, but it is close. We ffiight for our next job, for the next link in the chain of our future. My Kitra is a born leader. She looks beyond the horizon, searching always for what can make things better. She saw these rare-earth elements as a means to take a firmer hold on our destiny." Levi took a long breath. "On behalf of my daughter, my son, and my community, I am here to offer you an alternative future. I feel that what Marc has told you is correct. The world's hunger for these rare earths is too great. You will never farm this land again. And yet there is a chance we together could wrest back control. Form a coalition. And build a future. Together. For all of us."

Philip's uncle asked Marc, "This is your idea?"

"It is."

"Tell us what you plan."

"Extract the minerals here, refine them in Israel. Share the wealth, and the knowledge. Choose your young people, train them as engineers. Create a new future."

"But the land has been taken from us."

Levi said, "My community will invest in lawyers. And start an international public relations campaign. Your rights in the land will be defended. The extraction process used by the Chinese is the most polluting industry on earth. But there are new processes, none of which the Chinese have ever tried to apply. These reduce the pollution to almost nothing. The extraction process draws the elements from the earth. But they must be further refined, and separated, because most of these elements are joined and must be isolated before they can be used. We will form a joint corporation. We will train together, work together, and share profits equally."

The chief asked Marc, "Your government does not object?"

"I have spoken of this with my superiors. There are only two American companies who could be involved. Both have lost millions in the Congo, where these sands have also been found, but not at this level of purity. These two companies are not willing to invest more at this time. My government's greatest desire is to keep this new source out of Chinese hands. Their primary objective is to weaken their global monopoly. They wish for these Kenyan minerals to be managed by allies."

The council of elders pondered this for a time in silence. "We must speak of this among ourselves. We ask that you wait in the back for our decision."

Levi rose, stepped down from the dais, then turned back and said, "At the airport, my wife reminded me of something she had told our daughter and son before they left for Kenya. This great valley you know as the Rift. It extends all the way to Israel. It is underground in my region, filled with alluvial soil. But as a geological feature, it actually ends very near to my kibbutz. My wife said that perhaps this is God's way of signifying a deeper bond between our communities than either of us had ever imagined."

The chief rose to his feet. "It is good that our new friend Marc Royce chose to bring you. In our clan, the Luo, to call someone a teacher is a sign of great wisdom and authority. This word *teacher*, in Hebrew it is rabbi, is that correct?"

"It is."

The chief extended his hand. "Rabbi Korban. We salute you."

Chapter Thirty-Three

When the visitors were seated at the back of the church, a young man brought them cold drinks. Levi sipped his Coke and rubbed his eyes. Charles remained up front with the elders. He was bent over in his seat, taking part in the discussion. Occasionally the pastor glanced back in Marc's direction. He looked very worried. Marc did not share his concern, nor feel any need to know what was going on. He had done everything he could.

Eventually Marc and Levi were again called forward. Charles translated, "The elders speak with one voice. They have decided that official confirmation of this plan is required."

Marc pondered this for a moment too long, because the Kisii elder barked at him. It was not a bellow, but it did carry anger. Charles's translation, by contrast, hovered somewhere between toneless and ashamed. "The elder says, Why should we trust the future of our tribes to new voices from afar? How often have we been lied to by smiling white faces?"

Philip's uncle stared at the floor by his feet. He did not look up or speak.

Charles continued with the elder's charges. "This is not some group of angry tribesmen who oppose us. We were not evicted by some local gang. This was the government. For us to succeed, we must have powerful allies. All we see here are two men we do not know."

One of the other elders muttered two words, which Charles translated as "Philip's dream."

The angry elder dismissed that with a swipe of his hand. "We may have just this one chance. We must choose rightly. We must *know*."

Marc said, "Please tell the elder I should have thought of this before I showed up. I apologize. We've traveled all night and I'm weary. I have no other excuse."

The elders murmured appreciation of his answer. Oyango nodded gravely. The Kisii said through Charles, "It is good to know you treat our concerns seriously."

"Always." Marc pulled the sat phone from his pack. He had no idea how Walton would respond. But he saw no alternative. He remained in his seat as he punched in the number. The Kisii elder continued, "We are important to this process. We cannot give our earth away."

"No one is giving anything," Philip's uncle spoke in English to the floor by his feet.

Walton answered, and Marc showed the elders an upraised hand. He swiftly summarized the situation.

Walton showed no astonishment whatsoever. "How fast can you get to the embassy?"

"Hard to tell. It's an hour before dawn. I don't know when traffic—"

"Go there now. Take the elders. I'll arrange things from this end."

"It will be outside official hours," Marc reminded him. "Since the terrorist bombings, they totally shut things down—"

"I said I'll handle it." Walton cut the connection.

Marc traveled to the U.S. embassy with Charles, Levi, and Deb in the Tahoe driven by Joseph. The elders followed in two ratty taxis. They made good time.

As they turned onto Moi Avenue, they were halted by a convoy of Kenyan military guarding the embassy's main gates. Marc grew concerned that the guards might forbid this clutch of local nationals to enter the compound. Kenya had been the first sub-Saharan nation to endure terrorist bombings, including an attack against the U.S. embassy. As a result, the new American compound resembled a polite bunker system. But when the three cars pulled up, a trio of white-hatted American MPs stepped from the guardhouse and approached the lead Kenyan armored personnel carrier.

The MP officer saluted Deb Orlando, then asked Marc, "How many are you, sir?"

"Besides Ms. Orlando, myself, another American citizen, seven Kenyan nationals, and one Israeli."

The MP spoke into his radio, then said to the Kenyan officer, "We'll take it from here."

The Kenyan soldiers stepped aside. The elders rose in slow stages from the two taxis and stood in regal stillness as the compound gates rolled open.

Marc stood to one side and allowed the elders to enter first. The elders were dressed in a motley collection of cast-off clothing and headgear. Three of them supported their weight on ornately carved staffs.

Inside the main building, Deb handed each a visitor's pass and ushered them through the security station. When the duty officer saluted Marc, he thought he detected a hint of good humor in the marine's gaze.

Deb led them across the foyer and down a wide main hallway. She said quietly, "This has been a surprisingly good day, thanks to you and your boss. Long, but good."

Marc guessed, "Walton had another word with your superior."

"More than a word. When Walton's first request surfaced yesterday evening, my boss decided he'd had enough and complained to his main squeeze back in D.C." She made no attempt to hide her pleasure at the memory. "I don't know who phoned him back. But my boss left here with third-degree burns covering a hundred percent of his ego. Then, just to make sure there wasn't any question over the matter, the ambassador also got a couple of phone calls."

Deb opened a door marked only by a number. "I've also been invited to transfer into ops as soon as my tour here is done. I just want you to know, sir, whatever you need, all you've got to do is whistle. I'm there."

"Ops will be lucky to have you," Marc said. "But I'm grateful for the offer."

"That's no offer, sir. That's a promise."

"I have invited you here to confirm that I speak as a representative of the United States government. At the same time, everything we discuss is unofficial and off-the-record."

They were seated around one end of an oval conference table. The table's other end was dominated by a flat-screen monitor set in the rear wall. Sliding panels had been pulled back to reveal a battery of electronic equipment and speakers. On the screen, Ambassador Walton sat in a high-backed leather chair. The corner of a desk was visible in the lower portion of the screen. Marc had no idea where the office was located. But two flags were stationed behind the chair, framing a trophy wall of signed photographs, including three U.S. presidents. One was the American flag. The other had a pale blue shield on white background, but was folded so that Marc could not make out the insignia. It could have been military, or state, or some rarer form of ambassadorial corps. Whatever it was, the two flags and the battery of awards and photographs made for a very impressive backdrop.

"The United States government deems it to be of vital national interest to prevent the Chinese from extending their monopoly on the international supply of rare earths," Walton continued. "We therefore offer what support we can to your endeavors to develop these resources. We may, repeat may, be able to include the UN in the equation. Marc Royce will explain this further, if or when the situation materializes."

Marc sat with his back to the room's lone window. Oyango was seated to his left with Levi Korban across the table from them. The other elders formed a semicircle around the table's end. Charles was seated behind them and translated in a constant low monotone. Deb stood between Marc and the window. She had declined his offer of a seat.

Levi asked the man on the screen, "Why us? I mean no offense by the question. But I for one need to understand why you are speaking with us like this."

"Why not bring in an American group, you mean. Two

reasons. First, you are there and things are moving swiftly. Any action we take to insert a third party will mean taking this whole thing public. It then becomes a battle between nations. We don't want another cold war. We also have a greater chance of success if we match China's calculated strategy with our own. Getting a third party in place and up to speed in a hurry will necessitate a lot of noise."

He waited for Charles to complete his translation, then went on, "The second reason is simpler. There are only two U.S. rare-earth mining groups with any experience in Africa. They lost almost a hundred million dollars in the Congo when their operations were deemed part of the minerals fueling that nation's civil war. Because of Kenya's ongoing unrest resulting from your elections, they will under no circumstances become involved in this venture. I know. I have spoken personally with both companies' directors."

When Charles had caught up, Walton said, "Now tell me what you need."

For once, the elders were silent. Marc gave them a moment, then said, "For this to work, I need to know the extent of Lodestone's involvement in these forced displacements."

"We're working on that. So far, there is no evidence that their Nairobi operation knows anything at all. We cannot say the same for their Washington headquarters. Yet."

"What about who was behind the attack on us in Kibera?"

"Again, there is no evidence of Lodestone's direct involvement, other than passing on the message. Ms. Orlando, do you have anything further to add?"

"I checked with my sources just before meeting Mr. Royce at the airport, sir. Nothing yet."

Marc went on, "Any word about enlisting Sergeant Kamal and his men?"

"As you stated, he was pulled out of the refugee camp and reassigned. My contacts at the UN have located him. He has been issued orders to report for duty. Who has taken these soldiers' place at the camp?"

"We put together a group of young men and women from among the locals. They are standing guard, operating under the camp director and a local chief named Philip. But they are unarmed."

Walton examined him a moment. "This is the camp where the young man was abducted?"

"Serge Korban was taken at a different location. But he was stationed at this camp. His sister still works out of there." Marc gestured across the table. "This is Serge's father."

Walton nodded a somber greeting. "My sincere condolences and hopes that your son is soon rescued, sir. Speaking as one who has supervised a number of operatives in free-fire zones, I would urge you not to give up hope."

Levi's voice sounded strained. "I am trying."

"I would also urge you to extract your daughter."

"She is joining us later today," Marc confirmed.

"What is your next move?"

Marc sketched out what he had in mind. Walton studied him with grave intensity. He nodded once. "I agree with your assessment and your plans. I stand ready to support you in whatever way possible. Good evening, gentlemen, and good hunting. Walton out."

Chapter Thirty-Four

They left the embassy compound in the starlit hour before dawn. The moon was a soft golden globe hovering just above the horizon. The two taxis that had brought the elders from Kibera started their motors, clearly hoping for a return fare. Marc walked over and asked for the price to Kibera. The lead driver named a number. Philip's uncle spoke one word. The driver cut the number in half. Marc paid them both.

The Kikuyu elder patted Marc's shoulder before easing into the first taxi. He did not speak. He did not need to.

Philip's uncle was the last to enter. Oyango stared at Marc for a time. The other elders sat in silence and watched them through the taxis' open doors. The taxi drivers showed no impatience whatsoever. Marc found himself fitting into the African rhythm, where the passage of time was measured in the flow of shadows, the sweep of stars, the rising of crops, the growth of new generations, the carving of cliffs by wind and rain.

Finally Oyango asked, "What can we do to assist in making this happen?"

This was what he had been hoping to hear from them. "We need to find the Chinese processing facility."

"How will we know this thing?"

"It is large, and it is poisonous," Marc replied.

Levi stepped up alongside Marc. "If the Chinese operate it according to their standard methods, their runoff will pollute the entire region. Earth, air, but most especially the groundwater."

Oyango inspected Levi anew. "And yet you say your methods are different."

"Like night and day," Levi confirmed. "We have been involved in developing an entirely new method. Initially it was considered too expensive. And new extraction plants were not being built. But prices for rare earths have risen to where the difference between the poisonous method and the newer, cleaner method has become insignificant."

The chief mulled that over. "Then your daughter had the idea to come to Kenya."

"It is so," Levi agreed. "Our process is successful, clean, and cost-effective. But we could not find a buyer. The Chinese refused to either modify their current extraction facilities or build new ones. So Kitra had the idea to search out a new source of raw materials."

"This was what she came to offer," Oyango went on. "Not money. Not power. But a safe and clean method of building a future. With these materials."

"They are the gold and the platinum of the new millennium," Levi said. "We proved they could be extracted and refined without ruining the environment. We have carefully patented our discoveries. The Chinese dislike paying anyone for new technology. And they show total disregard for the environment, especially outside their own borders. They are after power and money and control. They care nothing for other peoples or their land."

Oyango turned back to Marc. "What do we say to those we send out searching for these facilities?"

"Tell them to seek a hidden camp. It may be disguised as a UN base. It will be well guarded. Trucks will enter filled with earth and leave empty. It will have a lab. And many Chinese men."

"And a toxic waste dump as big as a tall hill," Levi said.

"Nothing will grow upon this hill?"

"Nowhere near it."

"This we will do." Oyango made the pronouncement with the solemn conviction of an oath. He shook Levi's hand, then drew Marc to one side and asked, "You know of my nephew's dream about you?"

"He told me."

The chief cocked his head slightly. "You doubt that you are the one?"

Marc hesitated, then confessed, "No."

"Good." He nodded ponderously. "When surrounded by miracles, it is not proper to doubt the will of the Most High God."

Marc struggled to move beyond the resonance of that word *miracle*. "I prefer to think of myself as a servant. Not a hero."

Philip's uncle revealed an astonishingly bright smile. His teeth gleamed in the streetlights as he lifted one fist toward the stars overhead. "You will tell my nephew something for me?"

"Of course."

"Tell him I salute him. Say that I call him *Jatelo*. You can remember this word?"

Marc noted how Charles's eyes went wide, and he repeated the word, "Jatelo."

"My nephew, he will tell you what it means." He settled his hand where the Kikuyu's had rested. "It is an honor to pray for you, God's willing servant. And a friend to my people. An honor."

Chapter Thirty-Five

The embassy Tahoe went through another careful inspection before they were permitted to enter the Sheraton Hotel's parking lot. The hotel dated from the seventies and had started to show its age. In the U.S. it would probably have been sold off to a budget chain. But this was Kenya, and the definition of five-star luxury was often stretched. The Sheraton was safe; the staff were well trained, the beds clean.

Charles had called ahead, and Kamal was waiting for them in the lobby. Marc turned to Deb and warned, "You probably want to leave now."

"If it's okay with you, sir, I'll hang around a while longer."

"Then I need to make certain you understand, this is not exactly—"

"Part of my official remit," she cheerfully finished for him. "As far off the grid as Mars. Sir, some girls dream of prom night and frilly dresses. Me, I've been looking for this chance all my life."

"Nothing will be said to your embassy bosses?"

"The only person I'm answering to right now is Ambassador Walton. He asked me if I'd be willing to do whatever you needed doing. I said, 'Who do I have to kill?'"

"I hope nobody," Marc replied. "Okay, let's go."

Kamal was dressed in street clothes. The knit shirt was pulled taut over a muscled upper body. It was the first time Marc had seen him in anything other than military fatigues. Marc greeted the UN soldier with, "Man, are you a sight for sore eyes."

Even before Charles translated, the soldier was grinning. Perhaps he had seen the welcome relief in Marc's gaze. Perhaps it was just the African way of greeting. But his smile was brilliant, and his handshake began with a swing up past his shoulder, sweeping down as though he intended to swat Marc. Marc tried to match the elaborate handshake and felt warmed by the sense of belonging.

Marc said, "I really need your help."

Kamal replied, and Charles translated, "The sergeant says it would be an honor to assist one who seeks to assist others. I agree."

The warming at the core of his being strengthened. He asked Kamal, "Will your absence cause questions back at your base?"

"I have been given a document from UN headquarters in New York. This document promotes me to captain and orders me and my squad to go wherever it is you tell me to go. My superiors have never before seen such a document." Kamal's laugh enriched his every word. "My men and I, we were assigned to the depot. We guarded an empty godown. We were all so very bored. Five times I requested assignment to a camp, to the borders, anything but this. Five times they said no."

"They wanted you where they could keep watch."

"So we are thinking also. Then yesterday, my commanding

officer, he runs over. I have never before seen this man run. He says, 'I and my men, we must go.' I ask him, 'Go where?' He hands me the paper with these remarkable orders, and silver pins for my uniform, and extra pay, and travel permits. He says, 'You and your squad, you are ordered to Nairobi. The chopper is there waiting to take you.' Then he salutes me. I am still asking myself if any of this is truly real."

"Believe me, this is as real as it gets." Marc introduced both Levi and Deb.

Kamal inspected the man. "This is the father of the missing young man?"

"And Kitra."

"Your son and your daughter, they are a good evidence of the ones who raised them."

Levi managed a hoarse "Thank you."

Kamal resumed his grinning conversation with Marc. "My men say to tell you, they are rested and they are ready."

Marc resisted the urge to rub his hands in anticipation. "I have a plan."

But as Marc outlined what he had in mind, Kamal lost his good humor. He spoke a question, which Charles translated as, "You realize the officials behind stealing the village land and shipping the people to Kibera, this will reach all the way to the top?"

"We suspect that."

"This is more than suspect." Kamal's tone carried a lifetime's awareness. "Charles tells me of how you were ordered to leave Kenya. This was your only warning. Like my reassignment to the depot was a warning."

"I understand."

"Do you also understand that these documents in my pocket will not protect us? And the men who signed these papers, they are so very far away from Kenya." He fingered the silver bars on his lapel. "My promotion is no shield from bullets."

"You don't have to come," Marc said, though he feared moving forward without Kamal and his men.

"I am not refusing you," Kamal said sharply. "I simply ask, do you understand the danger?"

"As much as an outsider possibly can."

Kamal liked Marc's response enough to relax. "Then you will take advice?"

"That's why I need you."

"Soon, word will filter back to our enemies of me and my squad being reassigned. Our enemy will also come to know you are back and again asking the wrong questions."

"I returned to Kenya under a different name."

"They will know," Kamal repeated. "And if they find us, they will bury us all in a dusty grave."

Marc let the words settle a long moment. They were all surrounded by a different world, one of happy people and clinking glasses and rushing servants and safety. He studied each of the faces in turn, and found only grim determination. He said, "The stakes could not be higher. We're out to salvage entire villages and ways of life."

"You feel for their loss," Kamal said.

"With all my heart."

"As do I. Then I have one question for you and your companions, Marc Royce. Can you follow the orders of your guide through the jungle? For that is what you seek of me, yes? One who can lead the hunt and read the spoor."

Marc felt his own tension gradually ease. "That is exactly what I need."

Kamal leaned forward. He turned his head in a slow motion, hissing softly to each of them in turn. He spoke, and Charles translated, "That is the sound we make on the hunt. The one that tells our brothers, the prey is near and hunting us too. One false move, one broken twig, and we are all dead."

Kamal hissed softly once more.

Chapter Thirty-Six

They shared an early breakfast in the hotel restaurant. Marc's plan was dissected and worked over and walked through. Charles and Deb Orlando were both very tentative at first. Levi tended to bark his observations, then go silent for long spells. By the time the plates were pushed aside and various table items became components of their map, the three were fully involved. Which was what Marc had been after all along.

Then the bellhop appeared at their table. He asked, "Mr. Levi Korban, he is here?"

"That's me."

"A message has come for you, sah."

Marc tipped the bellhop and waited as Levi opened the note and declared, "Kitra is not coming."

Marc felt his breakfast form a knot in his gut. "Did she say why?"

"A flood of new refugees. An outbreak of some new disease." He balled up the paper. "She left a message so I couldn't argue."

"Go get some rest," Marc said. "This afternoon we'll arrange a transport to take you to the camp."

"I can rest on the way. I'm leaving now."

"We've flown all night, and been working straight since our arrival," Marc protested.

Levi rose from the table. "I've gone for weeks without sleep over this. I am going for my daughter."

Charles offered, "There's a Red Cross convoy leaving for the camps this morning. I can arrange transport for us both. But we must hurry."

Marc rose with them. "I need to stay. There are a ton of things we need to arrange."

"Do what you need to do. I'll phone you when we arrive." Levi shouldered his pack. "Let's go."

Marc walked Charles and Levi to the taxi stand and saw them off. Kamal then took his leave to gather and brief his men. Marc walked Deb over to where Joseph waited by the embassy vehicle. "We need a private location where we can prep and plan. Something near our target area and safe from prying eyes."

"I can do that." She gave Marc the clear-eyed gaze of a woman with a future. "Walton instructed me to check in whenever I could. Feed him regular updates. I didn't want you to think I was talking behind your back."

"This is Walton's way of observing you in the field," Marc explained. "Go do your thing. I'll grab a few hours' rest, then meet me back here."

Her smile was as genuine as the rest of her. "I just want you to know, sir, that I agree totally with the elders. When I look at you, what I'm thinking is, hero."

Her words stayed with Marc as he checked in and headed for his room. His sat phone rang while he was waiting for the shower to heat up. Boyd Crowder said, "We're about to see how good you are at staying alive, sport."

"Is it ever good to hear your voice." Marc cut off the shower and carried his grin and the phone over to the window. "Walton and the other white hats in D.C. have you written off."

"Yeah, well, reports of our demise are a little early. How're you?"

"Better now. What happened?"

"An hour after we landed in D.C., Karl caught wind of a possible hit on us."

"Lodestone?"

"We decided we weren't going to stick around and find out."

"Where are you now?"

"Azores. Refueling stop. Me and Karl hitched a ride with a buddy who's hauling a load of medical equipment to Nairobi. We're staying totally off the grid. Want to bring me up to speed?"

Marc told him about Israel and Levi and the embassy meeting with the elders. He explained how the elders were spreading the word, looking for the rare-earth extraction plant.

"Using the locals to find your smoking gun, that was a good idea," Crowder said. "Where's the rest of your team?"

"Two just left for the camp. Levi wants to see his daughter. Charles needs to bring Philip up to speed. Kamal is readying his team. I'm in serious prep mode, and I need your help."

"Why I called. Hold on." Crowder muffled the phone, then came back with, "My ride's ready. Got any idea how me and Rigby can sneak into Kenya on the quiet?"

"I have a lady at the embassy that might be able to help. Her name is Deb Orlando. I'll call her soon as we're done."

"You trust her with this?"

"With my life. She slipped me in under the wire earlier today."

"Sounds good enough for me. One word of advice, sport. Our buddies at Lodestone-Nairobi report Dirk has been given orders to take you out."

"They know I'm back?"

"At least they suspect."

"We need an out-of-the-way location for prep work."

"I'm on it."

"We're wheels down at six this evening. Crowder out."

The Red Cross trucks passed through Nairobi in the fresh light of a new day. Charles and Levi rode in the lead truck, on their way to the camp. Nairobi's main arteries thundered with traffic, but the vehicles managed a steady pace. In another hour, the streets would gridlock. All the truck traffic heading west from the Mombasa port raced through the night, pushing desperately to pass through Nairobi before the streets became parking lots.

As their driver made it to the hills forming Nairobi's western rim, the man grinned his satisfaction and turned on the radio.

The hills separating Nairobi from the Rift Valley were blanketed by tea plantations. The drivers and assistants leaned out the open windows and breathed the sweet air. The trucks ground their gears and powered through a series of sharp cutbacks; then suddenly the Rift Valley opened up before them. Charles never tired of the sight. His American family had once taken him on a journey across the United States. They spent two days hiking the Grand Canyon. The Rift held that same power and sense of wonder.

But the Rift was far larger than the Grand Canyon, and very green. The valley's opposite rim was visible through the morning haze like some mystical wall. At its widest point the Rift was over seventy miles across. Ancient volcanoes, their cones covered now in tropical growth, rose like islands in the midst of a vast emerald sea.

As the convoy traveled along the valley's eastern rim, it rounded a curve where below them sparkled a field of white. The driver and his three assistants grew somber. One of them cut off the radio. Together they watched in silence as irregular white shapes became row after row of tent tops. In the brilliant sunlight they gleamed like giant birds' wings, symbols of his country's tragic situation.

Charles turned to Levi, who stared morosely out the window. He wished to tell this man how much Kitra had meant to the camp, her healing way with children, the respect she had earned from the elders. But something held him back. As though right then what the man needed most was a reason to look beyond his sorrow and understandable panic, to get to know the country he traveled through.

Charles said, "This end of the Rift was assigned as pastureland to the Masaii, the nation's most ferocious tribe. The Masaii count their wealth in terms of the clan's cattle. They build no permanent dwellings. They live on the move. They graze and they hunt and they ignore the civilization that rises up beyond their traditional borders. They tolerated the game parks that surrounded the Rift's shrinking lakes, just so long as their ancient game paths and rights to use the lakes were respected. Then came Kenya's descent into civil war."

The driver grunted softly, like he had been struck in the

gut. Charles glanced over, then decided there was nothing he should not be hearing, and continued, "Four years ago, the party that had been in power since independence lost the national elections. The party leaders were not merely shocked. They were furious. They had always assumed their hold on power was permanent, and they would continue to take whatever they wanted. They answered to no one but their own party."

Levi's gaze did not so much clear as sharpen. He was connected to the moment now, which of course was why Charles was talking as he was. "After the results showed a landslide victory for the opposition, the ones in power refused to step down. They reworked the election numbers and declared themselves the victors."

"Not good," Levi said.

The driver barked a bitter laugh. "Oh yes, you are right, sah. It was so very not good."

"The population of Kenya exploded," Charles went on. "As the civil unrest spread, the party in power blamed the violence on tribal politics. It was a coldly vicious move, as emotions were already raw. By this point, politicians had already started confiscating tribal land. Villages held for centuries could show no written proof of ownership, and thus could be made pawns in the politicians' hunt for wealth. The politicians exacerbated disputes between the pastoral tribes, like the Masaii, and the clans who raised crops and became deeply rooted on one particular plot of land."

"A conflict as old as the Bible," Levi said.

"But new to our land. Tribes who fought against the party in power were ejected from their homelands. The Rift absorbed tens of thousands of displaced people, stuffed into camps that were rimmed by barbed wire and patrolled by the Kenyan army." Charles pointed toward the distant rows of white tents. "That is what you see there."

"Are those army vehicles by the gates?"

The driver nodded once. "The Masaii, they hate the new people."

Charles heard the driver's bitter anger, four years old and still fresh. "You have people inside?"

"Not this camp. Further north. My mother's tribe. Two villages. Same problem as here. The Masaii, they are very mad."

Charles explained, "The Masaii do not see these newcomers as victims. The Masaii do not vote. They care nothing for politics and the ways of the cities. The Masaii own no land. *All* the Rift is theirs."

"The Masaii saw these newcomers as invaders, not as refugees," Levi said. "So what's happening in the capital?"

"After nine tense months of negotiation, the parties reluctantly agreed to share power. New elections were scheduled, but far enough in the future for calm to be restored. And in the meanwhile the camps remain a tragic symbol of all that is wrong with Kenya."

The truck remained silent as they swept past the camp's entrance, flanked by Kenyan soldiers sweltering in the heat. No one said a word. Seeing the camp brought it all back, like tearing a bandage off an almost-forgotten wound. The violence, the fear, then months of political stalemate, and now a government that no one wanted.

Charles went on to say that Kenya had many refugee camps, and for a multitude of reasons. The drought, the

Angolan crisis, the war in Somalia, the upheaval in Ethiopia—Kenya had remained a stable place, a haven willing to accept and succor those harmed by bad regimes and worse mistakes. But these camps were different. They were utterly unnecessary.

Levi asked, "So what is the answer?"

"We must return to the ideal upon which Kenya was formed," Charles said. The answer came unbidden. "Our nation once represented Africa's shining beacon of hope. Many peoples, one nation. Under God."

The driver beat his fist on the wheel in time to Charles's words. "Yes, man, is true, all you are saying."

Charles shut his eyes and prayed—for the camp dwellers, the families, the future of his country. Charles prayed that a miracle would occur, and the hope be made real once more. He kept his eyes shut for a very long while, praying. He prayed until he fell asleep.

When he woke, the truck's radio was playing again and the sky up ahead was tainted by the volcanic cloud. The newscasters had repeatedly reported that the eruption was dying down. But Charles saw no difference. The plume formed a massive wall against the western horizon. The colors were mottled and sullen. Lightning bolts speared the cloud.

"Evil," muttered the driver.

Charles nodded. Certainly the displaced families thought so. His mind cast about and settled on the miracles, two of them. One inside a camp filled with refugees from the volcano, another at the Kibera church. Many tribes coming together, united by the one force great enough to overcome centuries of anger and fear. A force for good, only for good. A force strong enough to draw together the displaced villagers, the American government, and an Israeli kibbutz. Charles found himself humming along with the song on the radio. Perhaps the greatest miracle awaited them, up ahead at the end of this dusty trail.

Chapter Thirty-Seven

Marc slept late and woke slowly. The clock read half past five in the afternoon. He checked the sat phone, which registered both charge and signal. He assumed the fact that no one had called meant things were moving smoothly. Or not at all.

He ordered a meal and began a stretching routine, working out the travel kinks, readying himself for all the unknowns that the hours ahead might contain.

He was just coming out of the shower when Deb Orlando phoned from the airport, confirming that Boyd Crowder and Karl Rigby were inbound, and she was there to turn their entry invisible. Marc began putting together a written checklist, something they could all use to coordinate actions and timing. Only when room service knocked did Marc realize he was still in a towel. Marc called out for the guy to hang on and went to the closet for his clothes.

As he slipped into trousers, he heard the thump. It sounded like someone hit a note on a bass drum in the hallway beyond his closet wall.

Marc was moving before the sound died. A body had hit the wall and then the floor. Marc had to assume the room-service waiter had become the unwilling lure for an attack.

His actions were driven by years of what instructors had called live-fire simulations. In agency speak this signified the very real risk that field agents would face peril. The only way to determine whether they were genuinely meant for field-work was to present them with such risks under controlled circumstances. But this did not mean the agent was out of harm's way. In live-fire simulations the threat of injury was real and constant. The only way to gauge an agent's response to extreme conditions was to put them in extreme conditions.

Marc registered the adrenaline rush just as he did his own tight panting breaths. In the span of two accelerated heart-beats his vision and his mental acuity had taken on pinpoint clarity. He swept the room for his best chance of survival yet had space left over to recall his first training officer, a former field agent who started all live-fire exercises with the same words. *"Fear is just another tool to utilize,"* the agent had repeated. Courage is all about turning fear into success under impossible conditions.

The room's windows were sealed. The hotel's exterior wall was blank and free of balconies. If he broke the glass and tried to scale the wall, they would pick him off. As Marc searched the room's confines, there was another knock on the door, louder this time.

He called out, "Just a minute, I'm coming! I can't find my . . ."

The room did not contain a decent hideaway. The bed was nothing more than a mattress placed on a solid carpeted slab. Behind the sofa was too obvious. Ditto for the closet. The plastic shower curtain was transparent.

Which left him only one option.

Marc hit the sat phone's speed dial for Deb Orlando. He

placed the instrument on the glass shelf above the corridor sink, beside his key and money. Beside the phone he placed his genuine passport. Hidden in plain sight.

He called, "Give me two seconds!"

The narrow corridor leading to the bathroom held the closet and a miniature wet bar. Beneath the sink was a cabinet probably designed to hold a small refrigerator. At the moment there was just a coffee tray and a cramped empty space.

"Coming!"

As Marc set the coffee tray on the bathroom counter, he heard a tinny hello coming from the sat phone. He squatted on the carpet and through his fingertips felt the floor vibrate to the thump of many heavy boots. He had very little time.

He aimed his voice at the phone and shouted, "Be right there!"

The alcove was too small for a grown man. Which meant it would not be the first place they looked. Marc folded himself inside. He only managed to draw the door shut by exhaling and holding it in place with his fingertips. Each tight breath pushed the cabinet door open a fraction. If his sweating fingers slipped, all was lost. He would not be able to hold this position for long.

At that point the door to his hotel room exploded inward.

They hit the door high and low. Professional assault tactics. Shoulder above the lock, boot below, weapons hot.

"Freeze! You move, you die!"

They piled in. How many, Marc did not know. Four was his best guess. A fifth man left in the hall to secure their escape route. With each additional attacker, his advantage grew. They would be constricted by the proximity of their own men. Marc, on the other hand, would be held by no such restraint.

"He's not here!"

"Check the bed!"

"Negative!"

"Call it out!"

"Windows sealed!"

"Closet, check!"

"Bathroom, check!"

"Inspect them again!"

"Man, there is no place left to *look*."

"His keys and passport and phone are here. He's got . . ."

"What is it?"

"I hear something."

"There's a sat phone on the shelf by the—"

Footsteps shifted toward him. Marc took that as his signal. He struck.

He had wedged himself into the space at a twenty-degree tilt. This meant he could launch himself like a coiled spring both up and out.

The sudden assault from an impossible place momentarily froze them. They stared openmouthed long enough for Marc to strike the closest man, who thankfully turned out to be Dirk, their leader. Marc hit him first in the Adam's apple and then in the temple. The giant gave off a soft "ack" and fell to his knees. The floor thumped dully as he landed. Marc ripped the gun from the man's grip and slammed it into his temple. Dirk went down hard.

The men moved, but even now they were hesitant. They all carried silenced machine pistols. There were four of them in the room, three standing and one on the floor. The fact that Marc had laid out their new boss caused them to hesitate further.

Marc used leverage from the temple strike to catapult himself off the wall and directly at the man between the bathroom corridor and the demolished door. The two men on the bed's opposite side shouted and waved their pistols, but did not fire. The third attacker was shocked at both Marc's sudden leap and his speed. But this guy was also a pro. He lifted his weapon and tried to club Marc's face. But Marc had expected this, and his first strike had in fact been a feint. He shifted to his left and waited while the gun swept past. Then he used Dirk's weapon to hit the man twice on the ear. The second strike splintered the stock.

The attacker's own gun came back in another sweep, but more clumsily this time. Marc dropped his useless weapon and hit the man in that nerve axis where his jaw met his neck. The man grunted at the bright flash of pain. Marc struck him again. His body jerked spasmodically in an adrenaline battle against losing consciousness, and he accidentally pulled the trigger on his firearm. A line of bullets seared down the ceiling and the wall by the doorway. The man guarding their exit shouted a curse and flung himself away from the spray of death.

Marc gripped the machine pistol and hammered the man square in the forehead. The attacker started to fall, but Marc caught him and spun him around. Marc supported the attacker's enfeebled legs and pulled the man back a step, so the bathroom corridor offered more protection.

Marc aimed the machine pistol around his human shield and shouted, "Lose your weapons!"

The attackers by the window sneered, "You're threatening me with an empty gun."

Marc fired one round through the glass by his head. "Next round goes through your knee. Drop and spread. Now!"

The two guys still standing in the room were going for it. Marc no doubt sensed it before they did. If there had been just one, Marc could probably have talked him down. But the pair exchanged a look, ramping themselves up for the strike. Marc knew he was going down.

But before they could raise their weapons, the man in the hallway shouted, *"Cops! Cops!"*

The drumbeat of many feet had never sounded so good.

A deep African voice roared, *"Down, down, everybody face-down on the floor. Do it or die!"*

"We're Lodestone operatives!" But the attacker by the window had the good sense to lie prone before he shouted.

"And I am chief of hotel security, and I am telling you to lie down on the floor!"

Marc dropped his human shield and went prone inside the bathroom corridor, his bare feet against the tiles. A softly groaning Dirk and the second attacker formed a barrier between him and any random shot the attackers might try to get off.

A massive shadow fell over Marc and a barrel-deep voice demanded, "What are all these guns doing in *my hotel*?"

One of the attackers by the window said, "Sir, we have been ordered to apprehend a dangerous suspect."

"This suspect, was he the hotel staff I see unconscious in the hallway outside this room?"

The attacker by the window went silent.

"Yes, that is *exactly* what I am thinking."

"We operate under UN sanction!"

"And you do not think to inform hotel security first?" The shadow shifted. "Take these weapons and bind them up."

"I protest—"

"You be silent . . . What have you done to this wall here? And what has happened to *my window*?"

"The man we are here to arrest—"

"Who is in charge?"

"He is still out."

"Five sent to silence one man. But your leader and another are here moaning at my feet. This is very interesting."

"I'm telling you, this guy is a serious threat."

"Which one of you is Royce? Marc Royce."

"Here."

"Stand up, man."

The attacker by the window protested, "Marc Royce is a wanted felon!"

"I am not telling you to be silent again, you hear what I am saying?" The man was so large as to compress the room's air. He wore a neatly pressed uniform and a ferocious scowl. "You have ID, Mr. Royce?"

"On the shelf by the sat phone."

"You are armed?"

"No, I took the weapon off the man there."

"And you, the five brave men who come at an unarmed hotel guest. You have IDs?"

"At Lodestone."

"So you break into this man's room. And you do not alert hotel security. You claim you are a UN force. But I have been contacted by an official from the United States embassy. And she tells me that a U.S. federal agent is under threat from mercenaries." His voice rose once more to full roar. *"In my hotel!"*

"No, wait, that's not—"

"Take these men to the security cellar. No, leave Mr. Royce here with me."

"You need to call our director!"

"Oh, we will be calling all *sorts* of people. In due time."

Marc watched as the five were lifted up and dragged away. Their protests rang down the hall beyond his ruined door, sweet as a choir. The security chief must have seen his pleasure, for he smiled and said, "This lady from the embassy, she is most anxious for you to pick up your phone."

Chapter Thirty-Eight

Charles knew something was wrong even before he could see the camp. They rounded the final bend and the forest came into view. At first the vista looked just the same as always. The sun-bleached forest rose like a futile gesture, hearkening back to a time before the drought, before their world had exploded and been blanketed by ash.

Shadow figures flitted beneath the branches. Most were women, rags draped like shawls over their heads. They carried bundles of twigs on their backs, and more in their arms. They looked up as the trucks rumbled forward. One of the crones dropped her load of wood and waved what might have been a warning.

Then Charles spotted the others. "Hold up."

The driver did not like it. "These women, they will try and take our goods."

"I do not think so. And if they do, I will stop them."

"You are one man."

"I am their friend."

"But the camp, it is just ahead."

"It may not be safe." Charles reached over and gripped the hand holding the wheel. "I am known here. This is my home, as much as it is anyone's. And I am telling you to stop. For all our sakes."

The Red Cross driver grumbled, but he slowed and halted. One of the young men riding atop the load asked a question. Charles opened his door and called back, "Stay where you are!"

The women approached slowly. Charles understood the driver's concern. He and his men had seen other women gather like hyenas circling a wounded predator. Charles motioned for Levi and the others to remain where they were, and stepped onto the running board. He said to the women, "You know me."

The women hesitated, then one of the older ones said, "Philip, he says we are to warn you if you come."

Charles was about to question her when another voice barked from the trees. A man loped forward, joined by a young woman, and they by four more. All of them drawn from the teams put together by Marc Royce.

The man closest to Charles called, "The *shujaa*, he is with you?"

The word *shujaa* meant warrior, and so much more. It took Charles a long moment to realize the young man spoke of Marc. "He is not."

All four young people slumped in unified defeat. "Then all is lost."

"He will be here soon."

"Not soon enough."

"Tell me what is wrong."

"The men, they are here."

"The yellow ones?"

"Them and the others too. With the blue armbands and the guns. And their leaders. All here."

Charles turned and spoke through the open window. "You heard?"

The driver nodded. "Bandits?"

"The worst sort," Charles confirmed. "Thieves with uniforms and the law on their side."

"We will leave from here and go to the next camp," the driver said. "Half our goods are meant for them."

"Half will stay here," Charles insisted.

"But you just said—"

"These young people are here to help you off-load. They will see the goods are properly distributed."

"But the camp officials, they must sign my manifest or I lose my job."

"I am a camp official," Charles replied. "You know this, for you were ordered to bring me here. I will sign."

The driver nervously drummed the wheel. "I am thinking we should go now."

"Then think on this," Charles said. "The only reason you remain safe is because of my word. Try to leave and I will order them to stop you, and take everything."

The driver went sullen. "I am liking this less and less."

"And you will like this least of all. One of your trucks is to remain with me." Charles pointed toward the forest. "Pull your trucks off the trail and into the trees there. And hurry."

Levi slipped down from the truck and walked over, concern creasing his features. But Charles motioned for him to wait.

As two of the five trucks were off-loaded and their wares shifted deeper into the forest, the lead young man shared what he knew with Charles. Charles translated for Levi, though it pained him to do so. "They arrived yesterday evening."

"They?"

"A man with the UN logo on his chest. And guards. Many guards. All armed."

"By chopper?"

"This time by truck."

"The trucks, they were white with the blue lettering?"

"No, man. Khaki."

Which was impossible. The UN always traveled in white convoys. Even the soldiers drove trucks painted so that they shone in the sunlight and were known as noncombatants. Charles frowned. "You are certain of this?"

The young man nodded. "I saw them myself. They are imposters, yes?"

It was exactly what Charles had been thinking. And Marc had suggested. "Why do you ask this?"

"The lead man, he does not speak as the UN speaks, with kindness and concern. He stomps and he shouts and he points with his pistol."

"So they came in trucks."

"Not trucks like those that carry goods. Smaller ones, meant for people. With benches and closed up in back. They were stained with ash."

Charles assumed this was important, but could not think why. "What happened then?"

"The lead man, he speaks with the director. The director shouts back at him. The lead man, he strikes the director with his pistol." The young man swiped the air between them, like delivering a slap. "The director, he goes down hard, and when he tries to rise, the lead man, he points the pistol at him and smiles. It is not a good smile. It is the way a man looks when he enjoys bad work, you understand?"

"I have seen this look," Charles replied. "Many times."

"The director comes up slow; he is trembling. His face is wet and red. He takes the lead man to Philip and the elders. The lead man tells them what is happening, that the camp is to be moved."

"When?"

"Tomorrow. We are to take only what we can carry."

"I do not understand. We are to walk?"

"The elders ask the same. The lead man says there will be trucks for the young and the weak. Then he signals to his men, who go into the medical tent. They call back through the screen wall and say the woman, she is there. That is what they call her, 'the woman.'"

"Kitra," Charles said, dreading what was to come next.

"They bring her out, one man holding each arm. She tells the lead man the doctor is working at another camp. The lead man asks her name."

"No," Levi moaned.

When the young man glanced nervously at Levi, Charles urged, "Go on."

"The lead man says, 'She is the one. Bring her.' They put her in the third truck and drive away." When Levi moaned a second time, the young man asked, "This is the father?"

"He is."

"So now they have taken two of his clan." The young man's face was creased with experiences of his own. "The shujaa must hear of this."

"I will call him now," Charles said, though the prospect turned him leaden.

The young man made as to pat Levi's shoulder. "Tell this one, the shujaa of Philip's dream will know what must be done."

Charles translated the young man's words. He started to explain, but Levi did not seem to have heard what Charles had said beyond the moment he heard his daughter had been taken. Charles's head spun with all he had heard, and more besides. The word *shujaa* signified a warrior, one who rises within the tribe to save it in times of crisis. As he coded in Marc's number, Charles tried to recall if he had ever heard the word being applied to an outsider, most especially a white man. He listened to the phone ring, and knew this word meant Marc Royce was an outsider no longer.

Chapter Thirty-Nine

The call from Charles accelerated the group to a genuinely frantic pace. Crowder and Deb never left the Nairobi airport complex. With Walton's backing they had a chopper prepped and ready when Marc and Kamal pulled up an hour later. Kamal's men beat them there by fifteen minutes. Crowder's own team came in five minutes later.

The chopper flew west through the night. During the flight, Deb Orlando described their destination, a massive private estate on the border of Lake Victoria. A buddy with the DEA had made the arrangements. The estate belonged to one of the NBA's top scorers, who had been let off easy on a serious drug charge. The man remained extremely grateful.

The estate totaled nine thousand acres and was divided into three distinct parts. The largest portion joined with a national game preserve. Ninety minutes after takeoff they descended past a trio of luxurious towers called hides from which the compound guests could watch the wildlife. The hides fronted the lake's dark waters, where giraffes nibbled daintily at the leaves of trees. Lake Victoria, though, the world's second largest freshwater sea, had been hit hard by the drought. The lake was rimmed by vast fields of mud that glistened in the moonlight.

Marc thought he saw hippos wallowing in the slime as they landed.

The estate's second portion held five villages with cone-shaped huts. The villages were separated from the game preserve by a high barbed-wire fence. Beyond the villages rose the owner's private enclave, a two-hundred-acre hilltop domain with swimming pools and emerald lawns and seas of blossoms and a dozen guesthouses. Beyond the enclave stretched a landing strip built to handle a wide-bodied jet.

Levi and Charles arrived in the requisitioned truck while Marc and the others were settling into the guesthouses. Levi emerged from behind the wheel like a wounded beast, surveying the world in red-rimmed eyes. He endured the introductions and said to Marc, "I should not be here."

Marc replied with the same words that had convinced Levi to travel. "Kitra has already been taken away. The camp has been invaded in force. We don't even know how many armed opponents we will be facing. There's nothing to be gained by hanging around and waiting for the enemy to return."

Boyd Crowder stepped up beside Marc. "The worst thing about taking a fight personal is losing your clarity of vision."

"If we go in wrong-footed, we could wind up getting innocent civilians killed," Marc continued. "This includes you."

"That is the last thing Kitra would want," Charles agreed, looking almost gray with exhaustion. "The very last thing."

A servant emerged from the main house, wearing a starched white jacket, neat blue shorts and T-shirt, and no shoes. He handed out two more keys to the guesthouses without meeting anyone's eyes. Marc had the impression that the servant spent a lot of his time not seeing what went on here. Marc told his crew to shower and be back in half an hour.

They gathered on the rear lawn, seventeen in all, seated around a table that could have held three times their number. Charles sat by Levi, as though the pastor remained drawn to the man who needed him most. Kamal and his six team members sat across the table from Crowder and Rigby and his four. The Lodestone crew had responded swiftly to Crowder's call, especially as their new boss was still in police custody. They had arrived at the airport with a wealth of gear.

The household staff roasted an entire haunch of venison over a fire pit as big as a plaza fountain. Everything about the place was oversized. The main house's rear veranda was as large as a basketball court.

They planned as they ate. Marc felt Levi's burning impatience radiate across the table. He knew Levi wanted to throw himself immediately into whatever fight was within reach. But their plan was a good one, and for it to work they needed daylight.

Marc waited until the others had split up for their four hours of sleep before approaching Levi. He needed to say some things and preferred to do it when no one else was around.

Levi watched Marc's approach in silence. He had not spoken a word since the start of dinner. He stood slightly canted, his pain almost too much to bear.

Marc asked, "Can you hear me all right?"

"I'm standing right in front of you. Of course I can hear."

"I need to be sure you're paying attention," Marc said. "Either you pull yourself together or you're not coming with us."

Levi jerked as though Marc had slapped his face. Which, in a manner of speaking, he had.

"This is your one chance," Marc warned.

"I'm not staying behind."

"You won't have any choice. I'll have them chain you in the cellar before I let you risk another team member's life. And that's what you'll do, unless you can clear the fog in your head. I will *not* let you put any of this team in peril."

The man's features stretched out drumhead taut with the effort required to shape the words, "They've taken both my children."

"You're missing the point." Marc gave him a cold stare. Goading him away from the brink.

"What is it?"

"Go back to what Charles told us. What the young people from the camp said. Was it accurate?"

"I . . . Yes, I suppose . . ."

"Okay. So it sounds to me like they came for her."

"No, that's not . . . They're moving the camp."

"We know that. But look at what happened. They arrived at the camp in several vehicles. One carried the boss. The others, his security. Then what happened?" Marc gave him a beat, then, "One of the trucks left early with Kitra. Not headed for wherever they're taking the camp-dwellers. Do you see? They came *planning* to take her."

Levi screwed up his face, clearly frightened but clinging to any hope he might hear. "But . . . why would they do that?"

"We'll find out tomorrow." Marc stepped back, satisfied for now. "Tonight I need to know one thing. Can you focus and follow orders?"

His response was somewhat strangled, but clear. "Yes."

"Good. Go get some rest."

Marc did not notice Boyd Crowder until Levi headed toward his assigned guesthouse. The former colonel stood beyond the fire pit, where the flames and the flickering shadows hid him from view. He stared out over the thorn trees, to where moonlight rippled across the lake. To the south, cone-shaped hills humped up like the burial mounds of prehistoric beasts. The air was warm and close and filled with night sounds, buzzing insects and bird calls and the roar of animals.

"They've got forty, maybe fifty estates like this one dotted around Kenya," Crowder said without turning his head. "Little make-believe islands built with money. Movie stars, athletes, some rich business owners. They fly in on their jets, keep choppers in private hangars, maintain a staff of fifty. The villagers sing while they roast a buck. They spend a few days and fly back. Kings for a weekend."

Marc watched the horizon weave the night song and the rising moon. He was tired. But deeper than his fatigue was a rising power. He had never known such a thing before. It had taken him until now to understand it and give it a proper name. He was not angry so much as filled with a sense of reprisal. "They're not going to get away with it."

Crowder turned his back to the lake and nodded eastward, toward the unseen dawn. "Out there, in the real Africa, they do. All the time."

"Not with us," Marc replied. "Not here. Not now."

Crowder nodded again, either in agreement or because he saw no sense in arguing. "You really going to keep the girl's father off the hunt?"

"I hope I don't have to. But if that's the only way to keep my team safe, absolutely."

"Your team," Crowder said.

"That's right."

Crowder's grin was caught by the pit's final flames. "First time I saw you, I thought you just might be my kind of officer. Glad to know my gut was right."

Marc asked, "What does your gut say about tomorrow?"

"Same as yours, I expect." Crowder's grin grew larger still. "That we'll go out there and do whatever it takes."

Chapter Forty

They were awakened while it was still pitch-black. A servant was knocking on the guesthouse doors. Marc felt groggy from all the sleep he still needed. Levi and Charles emerged looking especially weary. And the worst was yet to come. The clock was against them. Marc inspected each man intently. They saw the stern message in his scrutiny and did their best to push their exhaustion aside.

The fire pit was lit and three cooks worked the biggest skillet Marc had ever seen, large enough to hold seventeen steaks and have room left over. The skillet was rectangular and had two long handles and two stubby legs. Young men gripped the wooden handles while a woman in a spotless white uniform stood between them and tended the meat. The air was further spiced by the aromas of coffee and fresh-baked bread and the blooming frangipani. The chef backed up so the young men could draw the skillet off the fire pit. She broke three dozen eggs so fast her hands formed a blur. The skillet returned to the fire for an instant; then the steaks and sunny-side eggs were lifted off and replaced with fat slabs of sourdough bread. It was a hunter's breakfast, intended to keep the guests filled all day.

The soldiers ate with the gusto of experience, not knowing

when they might have their next hot meal. Kamal and Crowder and Rigby went through the plans a final time with Marc. Levi remained alert and focused. Charles translated for Kamal and the troops between bites. By the time the meal was done, Marc felt they were as prepped as they possibly could be in the condensed time frame. Except for one thing.

Marc rose from the table and motioned for Charles to join him. He said to the others, "Those who would like, you're welcome to join us for prayer. The rest of you, we leave in ten."

Crowder and Rigby both stepped forward, as did two of Crowder's men, Deb Orlando, Levi, and three of Kamal's troop. When they had circled up, Marc asked Levi, "Will you lead us?"

Levi slowly drew a yarmulke from his rear pocket, settled the cap on his head, shut his eyes, and lifted his hands out before his chest. Marc did not hear the prayer so much as feel the words wash over him. Charles translated softly for the sake of Kamal's men.

After they were finished, Marc urged them to hurry. They grabbed their gear and split up among the three Land Cruisers requisitioned from the preserve. He saw how Levi and Charles had managed to move beyond the reach of their fatigue. Marc watched as they moved in fluid unity, heard the soft laughter and watchful tension of the team, and was satisfied.

They were ready.

They left the camp while it was still dark. The air through Marc's open window was crammed with the roar of predators, like a clarion call to everything that lay ahead.

They had the highway mostly to themselves. A few aid trucks rumbled past. Occasionally they spotted embers from cooking fires, and people huddled by the side of the road, sleeping where they dropped, waiting and hoping for a ride or food or just enough strength to make it to a camp.

The three khaki-colored vehicles were jammed with people and weapons and ammo and comm equipment. They reached the border zone where the volcanic ash began dusting everything just before turning off the main road. The trail leading to the camp was visible, but only just. Twin rutted tracks formed a straight indentation in the otherwise empty landscape.

Kamal drove the lead vehicle. Marc rode in the Land Cruiser's passenger seat. Deb Orlando was seated behind the driver. She held Marc's sat phone in her lap. Midway down the camp's trail it rang for the fourth time since the start of their journey. She answered, lowered the phone, and said, "Walton for you."

Marc shook his head. Did not speak. Orlando eyed him for a moment, then said, "Sorry, Ambassador, he's occupied now. Yes, sir. I'll pass on your message."

She cut the connection. "Walton wants a word."

Marc remained facing forward. The ash-covered trail extended out as far as the headlights' boundary, then disappeared into the night.

"Sir, he wants a word *now*."

"The ambassador tends to second-guess his field agents before any action," Marc replied without turning. "I told you back in Nairobi. Your job is to handle Walton."

They arrived at the forest fronting the camp in the first smoky hint of daylight. They off-loaded in absolute silence. There was no wind, no sound. After the thunderous din of wildlife surrounding the estate's water holes, the region held a funereal silence, a dirge to everything that had been lost.

Four figures rose from the first line of trees and shielded their eyes against the light. One of them waved tentatively. As he stepped forward, Marc recognized him as one of the young men he had chosen to help serve the camp. Marc said, "Hold here."

The young man stepped forward and peered through the open window. When he saw Marc's face, he sighed with both relief and exhaustion. "Shujaa. You have come."

The bare-limbed forest and its blanket of ash sucked out sounds before they were formed. The three young men and two women from the camp watched their preparations with solemn patience. Their bare calves were as white as the trees from the ash that had dried into their sweat. It was the hour before dawn and the air was utterly still and already very hot. The setting moon and the first wash of day cast the forest and the trees and the people in dim shadows, as though none of them were fully formed.

The Lodestone crew had all done long-term duty in-country. They did not know Kamal or his men. But they had worked with Kenyan soldiers and UN peacekeepers. The current situation, with a possible UN rogue executive using Lodestone mercenaries to create international havoc, did not affect the men's sense of professional harmony. Marc checked carefully. Crowder did the same. He caught Marc's eye at one point and nodded. They were good to go.

As they distributed bottled water and energy bars, Karl Rigby asked the leader of those from the camp, "How did you know to come now?"

"We have waited for you all night."

"What if we hadn't shown up?"

The young man replied solemnly, "Philip, he says the shujaa is coming. He comes."

Crowder asked, "Who's this Philip?"

"The camp's senior elder and chief," Marc replied. "And one of the best men I know."

Crowder asked, "What's that word you used for Marc here?"

"*Shujaa*. It means . . ." He turned and spoke with Charles.

Charles said quietly, "It means *warrior*. And a great deal more."

The young man nodded and pointed at Marc with his water bottle. "Yes. Is him. Philip, he says this is the shujaa of his dreams."

Crowder asked Marc, "Does that make a bit of sense to you?"

One of the women lifted her head, listened, then pointed toward the dawn. "The trucks, they come."

It took a few moments longer before Marc heard a faint rumble in the distance. He reached over. "Give me some kind of weapon and get your men in place." He accepted a pistol from Rigby and said to the young man, "You and your mates hide in the trees. Charles, tell Kamal it's time."

Crowder whistled for his men. Marc turned and waved to where Kamal stood with Charles and Levi and Deb. They drifted into position, spread down both sides of the track. Marc keyed his earpiece and said to Crowder, "Comm check."

The volcano was the loudest voice to respond, a hissing thunder that eliminated all radio contact beyond a distance of a few hundred feet.

When it was again quiet, Crowder whistled to the team a second time, and pointed at his ear. Marc heard a series of clicks and asked, "Charles, is Kamal with us?"

"And his men."

"Move only on my signal."

The trucks rumbled toward them. Marc waited until the first was within range, then said, "Now."

The drivers gawked at the men, who sprang from the pale ash and leaped onto their running boards. Marc aimed for the driver's side of the lead truck.

The driver raised his hands from the wheel and exclaimed, "We are empty! We carry nothing!"

"I know that. Where are you headed?"

The driver stared at him. "What are you thinking, man? Right there! The camp!"

Marc heard a soft chuckle through his earpiece. "I mean, where do you take the people when you leave here?"

"Who, man?"

"The camp occupants. The people you've been sent to collect."

"We are here for people? This I am not knowing."

"What were you told?"

"Be here for the dawn." He shoved pale palms toward the east. "It is dawn; we are here."

"Tell your trucks to turn around."

"But we are being promised much payment for coming on time . . ." He stopped because Marc aimed a pistol at his face. "This is a very bad thing."

"It's about to get worse," Marc said. "I'm taking your two lead trucks."

Marc, Charles, and Crowder watched the other trucks lumber away into the dawn light and the ash. Crowder said, "That wasn't nearly enough transport for the whole camp."

Charles replied, "They were here to carry the important supplies, the oldest, and the sickest. The rest walk. My people, they have much experience at walking."

Marc asked Charles, "Are you sure you want to be a part of this?"

"I am already a part," Charles replied.

Marc searched the pastor's face for fear or doubt, and found neither. Marc decided that after all Charles had witnessed in his life, assaulting a fortified refugee camp with a handful of men was just another day at the office. "Let's move out."

One of the troopers out of Lodestone's Nairobi HQ had brought two metal cases. Each held three long-range stun guns and portable charging units. The chargers were massive batteries that filled most of the space and made the lockers weigh almost three hundred pounds. The metal handle cut into Marc's hand as he helped maneuver one to the SUV's tailgate.

"Banned in all fifty states," Crowder proudly stated. "Claims to be good to eighty feet. But nobody I know can hit a cow past forty."

Six of them made up the first line of assault. They could have used more. The men assigned to backup duty certainly were eager to move into the hunt. But the Lodestone crew had only brought six of the special weapons requested by Crowder. Marc took one, gave two to Kamal and his chosen man, another to Deb Orlando, and the other two to Crowder. Crowder ordered Rigby to lead the second crew. Crowder's second-in-command didn't like it one bit, but had the good sense not to kick. When Levi started to protest over not being among the first in, Marc said sharply, "That's how it is, soldier."

The two requisitioned trucks were standard high-riding

transports with tattered canvas tops. Kamal drove the first truck and Marc sat beside him. They had checked carefully and found no sat phone in the trucks. With the volcano isolating the camp from radio and cellphone communication, there might be surprise over seeing a white face, but no objection.

At Charles's suggestion they asked the women gathering firewood to precede them into the camp. The young people had told them that two of the new security forces manned the front gates. Marc wanted to give the guards as much reason for distraction as possible. The women treated his request as a game. Their quiet laughter drifted through Marc's open window as they moved forward.

At the women's approach the two guards grinned sleepily and spoke between themselves. Their expressions caused the women to clutch together and move more swiftly. But that only made the guards laugh. One shifted the carbine to his left hand and reached out. Marc took that as his signal. He settled the heavy stun gun on the windowsill and took careful aim.

Just as Crowder had described, the trigger clicked twice. The first click and a laser target sighted on on the guard's chest. The soldier spotted the light playing across his fatigues, and whirled about, trying to brush the light away and bring his gun to bear all at the same time.

Marc pressed harder on the trigger. The bolt flew out with a softly hissing *zing*, like a miniature fly-by-wire missile. It struck the man precisely where the light had been. The electric hiss was powerful enough to cause the women to flee. The soldier entered a manic dance, his entire body arching to an impossible angle.

Kamal leaned out the other window and shot while the

second guard stood gaping at his mate. He fell as though poleaxed and sprawled on top of the first soldier.

Figures flitted forward from the second truck and bound the men with plastic ties. Crowder slipped onto the running board by Marc's window while Rigby joined them on Kamal's side. Crowder watched as the still-prone guards were hustled back to the rear truck. "Glad to know those suckers actually work."

"The latest in traffic-calming measures," Rigby agreed.

Marc asked, "Do you recognize those soldiers?"

"Never seen either of them before. Karl?"

"No. But they're wearing regulation Lodestone gear. Check out this label."

Marc keyed his comm link. "Deb."

She sprang from the third vehicle in their line, the truck requisitioned by Charles and Levi. "Here."

"Check these guys for IDs. Then photograph both men. Call it through to Walton."

"On it."

Chapter Forty-One

They halted about midway between the gates and the central compound. Marc clambered on top of the truck's cab and scouted in all directions. The light was still dim but strengthening steadily. He spotted a trio of soldiers patrolling the lane to his right and waved as though glad to see them. From this distance the color of his skin would not be visible. One of the soldiers lifted his rifle in response. Marc keyed his comm link and said softly, "Karl, we have three at your four o'clock, two hundred meters out and closing. Go."

Rigby and his men slipped over the back and vanished.

Another five soldiers came into view, walking the central lane. They ambled with the ease of men who saw nothing more than the end of a long shift. Marc waved a second time and keyed his comm link. "Crowder, you read?"

"In the green."

"We've got a crew headed straight down the road towards us."

"On it."

Marc slipped off the truck's roof and into the rear compartment. Charles took his place in the truck's cab, his face sheened like it was oiled. Marc said through the open window, "Tell Kamal to move up slow and easy."

Kamal did as he was ordered. Marc spotted another team patrolling to his left, but did not speak. He would need to use Kamal's men, and just then he did not want to take Kamal's eye off the target up ahead and closing.

Crowder's men appeared to either side of the five. One moment the lane belonged to the security forces, the next and they lay in the dust, a single tangled heap. Crowder checked in all directions, then gave Marc the thumbs-up and said through his comm link, "Clear."

"Rigby?"

"All down."

"Bind them and load them up." Marc leaned through the window. Charles looked like he was holding his breath. Kamal, on the other hand, looked almost serene. Marc liked that. A lot. "Ask him if he's ready for some action of his own."

Kamal's grin was the only response Marc needed.

"There's another team at nine o'clock and closing."

Kamal spoke briefly through the comm link as he slipped from the truck. Marc asked Charles, "Can you handle the truck?"

"I have driven them many times."

"Okay. Head towards the central compound at a dead crawl."

Marc dropped down from the truck to help Crowder and his crew bring back the supine soldiers. Their wrists and ankles were trussed with plastic ties. Two of them jerked spasmodically, the sign that they were coming out of wherever the stun guns had sent them. As they were hefted into the rear truck, Marc asked, "How many charges do those things hold?"

Crowder gave him a soldier's smile, all adrenaline and nerves. "Guess we'll soon find out."

Rigby and his team were loading the final unconscious soldier in when it all fell apart.

The morning calm was ripped open by a long burst of automatic gunfire. A pair of voices roared in fury. Then one screamed, high and shrill as a beast of the night.

Ahead of them, the central compound became filled with shouting men and whistles. Another pair of shots sounded to his left, then nothing.

Marc leaped onto the running board. "Pull the vehicles into the first lane. Go, go!" He jumped back down and waved the other truck off in the opposite direction. Before the two trucks had started their turns, he was down and following Crowder toward the shooting.

They arrived to find Kamal standing over two bodies. He tossed his stun gun to Crowder in disgust. Crowder hit the triggers and the gun merely fizzled. "Guess we've got our answer."

"We've got a man hit."

Kamal's man had his left arm stained black from the shoulder down. Crowder ripped away the tattered sleeve and probed. "Grazed."

The soldier grunted once as Crowder took a field dressing from his pack and treated the wound. Kamal touched the man's good arm and spoke softly. The man grimaced as Crowder taped the bandage in place and helped him to his feet. Kamal and Crowder half carried the man back to the lead vehicle.

Marc helped his team bind the two soldiers and load them into the rear truck. As he stepped back onto the running board, he said to Charles, "Tell Kamal I'm sorry about his man."

Kamal gave him only a slightly weakened version of his famous grin and spoke the first words of English Marc had heard from him. "Me and my men, we very much okay."

Marc hid the trucks in the shadows of two parallel alleys. As they off-loaded, two of the young camp dwellers who belonged to Marc's team came hurtling up the side lane. Through gasping breaths they said that all the remaining attackers had pulled back into the central compound. When Crowder asked for their number, they talked back and forth among themselves for a time, then shrugged. They could not say for certain. A dozen, perhaps more. Plus the four yellow men. And the two men in charge. Big men. One had a big booming voice. The other man did not speak at all. He had a scar on his ear and carried the shadow of death with him wherever he went.

Marc ordered them to clear everyone out of the first line of houses fronting the compound. The young men vanished. Crowder handed Marc a circular device of black metal. "Locator beacon. You know how to use this?"

"Yes."

Crowder handed another to Kamal and a third to Levi, then told them, "The gadget operates like a doorknob. Turn the top until it clicks. The light on the top goes on, see? Pull this tab off the back and jam it on anything metal. Don't use a bumper; they've got too much plastic. The body frame is best."

Levi asked, "What is the range?"

"Fifty miles, according to the book. But it operates by radio frequency, which the volcano jams."

Marc said, "Our job is to get these attached and follow the vehicles just beyond their field of vision."

But their chance never came. For while Marc was still speaking, the comm link hissed and Rigby said, "They're moving out."

The remaining assailants abandoned their positions in a roaring rush. Marc crouched by one of the huts nearest the camp's central lane, the locator beacon in his hand, and watched the dust cloud approach. The retreat had caught Marc totally off guard. The attackers were simply leaving behind a smooth operation that had worked numerous times in the past. He could only assume they had never before encountered stiff resistance. Marc had been fearing a number of retaliatory measures, reprisal killings, young hostages, anything. But not this.

There were nine SUVs in all. They sped past, clearly willing to run over and destroy anything in their way. The front bumpers were reinforced with broad black piping. Armed with automatic rifles, a man stood on each of these, using them like narrow guard platforms. Another two men rose from the roof windows, standing back-to-back in professional formation. One of these was armed with another automatic rifle, the other with an RPG. Their faces were grim, their muscles tense. They swept the camp with menacing glares.

Marc knew there was no chance for his team to get anywhere near the SUVs. It would have been a suicide mission, and pointless besides. Marc keyed his comm link and said, "Stand down. Do not approach, do not attack."

When the final transport had passed and the dust settled, Crowder eased in behind Marc and said, "So what's the plan now?"

"We've got allies among the locals," Marc replied. "The

Kibera elders are searching around where their villages used to stand, looking for the extraction facility."

"You're saying we wait?"

"Unless you've got a better idea."

Crowder squinted down the empty lane. "They'll be back."

"I agree."

"If I was in their position, I'd bring in a couple of gunships and heavy backup."

Marc nodded. He had been thinking the exact same thing. "We have to finish this before they return."

Chapter Forty-Two

They broke into teams, each made up of a few armed men and several of Marc's local crew. Together they searched the camp, ensuring all the opposition had fled. Everywhere he went, Marc was greeted with cheers and waving hands. Marc forced himself to put aside his worry over Kitra and what the next day might bring, so he could smile in reply.

Afterward they met up at the schoolhouse, where Philip had gathered the children. The main classroom shared the chapel's side wall and ran the entire length of the building. The young chief directed them to pile their gear by the baobab tree. As they entered, Philip made a formal process out of rising from his stool and shaking Marc's hand. He offered the rest of the men a solemn greeting. He then resumed his place before the children and started speaking. His words carried an almost musical tone, deep and resonant and calming. Which was good, because the children were clearly frightened.

Charles leaned against the doorway leading to the shaded front porch. Several of the men patrolled in slow circles, passing back and forth in front of the windows. The sun beat down hard, and the air inside the room felt very close. Charles regularly swiped at his face, not so much clearing the sweat as distributing it more evenly. Philip was seated on the stool at the front of the room. Between the young chief and the soldiers clustered at the back sat well over a hundred children.

Charles translated, "Philip is reminding the children of all the joys and wonders they have known over the past few days. They have all shared in a wedding feast. They have sung the wedding songs of their tribes for the newly married. Four tribes are here in this camp. Four different wedding songs. How many of the children remember the laughter and the joy of all the people?"

All the children raised their hands, but not together. Marc realized Philip was speaking in two different languages, back and forth in such a smooth rhythm that Marc had assumed it was all one, until he saw how half the children raised their hands, then the other half followed while Charles translated.

Philip's tone held a timeless cadence, almost a chant. Marc saw how smiles began to bloom. The atmosphere in the room changed. The men along the rear wall must have noticed it as well, for they settled down on their haunches. A few of the children glanced over at them, but not many. Most were too enthralled with what Philip was saying.

Charles translated, "There was once a time when God walked this earth. For we know, all of us, that Kenya is truly the place where Eden was made. The garden that our God created for all men was here where we live. How could it be anywhere else? Our land is the first land, the most special, and the most beautiful. Is that not so? Tell me that you agree."

The children responded with a soft *"yebo,"* a chant of their own.

"In the days after the fall of man, God watched as the

garden became tainted by man's sinful nature. This shadow of wrongfulness was everywhere. The flowers stopped blooming all the year long. The animals no longer lived in peace. There were even times when the rains did not come. And the people suffered with the animals and the plants. And our God, he suffered with them.

"But there was one tree that did not suffer with the others. And this one tree, it was the worst of all. A tree filled with pride and arrogance. A tree that even dared to defy God. Do any of you know what that tree was?"

The children shouted out a dozen words all at once. Philip silenced them with an upraised index finger. He leaned down, he scowled, and he snarled, "It was the baobab tree."

The children shrieked with laughter.

"You think that I am mistaken. But this is a true tale, told to me by my father's father, and to him by his father, back through time to the moment when the tree defied God.

"The baobab is the strongest of trees. Its roots go so deep it can drink even when all the world thirsts. The baobab's leaves remain green even when all the world withers away. It is strong and great and lives longer than any other tree. And the baobab knew this. He saw how he was the greatest and oldest and strongest of trees. And he said, I do not need God. I am my own tree. I can live without the help of anyone. I am king and lord of this land.

"And God heard the baobab's words, and he grew very angry. So angry, in fact, that he reached down and took hold of the tree. And do you know what God did? Can you imagine? He pulled the tree out, turned it upside down, and planted it back in the earth."

This time, some of the men laughed with the children. For everyone who spent time in Africa knew the baobab's curious nature. Now that Philip had spoken, they realized how the baobab's limbs did indeed resemble roots. Like the tree was planted upside down. The children saw how the soldiers laughed with them, and laughed all the harder.

Philip went on, "And now we come to the lesson my father's father told to me. I hope you are all listening, for this is a lesson to carry with you all your life long. God demands our allegiance above all things. We are to remain steadfast with him, even when things are the hardest, even when we are weakest, even when we are angry, even when we are afraid. These are all forces from beyond the boundaries of Eden. They exist, yes, and they test us. But we can carry the holy garden with us wherever we go, so long as our hearts remain true to God."

Philip disengaged himself slowly from the children. A kind word here, a hug there. As Marc rose to greet him, a child latched on to his leg and looked up. The wide-eyed expression said it all. Don't go. Stay here. Keep us safe. Philip moved over and touched the boy's cheek. He rumbled a soothing note.

Only when the child released Marc and stepped away did Philip say, "Walk with me."

Marc saw the look Crowder gave him and asked, "Can my friends come?"

"All friends of the shujaa are welcome everywhere."

Six of them went along with Philip: Deb Orlando, Levi, Charles, Crowder, Kamal, and Marc. Karl Rigby wanted to come; Marc saw it in his face. But he was enough of a soldier to realize someone needed to remain on post. Rigby stood on the school's veranda and watched until they disappeared around the first line of huts.

The lane they took became rimmed by faces. Watchful. Silent. Respectful. Marc assumed this was what Philip intended. Show the flag. Calm his people.

Marc murmured to Philip, "We must find the rare-earth extraction facility. That is the key."

"You will do so. Of that I have no doubt. With God's help."

"Could you ask your uncle if he knows anything more?"

"We have spoken last night and again today. He has nothing to report. His people are still searching. We will hear as soon as they do."

They walked on in silence for a while, then Marc said, "This name you're using for me."

"Shujaa, yes. A very old word. From the time before the colonials. When king and warrior and chief could all be described by the same one word. *Shujaa*."

"I'm not sure I'm comfortable with that."

"It is not the word that makes you uncomfortable. It is the call of your destiny." They continued their walk in silence, and after a time Philip said, "Now I have a question. One I have asked you before. Why did you come to Africa?"

Marc felt increasingly uneasy with all the listening ears. "I seek answers of my own."

"This is good. But it is not everything. What else does the shujaa seek?"

Marc felt his face redden. "A future."

Philip smiled his approval. "In my tongue, future and destiny and purpose are all one and the same. The question, Shujaa, is this. How will you know the future purpose that God has waiting for you to claim?"

Marc did not respond.

"Listen carefully, for here is the answer to the question that drew you to Africa. The rest of the world hears that word *hero*, and they think, oh yes, this is what I want. Call me. Make me a great man." Philip poked one rigid finger into Marc's ribs. "But you hear the different message. You know the true meaning of this word *shujaa*. The meaning that can be said in just one word. In all languages the one word is never changing. It is the eternal meaning behind a *true* hero."

Philip leaned in close and blasted Marc with his soft murmur. "That one word, my friend and ally, is *sacrifice*."

Chapter Forty-Three

An hour later, Marc left the camp through the front gates. The pressure of the ticking clock pursued him down the trail and into the forest. He walked in silence with Deb and Crowder, Levi and Charles and Kamal. His team. The French camp director and his staff had apparently been taken by the assailants. Marc's young crews were busy doling out rations. Kamal estimated they had two weeks' worth of supplies in the godowns.

They emerged from the forest just as the sun touched the western rim. Kamal and Charles continued their assessment of the camp's current situation. The problem, they said, was medical treatment. The clinic was empty, the medical staff evacuated with the director. Marc half listened to their summary. Most of his attention remained gripped by the same dilemma that had propelled him from the camp. They had run out of options. The Kibera elders continued to scour the regions surrounding their former villages, but the extraction facility had not been located. Time remained their greatest foe.

Marc faced south by west, directly toward the volcano. The sunset was stained a livid green by the looming dust cloud. Marc thought he could discern a very real change to the eruption.

The volcano still fumed, but the bone-shivering resonance was gone. The pillar of smoke and ash was thinner. Lightning streaked the high reaches only now and then.

Kamal was still talking and Charles translating. Together they predicted the first thing the camp would run out of was vaccines. Marc wanted to wave the words away, shout at them that unless they came up with the location of their enemies, the camp and all its problems would be wiped out.

It was not a matter of praying for guidance. He had been praying all day. He felt the pressure mounting with each passing minute. *Kitra. Serge. Levi. Philip.* All the outcast people. All the displaced villages. Counting on him, "the shujaa."

Then it hit him.

Marc froze on the spot.

Crowder demanded, "What is it?"

Marc said to Kamal, "Run through for me what you just said again."

Kamal frowned at Charles's translation and said, "Which part?"

"About the camp's newcomers. Repeat what you said."

Kamal's frown deepened and was matched by Charles's own confusion. "We said that the number of new refugees was declining because the towns threatened by the volcano are already evacuated."

"After that."

"Families with frail old ones or sick children might have tried to wait it out—"

"No. After that."

"The outlying regions are coming in now. People who might have thought to be safe—"

Marc snapped his fingers. "How do you know about this?"

Kamal said through Charles, "It is all they talk of at the regional depot."

"Okay, okay. What next?"

Crowder said, "I'm lost."

"Oh, good," Deb said. "I thought I was the only one."

"Hold," Marc said. "Go on, Kamal. What came next?"

"The depot medical staff, they are seeing new ailments. The locals report the newest arrivals suffer from the same thing. Very bad abdominal cramps. They first thought typhus or dysentery, but now these are ruled out. Violent purges of the digestive system. The depot doctors are now thinking a poison from the volcano has leaked into the underground aquifer system—"

"That's it!" Marc wheeled about. "Come on!"

"Where are we headed?"

He had to shout over his shoulder, for he had already left them far behind. "To catch the bad guys!"

Chapter Forty-Four

Hard as they pushed, it still took them the rest of the day to make plans and set things in motion. As they gathered for the evening meal, Marc stared into the sunset and fought against the temptation to depart immediately. Levi certainly wanted to. Though Kitra's father held to his resolute silence, a desperate appeal burned in his dark gaze. But so did the exhaustion, something they all shared.

Later, as Marc rose from his chair, every eye in the mess hall turned his way. He said, "Everyone turn in. We leave at four. Charles."

"Yes?"

"Have the mess staff understand we need a full breakfast ready at three. Rigby."

"Here."

"We'll travel in the SUVs from the game camp. Top them off from the generator's fuel tank."

"On it."

"Crowder, you and Kamal arrange watches. But I want you three to stand down. The team leaders need an uninterrupted night. There's no telling what tomorrow holds." Marc left the mess hall, entered the bunkroom, pulled the mosquito net around his bed, and lay down fully clothed. He fell asleep to the sound of the ticking clock. He dreamed of a woman's soft breathing, somewhere in the far distance. Waiting for him.

They left while it was still dark and arrived at the regional depot around midmorning. The full-on panic Marc had witnessed during his last visit was gone. The camps were up and functioning, the tide of refugees somewhat reduced. The only frantic people Marc spotted were the medical staff. The makeshift hospital tents were full to bursting, with canvas lean-tos sprouting yet more beds. Staffers rushed and shouted. Marc nodded to Charles, who drifted away with Levi. Their job was to find out the precise origin of these incoming patients.

Marc and the others headed for where the noise was loudest. He spotted the pilot who had brought him into the depot. It seemed like a memory from a different lifetime. He said to Crowder, "Let's talk with this guy."

The pilot leaned against his chopper's fuselage, making time with an off-duty nurse. The woman's surgical blues were stained, her expression very tired. They both looked over at Marc's approach. It took the pilot a long moment to recall, "You're that accountant. The guy from Philly, right?"

"Close enough."

The pilot took in the crew that gathered in a semicircle around Marc—Boyd Crowder and his men, Kamal and his squad, Deb Orlando. All of them armed. The pilot's smirk vanished. "Guess you had what it takes after all."

"We need you, and we need your chopper."

"Hey, I'd like to help. But—"

"Actually we need two. Got any suggestions?"

Boyd Crowder said, "I've flown with that crew juicing up the Sikorsky over there. They'll do."

"Okay, him."

The nurse slipped away with a casual, "Later."

The pilot scowled at her departure. "This is absolutely not happening. Look, I don't care how many guns you point at me, I'm—"

"Deb."

She scarcely stood tall enough to meet the pilot's rib cage. But something in her gaze jammed the guy up solid against his chopper. Deb said, "This document is from the chief of UN global security, authorizing us to requisition anything and everything we need."

"That's you," Marc said.

"And your buddies gaping at us over by the other bird," Crowder said.

Deb withdrew another document from her pack. "As you'll see from the letterhead, this comes straight from the White House."

Marc had not even noticed the copilot until her head popped out of the rear hold. "Is this a joke?"

"No," Crowder replied. "This is totally for real."

The copilot leaped easily to the earth and leaned in beside her boss. Together they inspected the page. The woman asked her partner, "Whose coffee did you spit in?"

"Hey, I only saw this guy *once*, and all I told him was 'be careful.'"

Deb said, "You are hereby ordered and authorized to do whatever Agent Royce commands."

"Agent who?"

"Royce," Marc said. "That would be me."

Deb continued, "You are also ordered to tell no one what you are about to do. Ever."

"Or we come gunning for you, your family, your pals, and your dog," Crowder said. "Joke."

Deb went on, "You are assigned to assist us for as long as Agent Royce requires."

The copilot said, "The spaces for names here are blank."

"Spell yours out for the lady," Marc said. "Then fill your tanks."

The pilot complained, "What do I put down for my flight plan?"

"Use your imagination," Marc replied. "We leave in ten."

Crowder and Deb and Levi and Charles and Kamal were in the first chopper with Marc. It made no sense to bunch them all together. But Crowder had insisted on going with Marc, and the others had simply piled in. When Marc objected, Crowder had replied, "Eyes are eyes." Marc had let it go.

They flew toward the volcano.

The cone-shaped mountain loomed above an otherwise flat landscape. The eruption had blasted away the cone's upper fifth, leaving a ragged-edged maw that spewed a constant evil fount. Fire gleamed about the rim, but no new lava spilled out. Just a torrent of ash that tainted the sky.

"You're lucky the wind is strong." The pilot had repeated this half a dozen times during their forty-minute ride. "I got to stay well clear of that gunk. Thirty seconds inside the cloud and my intake manifolds are clogged and we drop like a stone."

The wind pushed with steady force from the south. The

smoke pillar tilted slightly away from them. The sky directly overhead was a washed-out blue. The landscape below was blanketed by ash. Here and there the pale earth was riven by veins of frozen black lava.

"Okay," Marc said. "Begin your search."

"Tell me again what we're after," the pilot repeated.

"A camp that does its best to remain hidden. Beside it will be a small mountain, maybe several. Unnatural hills that shouldn't be there," Marc replied patiently. "Signs of recent truck activity will lead to and from the site."

"And the hills are . . ."

"Slag heaps. There will probably be some form of surface water nearby."

"In this drought?"

"Which will make any pool or underground-sourced lake highly visible."

"Any water around these parts will be polluted by the fallout."

"Not as polluted as it will be when they're done with it," Marc said.

The pilot's cabin had three fold-down seats that were occupied by Deb, Crowder, and Marc. They were connected to the others by headphones and bulbous mikes held directly in front of their lips. The volcano's static formed a constant background hiss. The pilot's voice crackled with each word as he asked, "Anything else?"

"Factory-type buildings," Marc said. "Again, they'll try their best to be hidden away."

"Hidden," the pilot repeated. "As in, hard to spot."

"Exactly," Marc said. "Your target is what they can't hide so easily."

"A mound of dirt," the pilot said. "In this."

"Far enough away from the destruction that the workers can breathe when the wind is against them," Marc agreed. "Close enough to hide beneath the ash."

Their pilot had to almost sit on top of the other machine to communicate through the volcanic hiss. Every time lightning sliced the cloud to their north, the static crackled like gunfire. Everyone winced and focused grimly on their hunt.

The two choppers had worked in tandem before. The pilots both had military training, and adopted a standard search-and-rescue pattern—tight weaves that coiled around the border zone surrounding the mountain.

Ten minutes into the search, Crowder said, "Explain to me how you got this idea."

Deb replied for Marc, "He's been through all this."

"Hey. Where else can I go for my entertainment?"

Marc didn't mind. It filled the empty spaces and helped clarify the situation. "It started with something Levi told the Kibera elders. The Chinese don't care. They will pollute and destroy without a backward glance."

"If you need evidence," Levi said from the rear hold, "look no further than the air over their own cities."

Crowder said, "So they hide their extraction plant by the volcano, and the volcano makes them sick. Just like this latest stream of refugees."

"No," Marc replied. "That's not it at all."

"Explain."

"The Chinese use the most primitive extraction technology because it's the cheapest. Even though cleaner systems have been developed, right, Levi?"

The wind through the open rear door buffeted Levi's microphone as he replied, "Our system releases no toxins into the environment. None."

"So the volcano—"

"Forget the volcano," Marc said. "It's not the volcano causing these people to grow ill. Their extraction process has poisoned the groundwater. Maybe they didn't plan to. Maybe the tremors created a leak between their retention pool and the underground water system. Maybe they just don't care. Whatever the reason, the poisons resulting from their outdated extraction process have worked into the water supply."

"And the people are showing up at the camps and the depot," Deb Orlando said, "and they're sick. But the doctors can't figure out what it is that's affected them."

"Because the doctors are looking for a tropical-based ailment, or they're thinking maybe it's something from the volcano." Marc confirmed. "That's what Levi and Charles went asking about. That's why we're focusing on this region between the mountain and the three cities from which the sickest of these new patients are arriving."

"But the illnesses they're seeing don't have anything to do with the volcano, so they're misdiagnosing the problem," Crowder said, nodding slowly. "This makes sense."

Levi's worry resurfaced as he asked, "So you think my Kitra may still be alive?"

Marc rose from his seat and folded it back against the wall. He slid open the metal door separating the cabin from the rear hold. The pilot glanced over his shoulder at the wind and noise, but did not speak. When Levi met his eye, Marc said, "*Think*. Why would they have taken Kitra?"

Levi just stared at him.

"Someone had to have told them."

Levi sat immobile in the jump seat beside the open rear door. He tasted the air. "You think . . . Serge?"

"Imagine how that conversation might have gone," Marc pressed. "Serge tells his captors, 'There are all these staffers getting sick. I need help. I need a trained nurse, someone who has hands-on experience with regional ailments'."

Deb leaned back to observe them. "Whoa."

Marc went on, "He says, 'I know this great nurse. She's got exactly the skill set we need. You've got to get into this camp and bring her here. If anyone can make them better, it's her'."

Levi groaned, "Why would he have them take his own sister?"

"*Think*," Marc repeated. "It was *never* about taking Kitra. Serge was sending us a message."

Crowder cut off Levi's reply. "Heads up! I think we've got us a match."

Chapter Forty-Five

Two days later, Marc stood at the tall window and surveyed the empty reaches. Surrounding him were the skeletal remains of a town that was no more. But he did not see the ruined structures or the ash-strewn roads. Here in this dusty room he sensed a clearer understanding of his calling. He was being asked to lead, to face danger, to protect the weak, to give voice to the powerless. Marc stared out the window and glimpsed something he had doubted he would ever see again.

A future.

The second-story room had once been an executive's office. The room was large with windows on two sides, a modern desk, and part of a sofa set. The chair from behind the desk was missing, along with the coffee table and all the electronics. From the screw holes and the dangling cables Marc assumed the office had once held a flat-screen television and a phone network and computer and several monitors. All no doubt taken by looters.

In the far corner, on a shelf built at what was knee-high to Marc, sat a collection of porcelain dolls in Victorian clothes. Some had black faces, some white. Two more dolls wore Indian saris, and beside them sat a cloth doll dressed in Bolivian ceremonial robes. Marc liked the idea of a busy executive making a space where his daughter would feel so welcome. It was why he had made this his headquarters. That and the view from the front window.

The extraction facility was so well hidden, the choppers had flown past before Crowder had identified the sharp-edged shadows for what they were. Marc had ordered them to keep their distance, and inspected the site through binoculars. What at first appeared to be merely another empty trail leading nowhere proved to be furrowed by heavy tracks, suggesting trucks bringing in the raw materials, traveling at night.

They had landed eight miles away and hoofed it back. Marc went forward with two spotters, taking utmost care not to be seen. Their first glimpse confirmed what they had sighted from the air. The facility melded with the ash-covered landscape. The open-air parking areas and supply depots were draped with tent canvas. The buildings were painted the same pale wash as the surrounding region.

Marc had held them there, scarcely breathing, until he had spotted the first Chinese. The man had emerged from a door Marc had not even noticed until it opened. The man had been deep in conversation with Frederick Uhuru.

They had made camp in the neighboring ghost town. Then as now, heat baked the road leading out to the extraction facility. Throughout the two nights since their arrival, they had listened to trucks rumbling down the road, delivering the earth that was not theirs to claim.

The town was silent in a way that made the emptiness even greater. They had been waiting there for all of one day and part of another while Kamal returned to the depot for trucks and then traveled to the refugee camp, and the two choppers had been sent back to Nairobi. All part of the greater plan, which was now on the verge of unfolding.

Marc heard Deb's voice from the next room. He assumed she was catching it again from Walton. Once more Marc gave silent thanks for this woman being brought into his orbit. Walton was obviously facing a lot of pressure at his end. The ambassador's natural tendency was to pass it down the line. Ever since Washington had identified the soldiers they had captured and photographed in the camp, Walton had been pushing them. Marc could understand why. But everything depended on holding tight a little longer. Which was why Deb was on the line and not Marc. He was determined to keep a firm distance between himself and the frustration boiling over in D.C.

The troops they had captured at the camp were indeed Lodestone operatives. But they had been drawn from the Angola contingent and slipped secretly across the border. Marc had expected something like this. Crowder and Rigby, however, had bristled at the news. They had counted the Angola directors as trusted friends.

Not anymore.

Walton and the UN security chief had both gone into low-altitude orbit at the revelation. This cross-border operation violated international agreements, UN mandates, and the laws of three nations. Walton's superiors in Washington wanted to strike and strike hard. But Deb had done a masterful job of relaying Marc's refusal, and talking them down. At the moment, all Lodestone knew was that their Angolan troops had gone missing while clearing out a camp. They had no evidence tying this to anything other than locals defending their own. They might suspect Crowder and Marc were back and playing a role, but they had no proof.

And that was what it was all about, Marc had instructed Deb to tell Walton. Proof.

If they arrived with warrants at Lodestone's Washington headquarters, the Chinese would hear and roll up their operatives and flee. Deny everything. Go through official channels and apply for legal permits to extract and process rare earth. Grease the palms of their allies in Nairobi and New York. And win it all.

That was not going to happen.

Marc turned as Deb knocked on his open door. Like all his team, she wore a surgical mask. They had requisitioned six cases of these back at the depot to protect from the ash. Deb's voice was slightly muffled as she said, "Walton can't last much longer. I'm thinking stroke and seizure and heart attack, all within the next couple of hours."

Marc asked, "The elders are gathered?"

"Both from the camp and Kibera."

"What about Kamal and Crowder and their teams?"

"Fully prepped. Safeties off. Green light."

"The trucks?"

"Refueled and ready to roll."

Marc stared a moment longer at the dust drifting down the street. The ash was lifting higher now, up to where it could rattle against his window. "It's time."

She brightened. "Can I be the one to tell Walton?"

"Do it."

She started from the room, then turned back to ask, "What has changed?"

Marc replied, "The wind."

They gathered in the warehouse behind Marc's temporary office. The vast structure had been used for roasting coffee and packing spices. The building was the largest and certainly the cleanest of those they had searched. Even when crammed with a startling mix of humanity, Marc could still smell the roasted beans and vanilla and thyme. It was a heady, exhilarating blend.

The main hall was probably a hundred and fifty feet long and forty wide. High louvered windows opened on pulley chains. The ones along the windward wall were shut, which meant the air was close and hot. A sizeable crowd drawn from the refugee camp and from Kibera milled about, most of them wearing the masks.

The elders were grouped in a semicircle beneath the open windows on the building's far side. They had selected which ones would be brought in—from Nairobi by way of the requisitioned choppers, and from the camp by trucks. The two sets of elders were all seated on small stools, the elders from Kibera intermingled with those from the refugee camp. A gentle snow of ash filtered down, flaking their heads and shoulders. The elders did not brush it away. They watched motionless as Marc approached.

Marc stopped in front of them. He felt the pressure mount, but still he waited. He could observe them with a singular clarity, and he saw a depth to them that he was only beginning to fathom. They had waited for weeks and months and years as all their world had been stripped away and their clans relegated to slums and camps. They had waited while governments and bureaucrats had lied and deceived and let them down.

The entire warehouse was silent now. Waiting.

Marc removed his mask so his voice would carry. "The danger is very great," he began. "But the time has come for us to act."

From his position behind the elders, Charles translated. His voice resonated and echoed through the vast hold.

"Our plan is a good one." Marc went on. "If we're successful, this will result in an international public outcry, one large enough to force the proper governments to respond. Our aims are twofold. First, to find you new villages. Second, to peacefully resolve the rare-earth crisis in a way that benefits us all."

The people did not speak or move. The only sound was the gentle sigh of falling ash. Marc finished, "I would be grateful if we could all join together and pray."

Philip's uncle rose slowly from his stool. Oyango stepped forward so that he stood midway between the elders and Marc. He addressed the people in his own tongue. When Charles started to translate, Philip rose and motioned to the pastor that he would do the English translation himself. Philip stepped forward to stand beside his uncle. He lifted his voice, matching Oyango's fierce power. "We will pray for you, for our success and for our future! Not many futures for many tribes, but *one* future, and for *one* nation bound together by our God. The same God who waits for us to call upon him! The same power that brought victory to Joshua! The same power that destroyed the walls of Jericho!"

Oyango settled a hand on his nephew's shoulder. Together they continued to speak, one in Swahili, the other in English,

"We will march forth armed with God's might—the same power that restored my soul! The same power that spoke through to my nephew through dreams. The same power that promises us a green and verdant land."

Oyango wheeled about and aimed his ceremonial staff at Marc. "Shujaa!"

The crowd echoed back its shout, "Shujaa!"

"He is the *mashujaa wa Mungu*. The hero of God. He is called as *we* are called," Philip said in Swahili, then in English.

The crowd roared again.

Oyango now placed his hand on Marc's shoulder, an act of benediction that burned like fire through his soul. The man cried out some phrases in Swahili, and afterward Philip followed with, "Go forth, Mashujaa wa Mungu, and remember that God's power is with you. And with us all!"

Chapter Forty-Six

I don't like moving forward unarmed," Crowder complained. "Not one bit."

Marc did not respond. On his other side, Charles followed Marc's lead and remained silent. There was nothing to say.

"I might as well walk down this road without my boots on," Crowder said.

Their footfalls made no sound. Somewhere below the inch or so of ash was a road of gravel and old asphalt. Marc walked in furrows laid down by numerous trucks. His stomach growled. They had subsisted on energy bars and cold C-Rations since their arrival. Marc had not wanted any odor of cooking to alert the enemy. He was full but never satisfied. And everything tasted of ash. What was more, he was always thirsty. The ash sucked the moisture from his skin, his eyes, his breath.

He approached gates fortified with steel crossbars and coils of razor wire. To either side rose claxons mounted on concrete stanchions. But Marc was aware of only one thing. He felt a growing sense of anticipation. An electric current surged through his body, a fierce power propelling him forward.

Up ahead was humming and hidden activity. Otherwise there was nothing. No life, no sound.

Marc halted.

Crowder demanded, "What is it?"

"The wind has stopped."

"Is that bad?"

He hesitated, then decided, "Not so long as the ash keeps falling." He spared a glance upward. There was no sky. Only the seamless gray blanket and the false dusk and the gritty snow. He continued on. "Try your comm link."

"I already did. We've got nothing but static. Which means we can't get hold of backup if things go south." Crowder kicked the ash at his feet. "This is nuts. We're totally exposed."

Marc knew Crowder was just letting off steam. He asked Charles, "You okay?"

"What is it you soldiers say, in the green?"

Crowder snorted. "Shows how much you know, preacher boy."

"I know I am surrounded by miracles, soldier man."

Marc asked the colonel, "When was the last time you went into action without a weapon?"

"Never, that's when. Which is why I'm here to talk about it. My momma wasn't big on stupid." He caught the grin Marc shared with Charles. "I say something funny?"

"No, it's just, I'm glad you two are here with me. Finally doing this."

"All in God's time," Charles said. "The words have been ringing my chimes for hours now. And God's time, it has come."

Crowder didn't say anything more until they arrived at the gates. "What now? I don't see a doorbell."

"We'll give them five minutes," Marc said.

But they only needed two.

Frederick Uhuru appeared through the veil of falling ash.

The rogue UN executive suited this region of isolation and empty death. He was the kind of man who made friends of the silence and the absence of light. He even seemed comfortable with the volcano and the smoke. He wore no mask. His grin was tight and angry. He dismissed Charles with a snort of derision, then said to Marc, "You, I can understand. The Western idealist. The one who thinks he will find a reason for his empty days. Here, in darkest Africa." Uhuru turned the last two words into a mockery: *dahkest Ahfrica.*

Marc said, "Open the gates."

Uhuru sneered and turned to Crowder. "You, I do not understand. You have the experience. You have fought many battles. Why did you come, I wonder? Perhaps you are tired of the struggle. Is that it? Do you seek the bullet etched with your name? So you accompany this idiot with his futile cause?"

Crowder replied, "I've come for the bodies of my men."

Uhuru squinted, confused. "There are no bodies here."

"Then I guess I'll have to settle for you." Crowder stepped forward. "I'm making a citizen's arrest."

Uhuru turned and barked over his shoulder. The falling ash parted a second time to reveal Uhuru's gunman, the slash-eared killer who had threatened the Kibera elders.

Uhuru turned back and said, "You forget how close you are to death here. And you, my foolish Western friend, you will never have a chance to learn."

Marc said, "The United Nations security chief has been alerted to your actions. And the White House. Your operations are to be shut down and—"

"My actions are only *starting*. The Chinese *dominate* the trade in rare earth. It is *theirs*. And I am their ally."

"You're finished."

"No, no, my stupid boy. You are the one who is finished. You will fall and be buried and forgotten. My allies and I will fly out. When the noise dies off, we will return—"

"You can't leave."

"Your threats are empty as your head. We will leave today and come in force tomorrow. But not before we dispose of you. You think you will shoot our helicopters from the sky and ignite an international incident?"

"I don't have to." Marc lifted a hand to the day. "The ash will do it for me."

"What are you saying?"

"Check with your pilots. They won't take off. Five minutes in the air and their manifolds will be clogged."

"This is absurd. And it is over." Uhuru turned to his gunman. "Kill them."

Then it happened.

Chapter Forty-Seven

The sound started with a single voice.

Oyango half sang, half shouted the words. He called from behind the nearest ruins, beyond the slender river that ran black and putrid by the right-hand fence. The storm and the stillness seemed to open for this one voice. The tone was not softened by the ash. Instead, it was magnified. It went on and on. It grew louder with each passing second.

Oyango's final word ended in a long drawn-out hum. When he finally went silent, the response came from all around them.

Yebo. Affirmative. More than yes. A unified declaration. *Yebo*.

Oyango spoke again, only this time the words were shouted by two voices. Oyango on the hill to Marc's right, Philip to his left. The half-sung words lasted maybe thirty seconds.

Yebo.

The assassin weaved about, aiming his gun at ghosts.

Uhuru demanded, "What is this nonsense?"

The third time Charles joined in as well. As did a hundred other throats. Or perhaps twenty thousand, who could tell?

Marc knew what they were saying because Charles had told them as they left the warehouse. The words came from the third chapter of Joshua, "This is how you will know that the living God is among you."

Yebo.

Then silence. Even the humming inside the encampment was gone.

"Open the gates," Marc said.

"Get *away* from here!" Uhuru spun around and yelled at his gunman. Or rather, he tried. For at that moment the heavens were split by a blast of sound, a detonation that shook the earth, or so it seemed to Marc. Uhuru and his assassin cowered down, heads covered by their hands. And then the sound struck again.

All around them, the villagers came into view. The numbers were no longer important. The falling ash magnified their numbers and heightened the moment's intensity. Each of them carried long, slender instruments made of plastic. They were called *vuvuzellas*, infamous noisemakers that disrupted soccer matches and political gatherings across the continent. Marc was aware of all this, and yet down deep, beneath the veneer of modern logic, he saw something else entirely. He witnessed a multitude beyond count, all of them armed by a force that turned their puny instruments into a conduit for holy might. And divine vengeance.

Marc's entire being resonated with the next trumpet sound.

He watched the people begin to march. They moved about the encampment, snaking through the ruins and the poisoned stream and the slag heap. Blowing their vuvuzellas as they marched. The falling ash turned them into spectral shapes, making it seem as though a hundred thousand others had joined them. That was true of their noise as well. As though they were no longer the source of the sound. As though it were not a sound at all.

It was power.

It surrounded. It assaulted. It dominated. There was room for nothing else.

Up and down the encampment's central lane, the doors opened and people spilled out. The Chinese wore distinctive jumpsuits of pale blue. They rushed over and clustered by the open-sided warehouse containing the four transport choppers. They shouted and screamed and waved their arms. The pilots shrugged and pointed, first at their engines and then at the falling ash. They could not fly.

Then the earth joined in the blasting, resonating din.

That was how it seemed to Marc, like the earth had decided to sound its own trumpet.

The volcano expelled a massive blast of flame. The fire shot up, spearing the clouds overhead. And then a seam opened, which spilled a river of fire. Straight toward them.

The Chinese technicians quite literally freaked out.

They poured over Uhuru and his gunman. They clawed at the gates. There were so many of them, they could not work the gates' lock.

Marc did not care whether they could hear him or not. He shouted, "You are all under arrest."

As soon as the gates opened and the tide of blue-suited Chinese started pressing forward, Levi and Karl Rigby and a team drawn from Crowder's and Kamal's men rose from their hiding places beyond the first trench. Levi was the first inside the gates, followed swiftly by Marc. Crowder and Kamal directed their team to snare the fleeing Chinese, wheel them about, and lash them with plastic ties.

Levi shoved his way through. Marc ran at his side. He had to force the name from his constricted throat.

"Kitra."

They found her in the fifth building they searched.

The medical unit was jammed with extremely ill patients. Kitra and Serge and a local doctor worked the rows. They rose from their positions over various beds with weary reluctance, as though they had heard neither the trumpets nor the eruption.

Levi embraced his daughter first because she was closer. Marc stood just inside the doorway, halted by the swell of emotions.

Serge was a taller version of his father. But his broad shoulders were supported by a rail-thin frame, and his face looked almost skeletal. Deep plum-colored patches were dug into the skin beneath his eyes. He watched his father and did not move or wipe the tears streaming down his own face.

When Levi turned to his son, Kitra started toward Marc. Hesitantly at first, then in a rush that ended with her flinging herself into his arms. Marc buried his face in her hair. This was the feel of her, strong and feminine and warm and weary. He felt her heartbeat racing against his own. And never wanted this moment to end.

Chapter Forty-Eight

They needed only a week to build the second camp.

The fields on the other side of the forest were transformed into a hive of activity. Temporary structures and generators and satellite dishes sprouted from this new virtual city. The drone of choppers formed a constant backdrop to every passing day.

Marc stayed in the old camp because that was where the elders chose to remain. Kitra occasionally returned to the medical facility but spent most of her time at the new camp. Levi helped oversee the camp's development. Serge did what he could to help his sister, but his captivity at the extraction facility had left him brutally exhausted. He spent a lot of time in one of the new portable cabins, resting and eating and resting some more.

At Philip's request, Kitra served as a key negotiator in the settlement talks. These discussions grew to where they included representatives of the United Nations and the Kenyan government and the elders of almost three dozen displaced villages. The Americans were there as well, yet officially they served only as observers. Still, everyone involved knew the senior man represented the White House, and his word carried sufficient weight to move things forward.

The Chinese government lodged official protests. When the press used this as a lever to pry more deeply into the entire affair, the Chinese went oddly silent. For Marc it was like watching a predator retreat inside its cave. Waiting.

The negotiations took place at the new camp, because Philip and Oyango and the other elders insisted, and the Americans backed their request. The elders and Kitra and Walton and Marc all wanted to keep Nairobi at a distance. And the newcomers to the Kenyan government agreed. The risk of corruption and illicit underhanded acts were still very real.

The meetings dragged on and on. But Kitra did not mind. In fact, despite the long hours, Kitra seemed to grow more alive and energetic with each passing hour. By the eighth day, Levi had taken to sitting with the elders beneath the massive baobab tree while his daughter remained sequestered with the committee, poring over documents and arguing the minutiae of several agreements. Marc remained with Levi, or walked the perimeter with Kamal's and Crowder's combined team.

Lodestone was under investigation, their worldwide assets frozen, their operations in Africa shut down. Boyd Crowder had personally accepted assignment as head of all commercial security forces operating in Kenya. He had taken over one of the new camp's square white huts as his temporary headquarters. Kamal was to become one of his senior officers, while Rigby was promoted to chief of operations. Marc saw less and less of them.

Everyone felt the press of silent foes, the pressure to either complete this or face defeat. The threat of attack spurred them on. On the tenth day, word filtered out that it was done.

A feast was held beneath the forest's dead limbs. A combination of nations and peoples joined together as first the Kenyan delegate and then the UN security chief and then Philip and finally Oyango spoke. They asked Marc to say a few words as well, but he declined. As did Levi. It was left to Kitra to address the gathering. Marc only half heard her words. She sounded so authoritative. So much in her element.

A Kenyan corporation had been formed. It would hold all licenses for the extraction and refinement of the rare earths. This would be done in joint venture with an Israeli corporation. Kitra and Levi Korban were to be designated as officers. The Israeli shares were to be held in trust by their community.

The evacuated villages would be relocated and restored. The process of returning the people from the camps and from Kibera had already started.

One third of all profits from the corporation were to go to the villages. And their children. And their children's children.

As Kitra spoke, Marc watched another chopper rise off the new landing pad and disappear. He knew it was only a matter of time before hers took off as well.

Which meant that he was ready when she approached him that evening and asked if they could take a walk. As ready as he would ever be.

A gentle sunset wind blew steady from the east, pushing the volcano's cloud away from them. They passed under the first dry limbs, and she said, "This is where it all started. You enlisted the help of men who had no reason to trust you, and you brought order to the camp's chaos. You protected the weak. You made friends where the people had been taught to treat all outsiders as threats. As enemies."

Marc took her hand and did not speak.

"I have watched you time and again, Marc Royce. And each time I feel more strongly what I sensed the first time I laid eyes on you."

He wanted to ask, but decided silence was better.

She said, "I knew that you were the man I had thought I would never meet. A man strong enough to accept me for who I am. A man who would not be threatened. Who would love me as I am, and as I hope to become."

"I couldn't help but dream of hearing you say those words," he said.

"And I lay awake through all the nights since meeting you," she replied, "fearing we would never know a time that was truly ours."

He said, "The whole time I was in Israel, I listened to you speak. Not in words, but to my heart. And I knew I had a choice. Either I came with you, or we would not have a future."

"You cannot ask me to live anywhere else. I would despair. Our love would die before it had a chance to live."

"That was the most important lesson I brought back with me from Israel," he confirmed. "Understand the move and do it with my eyes wide open or not at all."

They drifted through the trees, taking their time. Knowing each step was vital, each word. Overhead, the white limbs reached out and carved a secret scroll upon the sunset. He wanted to sweep her up and promise her the world and his life both.

Finally she said, "You have touched the secret parts of my soul, Marc. The parts no one else will ever know exist."

He shivered through a long breath. "I am bound to a different land, Kitra."

"I know," she said with mournful softness. "So well. I know."

He stopped walking and turned toward her, but she did not meet his gaze until he cradled her face in his hands. "I feel a calling to my own homeland, as strong as what you have for your own."

"I know this also," she whispered. "All too well."

"I have to do as God calls. I have spent the days since we returned praying. So far, he has not answered."

"He will. This I know. And when he does, I pray he changes your heart." Her smile trembled. "I know it is a selfish desire, and I don't care. Know this also, Marc Royce. I will wait for your decision."

He was still trying to shape his response when she leaned forward and kissed him quickly.

When they parted, it was to hear her say, "Only do not make me wait too long."

 **Davis Bunn**, a professional novelist for over twenty years, is the author of numerous national bestsellers with sales totaling more than six million copies. His work has been published in sixteen languages, and his critical acclaim includes three Christy Awards for excellence in fiction. Formerly an international business executive working in Europe, Africa, and the Middle East, Bunn is now a lecturer in creative writing and Writer in Residence at Regent's Park College, Oxford University. He and his wife, Isabella, divide their time between the English countryside and the coast of Florida.

You will find more about the author and his work on his website, *davisbunn.com*. Sign up for newsletters and live chats with Davis, along with information about upcoming books and films.

More from Bestselling Author Davis Bunn

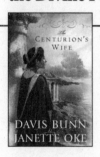